Seeds of His Evil

by Emersyn Park

Seeds of His Evil, 1st Edition

Cover image by Alan Shapiro. Designed by Julie Frank.

Editor: Caramie Malcolm

ISBN: 9798987902233

Library of Congress Control Number has been applied for.

Website: https://www.emersynpark.com/

Instagram: https://www.instagram.com/EmersynJulesPark

Facebook: https://www.facebook.com/EmersynPark

Seeds of His Evil is the third novel
in the Normal Scandal Series
following *He Loves Me, She Loves Me Not*
and *Roots of His Evil.*

Other novels by Emersyn Park:

Puppet's Shadow

Secrets Maple Keeps

The Last Arrangement

Your mind is your garden.
Your thoughts are the seeds.
The harvest will either bring flowers or weeds.

~William Wordsworth

Nature vs. Nurture

by Tara Brady

Midwest University

Abnormal Psychology

Professor Beth Doyle

May 10, 1993

Life is defined by a series of moments. If a moment is laced with a strong emotion–happiness, fear, or sadness–it takes your breath away and becomes engraved in your heart and mind. These seconds in time mold you and influence your natural responses. They define your future. Each weighted moment affects the choices you make.

Every scientist understands that adding variables to a formula will alter the results. In life, heredity is a variable. Depending on which is stronger–genetics or experiences–each person will choose a different path when given the same options. Did you make that decision based on your past experiences, or did it stem from the genetic makeup of your DNA? The question of nature versus nurture is one of the oldest debates.

In 1859, scientist Charles Darwin suggested that people are prone to violence based on their biological rather than environmental influences. The National Library of Medicine concurs with Mr. Darwin's theory, even after a century and a half.

> ... human genetic variation and the genetic basis of prosocial traits focus on the recent and mounting evidence that points to genes for antisocial behaviors, genes for criminality, and genes for violence. All of them contribute to discredit further the scientifically untenable cultural dogma claiming that human behaviors reflect nurture, represented by social environments, not nature, in the form of biological factors.

> The National Library of Medicine's January 1993
> Newsletter, Page 12, Bethesda MD

Most often when someone refers to their heritage, people assume they're talking about how they look. Genetics are present in physical characteristics. The long, narrow nose or the intense blue eyes can be traced through generations without much thought or consideration, but behavior patterns continue to cause professionals to debate the true origin. The debate has been going on for centuries, but the findings often differ. Research on identical twins has demonstrated that despite their physical similarity, their brain's wiring causes them to react differently to the same stimuli. Behavioral genetics inherited by a family member are harder to trace.

Nature refers to the heritable traits that are passed down by parents, while nurture refers to the environmental factors that influence behavior. For example, when a child is well-behaved, parents often brag that their child inherited excellent manners from them. However, is the child reflecting behavioral patterns that they witnessed, or is the child behaving well because they possess a calm demeanor that was inherited from the parents? It leads to the question: Is a baby born a clean slate, or is their path already defined by their chemical makeup?

At the beginning of my research, I'll admit that I believed nature versus nurture was a black-and-white issue. I held the simple–but also very popular–opinion that a person was born either good or evil. Simple studies show that if a person is born in poverty, they will most likely remain in poverty. If a person is born into a highly disciplined, educated family, that person would set lofty goals and strive to impress their parents with their accomplishments. However, these basic studies don't take into account environmental factors. For example, a person born into poverty may have suffered trauma that affected their ability to maintain a full-time job. Or perhaps the wealthy person who is considered successful had their life choices defined before birth, and they simply needed to show up.

In my paper, I'll convince you that even when genetic makeup shows predisposed patterns, you can alter the chemicals by collecting knowledge to make an informed decision based on facts and not behavioral patterns. I'll prove that a person can overcome a strong, dominant hereditary trait by searching for understanding and knowledge. Knowledge is power.

While conducting research for this paper, I interviewed an inmate in Fort Madison's Correctional Facility, where he is serving twenty years for his role in a sex scandal that rocked many communities in the Midwest. The secrets that were uncovered during his trial exploded like a bomb. In the wake of this discovery, ordinary people were left wondering how it all happened under their noses. Everyone wanted answers and to understand how they were duped into believing that the words he said were truth, literally the Gospel.

When Pastor Tony Shade was arrested for soliciting sex from a minor, the authorities uncovered an underground secret sex ring happening in the small town where I grew up. It was occurring in the pastor's home. Throughout the investigation and subsequent trial into these charges, so many unlawful things occurred.

During my eight-week interview process, we discussed his family history, environmental factors, and his current mental health. Unfortunately, I was unable to interview Mr. Shade's parents or grandparents to confirm his side of the story, and he has no siblings that he knows of. But luckily, I was able to collect evidence from a couple of his offspring to prove my points made in this paper.

Even though genetics suggest a pattern of behavior, environmental factors can correct or bend a desired outcome.

Chapter 1

"**K**nock-Knock. Knickety-Knock."

My mother's sweet, it's-time-to-get-up greeting on the other side of my bedroom door stirred me conscious. When I turned twelve, she adopted a new rule—not to enter my bedroom without announcing herself. "Young boys need their privacy, and I respect that."

She had no idea how much I appreciated her newly adopted rule.

"Your breakfast is ready, honey. I made your favorite—egg in the hole. Are you awake?" She gently tapped on my bedroom door with her knuckles.

I quickly mumbled a response, acknowledging that I'd heard her through the thin, core door. I didn't want her to feel the need to break her new rule by entering my room to see if I was still alive. Over the past two months, as raging hormones coursed through my veins, I woke every morning with a severe cramp in my privates that made it impossible to get out of bed. Instead, I lay in my twin-size bed, thinking about my middle school science teacher, who referred to what I was experiencing as 'morning wood.' The mole on his lip had started sprouting two dark hairs. As my brain focused on the memory of the ugly, protruding anomaly on Mr. Johnson's face, my cramp began to dissolve slightly until suddenly I remembered what I'd been dreaming about before my mother's voice woke me.

A smoky fog surrounded the edges of my vision of a beautiful girl. Everything except her was out of focus. Her big brown eyes stared longingly at me as she shook her long, wavy, golden-blonde hair out of a ponytail. Sitting next to me on the edge of my bed, she was completely naked except for a sparkling gold chain hanging around her neck. If I pull her necklace tight, will she choke? Would she like that? The nipples on her apple-sized breasts stood at attention, and I wondered if she would scream if I bit one of them. How hard would I need to bite down to draw blood? I watched her lick her full pink lips.

Mr. Johnson's mole! Mr. Johnson's mole!

To make the cramp dissolve, I needed to think of something grotesque. The mole was the size of a large pea. A large, brown pea that wiggled when he talked fast. Disgusting. I wondered if the hairs were an inch long yet. I wondered if it was cancerous. If I flicked it, would it hurt?

When I was twelve years old, I realized that I was different. Every awkward middle school boy could claim that he felt he didn't belong, was odd, and felt like his body was sometimes possessed by an alien. However, in my case, it was true. My 'difference' wasn't unique and eccentric. My 'difference' was strange and deviant. From the outside, I looked like the golden child with curious, big eyes, straight white teeth *without the need for braces, and an approachable, friendly, natural charisma. I hadn't earned these traits. They were genetic gifts from my attractive and well-mannered parents.*

I checked all of the boxes on the outside, but inside I was a fraud. I was not like everyone else.

I'd been invited to a slumber party with a group of boys from my sixth-grade baseball team. After the last game of the season, ten sweaty, stinky pre-teens piled into a parent's station wagon and headed to Greg's house for pizza, cake, and movies. The chatter in the back of the car was laced with testosterone and excitement. Greg's parents owned a huge house, and we'd have the basement to ourselves. We looked forward to stuffing our faces with greasy pizza, staying up all night watching horror movies, and causing a little trouble.

"Dudes, my mom rented a VCR player and a ton of movies to watch. But if you get sleepy during the movie, don't blame me. I provided enough caffeine and sugar to make a sloth run in circles for hours. Be sure to chug a couple of Tabs, Carson." Greg slapped Carson on his back. A few chuckles rose from the group.

Carson shook his head and subconsciously rubbed his top lip. "My mom almost didn't let me come tonight because of what you did last time, Greg."

We laughed because we remembered the legendary story from a previous sleepover. Carson fell asleep with his mouth hanging wide open, drool threatening to drip onto his pillow, while his friends used a permanent marker on his face. Carson was the first and last victim.

No one dared to fall asleep anymore. Most of us chugged caffeine and vowed to sleep when we got home the next day.

"Your timing on that prank sucked, man. It was Good Friday, and your lame attempt at a mustache hadn't faded much for Easter church service a couple of days later. When we were sitting in the pew, my eighty-year-old grandma thought a huge, ugly caterpillar was crawling on my face. She slapped me right during the sermon trying to get it off of me."

Everyone laughed so hard that our bellies hurt and we earned side aches. Time with my friends was what I needed after feeling so strange lately. Crazy, absurd thoughts kept popping up in my brain without warning. For example, I'd biked to the grocery store for pop and snacks for the slumber party. As I pulled out my money to pay the cashier, a random thought exploded in my head.

If I tied her hands together behind her back and taped her mouth shut, I could force myself on her. I should buy some duct tape.

As a cramp threatened to rise beneath my jeans, my eyes shot wide open. The cashier, noticing my surprised expression, asked, "Is everything okay?"

Where did that violent thought come from? I'd never even had sex before or watched a dirty movie. Why did I even think of something as evil and disgusting as that?

"Young man, did you forget something? I can wait a minute if you need to go grab it."

The grocery cashier was average-looking and at least ten years older than me, but it was the fact that her breasts were exploding out of her uniform shirt that caught my attention. The buttons of her blouse were straining to hold in its contents.

"No. Sorry. I'm good. I only need these things for right now, but thank you."

I wonder what time her break is. I could sneak into the breakroom and wait for her.

I snagged my bags and rushed out of the grocery store. I gasped for fresh breath as I unlocked my bike from the rack. What was happening to me? I noticed changes in my physical appearance, like the growth of dark hair in my armpits, the emergence of stray curly hairs around my manhood, and random arousal. But these thoughts were scary.

Do these strange thoughts come with puberty? I wanted to ask someone, but something held me back. Maybe it was the violent nature of the thoughts. They had not been discussed in health class.

We'd learned through the sex education discussions at school that both boys and girls would experience a change in their minds and bodies at this age. I remember Mr. Johnson telling the class of boys, "When puberty hits, the hormones surging through your bodies cause new wiring in your brains to develop. Last year, you thought Lisa was annoying and loud, but suddenly she's a total fox. That's puberty."

Giggles erupted from the class. We were all sitting on the edge of our seats yearning for more information while still being embarrassed and repulsed by an adult talking about sex. Our class of one hundred kids had been split into two rooms—the boys in one and the girls in the other. I wondered how the talks differed. What were the girls being told about what we were going through, or did they only learn about their own bodies?

Mr. Johnson continued, "You need to remember a few things, boys. First of all, this change is completely normal. It happens to every one of us, just at different times. Your dad, your uncle, and your grandpa experienced it. It even happened to me. Far too many years ago for me to count, but we all go through it.

"Physically, our bodies flex like rubber bands. Boys go through an awkward stage where their feet grow so much that their parents can't keep them in shoes that fit. Not only is your outward appearance changing, but emotionally your wires are being ignited. Things that didn't bother you before, like losing a baseball game, totally enrage you now. Intense feelings accompany the chemical change occurring in your body. The most important thing to remember is how you act. You can't control everything in life, but you can control your reaction. Never hurt someone else when you feel a testosterone surge pulse through your body. Don't throw your bat when you strike out. Don't punch Scott because he said something stupid. Part of becoming a respectable, charming man like me," he earned a few giggles, "is learning to channel your feelings into positive outcomes."

Not only was Mr. Johnson our science and health teacher, but he also coached baseball. We respected and listened to his advice because he had a down-to-earth approach to dealing with kids. Plus, he made learning fun.

"A real man learns to focus these foreign energies into something productive."

If I asked Mr. Johnson, I worried he'd feel obligated to mention it to my parents. I didn't want that. I was embarrassed enough about what was happening that I didn't need my parents looking at me strangely. I'd see how the slumber party went with my friends. Maybe one of my teammates would bring up weird, sexual thoughts that popped up in his head, too.

Chapter 2

Midwest University

March 1993

"This semester's final project will be a twenty-page paper worth seventy-five percent of your grade. I'm not going to give you a list of topic guidelines. In fact, I'm going to do the opposite. I'm going to tell you what *not* to write about." Professor Beth Doyle was approachable, honest, and knowledgeable, and her Abnormal Psychology class was by far my favorite this semester. If she didn't know the answer, she'd admit it and promise to find out. Her enthusiasm for the course was obvious to her students, and her energy made her a popular professor.

She looked comfortable behind a small wooden podium, facing approximately sixty college students who were either hungover or bored. With her index finger, she pushed her large black-rimmed glasses up the slope of her nose. I wondered if they were for show. Her dirty blonde hair fell to her shoulders. She always wore clothes that looked like they were borrowed from her father's closet—nonsexual and three sizes too big. The only jewelry she wore was a pair of diamond stud earrings.

"Do not write a paper on nonverbal communication, sexism, racism, or eating disorders." She paused for a moment, trying to recall one more subject she wanted us to avoid. Before continuing, she pulled her hair back as if she was going to put it up in a ponytail and then let it drop to her shoulders. It was one of her habits that my classmates kept track of during her lecture. They'd take bets before class, and whoever lost would be buying drinks that night at the bar. Today, according to the guy next to me, she'd gathered her hair twelve times already before letting it drop back onto her shoulders. "Oh, and don't do depression. I can't handle another paper on depression. I've read and critiqued hundreds of papers on these topics from your predecessors, and I've grown incredibly bored. Wow me. Give me something new. Discover a new perspective about a hot topic." As she glanced at the large clock on the side wall of the lecture hall, she added, "One more thing: don't stop me after class to pick my brain. Even though you've slept through a good portion of my lectures, you know I'm not interested in holding your hand through this process. Get to work. Class dismissed."

With that closing, she slapped the book on the podium shut and packed up her belongings. There was a slight hush in the room as she made her way to the door. The noise and adrenaline in the room made me think of a beehive. Professor Doyle was the queen bee, and we were her worker bees who buzzed around the honey she sprinkled.

Normally, she didn't rush out of the room. She lingered and conversed with her little bees. After every lecture, a handful of students walked her back to her office, picking her brain along the way. This time she flew off alone.

When the door closed behind her, the humming intensified. Everyone wanted to come up with a topic to impress her and pique her interest with a unique point of view. I listened to the excited chatter around me as I finished putting my books in my bookbag.

"Do you think she wants more of a political piece?" asked the guy next to me who'd been keeping track of her nonexistent ponytails. He wore a wrinkled, light blue Oxford shirt that was only buttoned halfway up, exposing his hairy chest and the thick gold chain around his neck.

"I think she's looking for something new and relevant to current social tendencies," responded his friend, who looked like he rolled out of bed and shuffled to class. He wore gray sweatpants, a white T-shirt that was inside out, and a baseball cap that read Midwest University.

"Is she single?" I heard the first guy–Oxford–ask, and then quickly he added, "No, no, not like that. I wonder what she'd think of a paper on a unique perspective on online dating. Like an inside scoop."

Sweatpants laughed and slugged him on the shoulder, "I'm imagining your personal ad: 'Looking for a weak, unintelligent, broke college boy who irons his jeans? I'm your man.'"

"Some women like projects," defended Oxford.

***

I decided to walk the long way home. A good, brisk stroll would clear my mind and generate a good idea for this paper. Professor Doyle's class was housed in the center of campus, so when I exited the building I turned west to walk around the outermost perimeter. It was one of the days at the end of winter when all Midwesterners remembered why they chose to live here. Mother Nature blessed Canby, Minnesota, with an untypically warm day. The snow had melted, which left moisture on the ground, causing a fresh, wet scent. The brisk winter had lessened, allowing the first signs of spring to blossom.

It felt good to be outside again. Winter was my least favorite season by a million miles. I hated being cold. I hated wearing boots, scarves, mittens, and hats. I hated to warm up my car before going anywhere. And don't get me started on how much I hated shoveling.

As I unzipped my winter coat, I started my brainstorming.

Unplanned pregnancy. Sixty years ago, if a woman became pregnant outside of marriage, her family shipped her off to a long-lost relative so she could have the baby in secret and give the newborn up for adoption. She'd return to her life as if nothing ever happened. Now, we have clinics in big cities called Planned Parenthood. Were these clinics started by women who were forced to give up their babies when they were younger? I could interview and research the possibilities, but is the topic interesting enough?

What if a single woman planned her pregnancy? In my mother's case, it was a planned pregnancy because she visited a sperm bank to become a parent. Because my mother's choice to start a family on her own wasn't a popular choice, we didn't talk about it much outside of our home. Kitty–the nickname everyone used for my mother–didn't share much of her personal information with anyone. She chose to let rumors spread, which bothered me when I was a teenager. I wanted her to set the story straight and tell the small-town gossip that she wasn't a tramp. She was picky and selective. I mean, what is more exclusive than picking the father of your child from a binder? However, I never won that argument, and I doubted she'd be thrilled if I shared that information in a paper that could be published.

An hour later and no closer to a thesis, I arrived home. Not only did I want to ace this class, but I also wanted to impress Professor Doyle. Sometimes, she would submit an undergrad paper to one of the popular psychology magazines, which was like earning an Oscar for an actor. I needed to be patient with my brainstorming process. Having a solid, meaningful topic would be the catalyst for achieving my goal. I wanted to see my name in the byline of an article published in *Psychology Today*.

When I dropped my book bag onto the entryway table, I noticed the red light blinking on the answering machine.

"Tuesday at 3:33 p.m." The robotic machine labeled the day and time of the message. "Tarasue, it's Mom. Can you give me a call? I need to see you. Well, I need to talk to you *about* coming to see me. It's important. Call me."

After a ten-minute conversation with my mother, I made plans to visit her the following weekend, under the condition that I was only scheduled to work one lunch shift. She owned a cafe in my hometown, Normal, Iowa. Kitty was notorious for scheduling me to work whenever I came home for a short visit, often blaming Hank, and saying that he wanted to see me. I loved working with Hank. He'd worked for my mother as a full-time cook since I was a child. Our refreshing back-and-forth banter made me feel at home. Hank was the closest thing I had to a father figure, but sometimes he acted more like an older brother. Just like my hippie, free-spirited mother was a staple at the cafe, so was Hank, who completed the majority of the cooking and prep work. The two of them had a bond that no one understood, but it worked for them. I never witnessed anything more than a friendship or a working relationship, but rumors around town always circled back to the idea that there was a secret love affair between the two of them.

Love affairs in the office place–do they ever last? Do they lead to promotions? What happens when the relationship dissolves? Could this be a potential topic for my paper? I might have to ask Hank what he thinks about this matter. I didn't even consider asking my mother these questions, because I knew her answer. She'd be appalled and give me the silent treatment.

My eyebrows rose at the possibility. Maybe that wouldn't be such a bad idea after all.

At least I'd have some drive time to brainstorm on my paper. Maybe going home to my roots would ignite a fresh idea.

Chapter 3

Growing up with a single mother in the 1980s wasn't as difficult as people like to think. I can't lie and say I missed having a father figure because I knew nothing different. Kitty was my everything.

She was a teacher. When I was six, she taught me how to ride a bike. After the training wheels were removed, she encouraged me to take a dozen deep breaths before I pushed away from the pavement. She raced down the road with me as I finally figured out how to balance myself on two wheels. When I peeled my eyes off the road in front of me to look over at her running alongside me, she was grinning from ear to ear and running barefoot, because her flip-flops had flown off as her feet pounded the pavement trying to keep up with me. She was so proud of me. She was as excited for me as I was.

"I knew you could do it, Tarasue." She shouted at me as we raced down our neighborhood street. "You can do anything you set your mind to."

She was a ruler. The whole town of Normal assumed that because she dressed like a hippie, she was lackadaisical about rules and parenting. Untrue. While she was open to discussing opposing beliefs, Kitty was strict and not someone you wanted to mess with. When I was a senior in high school, my weekend curfew was midnight, and she would not budge.

"Kitty, even Carrie's curfew is one o'clock, and her parents are the lamest." My mother didn't respond to whining, but she was known to change her decision if I made a good argument.

"Are you Carrie?" She didn't even look up.

"Kitty. I'm just making a point."

"Point heard." She flipped a braid over her shoulder.

"And?"

"And what? You're Tarasue, and your curfew is midnight. End of story."

"You're ridiculous."

She was sitting at the kitchen table paying bills when I'd blow in after school and once again complain about my curfew. I'd been invited to a party at a classmate's lake home. It didn't start until ten, and it was an hour away. It wasn't worth the trip for anyone if I had to turn around and drive home an hour after arriving. If I tried the 'I'm-staying-at-Stella's-house' line, she'd call and verify with her parents, blowing our cover. I'd learned that the hard way.

She pushed her checkbook away, put the cap on her pen, sat back in the kitchen chair, and crossed her arms across her chest. "Alright. Let's hear it. What will you do with sixty more minutes on a Friday night?"

"I dunno. That depends on where I am and who I'm with."

"One more Mary Jane? One more stiff Malibu Diet Coke? One more quick bonk with Tommy in the backseat of his cum-crusted Toyota?" My mother often used shock value to make her point.

"Kitty! Why can't you be normal? I'm not doing drugs. I'm not drinking... much. And Tommy and I have *not* had sex. We aren't even dating. That was like in middle school. So, stop that. I just want to be like everyone else."

"You want to be like Carrie? Just yesterday, you complained about her being a pampered, selfish brat. I think those were your words, right? If I recall, you said you were glad I have higher standards." Her memory was often an annoying quality. "Someday, you'll thank me. You'll appreciate that I instilled morals and values. One day, you'll realize that being like everyone else makes you boring and forgettable. A weird mom builds character."

In a deflated voice, I said, "I have enough character. I don't want any more. I just want a later curfew so I can go to a party." I stared out at the backyard through the window above the kitchen sink. Kitty came up from behind and hugged me.

I'd lost the fight and many more that followed. My midnight curfew remained. Looking back on my childhood, I no longer noticed opportunities I missed because I had to be home early. I recognized a mom who cared for me and did the very best she could. Alone.

Kitty was a friend. In my college courses, I read about how parents aren't meant to be their child's friend. However, I can speak from experience that having my mother be my friend was the icing on the cake. When I came home from school upset that Carrie called me uptight, it was Kitty who consoled me and told me that Carrie was a bitch. She was the one who rubbed circles on my back as I cried uncontrollably because my boyfriend broke up with me before graduation. It was Kitty whom I ran home to tell that I'd gotten a full-ride scholarship to Midwest University.

Kitty was my everything. I didn't miss a man who'd only given me chromosomes and was biologically connected to me through science. How could I miss something I never had? Sure, I felt left out when my best friend Stella and her dad attended our eighth-grade father-daughter dance. Her dad had given her a big bouquet of red roses and wore a bright yellow bowtie that matched her dress, but Kitty made that night special for me too. We rented a VCR player and watched the movie *9 to 5*, starring Jane Fonda. We laughed until she peed her pants, danced on the kitchen floor in our socks, and watched a few scenes over and over again.

And still, as an adult, I don't feel like I missed out on having a father figure because I had Hank. He attended all my birthday parties, taught me how to drive a car, and even introduced me to Nirvana. We shared a love of hard rock while Kitty rolled her eyes and insisted that Johnny Cash was the only man for her. Hank was an overprotective uncle, and so much more.

Walking through the front door, I smelled the ingredients of all my favorite foods–Swedish meatballs, homemade gravy, and mashed potatoes. Even though they were my favorite comfort foods, alarm bells ignited. Something was going on. She made the same meal when she had an abnormal breast exam, her mom/my grandmother died, and now... I wasn't sure.

Plus, she'd asked one of my high school classmates, Lily Armstrong, to help at the restaurant so we could spend quality time together. Kitty hardly ever took time off from work.

Is she moving? Did she and Hank finally cross the friendship line? Was she selling Kitty's Cafe? Has the breast cancer come back?

To announce my arrival, I fired off a question that had been bugging me since Christmas break. "Why do you tell everyone I'm attending college to become a nurse?"

I should've greeted her with a friendly hello, but old habits die hard. I was nervous about why she'd called me home, so I fired off a question to sway the balance of power in my favor. I put her on the defensive right away.

"Well, hello to you too, Bug. I don't know. Since you hadn't declared a major yet and expressed a desire to help people, I assumed you were interested in becoming a nurse or at least a profession in the health industry."

"You assumed wrong. Plus, people change majors all the time, and nursing isn't the only occupation that helps people. You could've corrected them." As I dropped my purse onto a kitchen chair, I continued. "Over Christmas break, Nurse Jenny asked me how I got over my fear of needles because she remembered the time I passed out when Dr. Opland gave me a flu shot."

She waved her hand at me as if my comment didn't matter. "As soon as you tell someone you're a therapist, they'll worry that you're analyzing them." Finally, the real reason. It didn't take as long as I thought. Usually, our back-and-forth banter to get the truth took at least half an hour. Either Kitty was losing her edge, or she did have something important to tell me and didn't want to waste time arguing.

"I will be, and who cares? That says more about them than about me."

"Tarasue! That isn't polite and probably unethical."

"Kitty, it isn't like I'm a mind reader. My job will be to help people, not discover their secrets to use against them. By counseling them, I'll help them see what they can't or, in most cases, refuse to acknowledge. If you'd ever been to therapy yourself, you'd understand the benefit."

Conversations about the weather, small-town gossip, and spring break plans continued for a few minutes while she finished preparing the meal. After she set the table, she clapped her hands together to announce dinner was ready. I sat down in my designated spot at our kitchen table. Unlike most kitchen table sets, our table only had three chairs, and the only people who ever used the guest chair were Hank and Stella. On normal days when we weren't expecting a guest, the chair was pushed up against the wall, because our kitchen was so small.

"Tarasue, what I need to tell you isn't going to be easy to hear or for me to say out loud. Honestly, I never wanted you to know, but I've decided that omitting the truth is the same as lying."

"Can we at least take a few bites before you break the bad news? I want to enjoy this mouthwatering meal that you went to all the trouble to make."

"Why do you think it's bad news?" After stabbing a meatball, she blew on it to cool it down.

Kitty and I've had lots of serious, hard conversations before–birth control, suicide, and sexuality–but during those conversations, I'd never seen an internal struggle in my mother like the one I was witnessing now. She wouldn't hold my gaze, and her answers to everything were short and crisp. For some reason, this discussion was difficult for her. I decided that now was not the time for one of my typical sarcastic comments.

"In the last five years, you've cooked this same meal every time you've had to tell me something you knew I wouldn't be thrilled to hear. I'm surprised that subconsciously the smell of Swedish meatballs doesn't cause me anxiety." My decision to not be sarcastic lasted about thirty seconds.

"You're not a test tube baby," Kitty blurted.

"What?" I almost choked on my meatball. I hadn't expected that declaration.

Her words were rushed, as if she needed to get them out before they ate her alive. "I didn't pick half of your DNA from a sperm bank. I know who your father is. I just didn't want *you* to ever find out."

Chapter 4

Kitty's words scratched at my brain, trying to infiltrate into the process of making sense of her words. However, my stubbornness wouldn't allow them in. No! I would not accept this bombshell, and I didn't want to try to make sense of it. I wanted to go back in time and be ignorant of this mess that was now my life. I worried about how it would change the course of my life, how I viewed myself, and my existence. No! This wasn't fair. Believing I was a product of my mother's initiative to have what she wanted without succumbing to society's pressure had been the driving force in my life to do what I wanted without feeling the need to satisfy others. Like mother, like daughter, or so I'd always thought.

As I swallowed the last of my bite, I rose from the kitchen table and paced around the room. My heart beat rapidly against my chest. I didn't understand. From the moment I could ask why I didn't have a daddy, I'd been given the same answer. Kitty expressed her desire for a child and made the inconvenient choice to have one before meeting her husband, whom she never found. She insisted she was born before her time and didn't believe in soulmates. Being true to her free spirit, she didn't follow society's rules and did what she wanted when she wanted. She marched into a sperm bank, picked my biological contributor from a catalog, and had me—her pride and joy—nine months later.

Her story was easy to believe. Her reasoning fit her personality to a T. But now as I tried to process her announcement, I wondered what part, if any, of the original story was the truth. If she'd known this whole time who my father was, then maybe she was also lying about her belief system. Did she really not want to be tied down to any one man? Did she truly believe that she'd never marry?

Was this man someone I knew? Was it the friendly man from the grocery store who always offered me a free apple to eat while Kitty and I were grocery shopping? Was it Stinky Dave who ate breakfast at the cafe every Wednesday? He claimed, "Hump day is my favorite day of the week." Then his crazy eyebrows would quickly go up and down. Or maybe it was one of my teachers from high school? Coach Knight, with his movie-star looks, seemed to be every mother's favorite.

I needed Kitty to just spit it out. My brain was going into nonproductive overdrive.

My nostrils widened with each inhale as I tried to calm myself down before I responded.

Don't say something snotty. Don't be passive-aggressive. Seek to understand, whispered the rational part of my brain.

But she lied. Lied for years! Not one little black lie. She fabricated a whole story about my existence, screamed the louder impulsive internal voice.

She must've had a good reason.

I don't care. A lie by omission is still a lie.

My internal communication silently argued. Patterns in a relationship are difficult to deny when they feel so natural. Unfortunately, now wasn't the time for me to challenge a pattern. I was angry. I'd been deceived for my whole life. My feelings were valid. I couldn't hold my tongue.

"Are you kidding me right now? Miss I'm-too-good-for-any-one-man so-I-picked-your-father-from-a-catalog is telling me that my whole existence, my whole life, has been one gigantic lie?" I laughed. Not an I-found-this-situation-hilarious laugh, more like a this-was-actually-happening laugh. "You're a piece of work, you know that? My whole life, you've taught me that honesty is the most important quality. And now, *now*, when I am twenty-three years old, you decide to tell me that my whole existence was fabricated. It was a lie!"

I hit a nerve. Her shoulders sagged, and she couldn't meet my gaze. Despite the obvious pain this revelation was causing her, I was furious. Not only had Kitty taught me to always be honest, but she also taught me to speak my mind. I bet she regretted that lesson now.

Serves her right. She hurt me, so it didn't bother me that my words hurt her. Eye for an eye.

You're lashing out at her because you don't know how to handle the news she delivered, whispered my rational voice.

Shut up!

"You know this makes me second-guess everything about my life, right? If you can lie and lie really well about this enormous fact of my life, my brain is trying to decipher what other lies you told me. Are you my real mother?" Visually, that question seemed silly, as we resembled sisters, but I was attempting to convey a point. "Is my grandmother Tammy truly dead, or do you just not want me to see her? Are you and Hank having a torrid affair?"

Is that it? Is Hank my father? Maybe that is why this is so hard. Either way, I'm going to make her say it.

I stopped pacing and stared at her. I paused my rant, allowing her to fill the silence with the truth, her truth. I attempted to catch my breath.

"I know you're upset right now–"

"Is it that obvious?" I could feel my blood boiling in my veins.

"You have every right to be–"

"Thank you for understanding my feelings," I uttered with unbridled sarcasm through my clenched teeth.

" —but hear me out, please. And then maybe you'll understand why it was hard for me to tell you the truth."

I sank back down into my designated chair at our kitchen table. My anger was causing me to sweat. I shook off my jean jacket and draped it over the back of my chair. I'd only taken one bite of my favorite meal, yet I'd suddenly lost my appetite. I pushed the plate away.

I crossed my arms over my chest, a sure sign that I wasn't open to her excuses. I'd expected a revelation today, but not one of this magnitude. This was a nightmare.

"When I was fifteen years old, my mom, your Grandma Tammy, met someone, but rather than date for a normal amount of time to get to know him, she up and married him."

The snotty, spoiled me wanted to say, *So, you're blaming your mother for your lack of morals,* but I held my tongue to let her finish. I'd save it for the moment before I stomped out the front door, which I imagined happening within the next fifteen minutes. Kitty hated when people blamed their upbringing for their behaviors, so I was curious to see where this conversation would lead.

"I should go back a little further. As you know, my biological father, your grandfather, died when I was a baby. Like you, I grew up without a father. But unlike me, my mother did not know how to be alone. She'd never been alone. As soon as she moved out of her childhood home, she married her high school sweetheart and imagined growing old with him. She was a hopeless romantic. When he died tragically, my mother was never the same. It was like half of her heart and soul died with him. She yearned to be in love again, so she went hunting for it wherever she could. But let's just say she wasn't a very good hunter. The quality of the men reflected the lack of value she had for herself. She was used, abused, and never cherished like she yearned to be.

"Years later, when she announced she met someone who was different, I was on guard. In her big brown eyes, I recognized her excitement and hunger to be loved. She wanted me to be excited and accepting of her newfound love. I remember taking a deep breath and telling myself to be happy for her. I was a teenager now, and I knew she was worried about when I'd leave for college in a few years. She'd be completely alone. Her biggest fear. A beat later she added that they were already married and he was moving in with us the following weekend. And if that information wasn't shocking enough, she told me that he had a teenage son. I went from skeptical to furious. I hadn't asked for this intrusion in my life. I didn't want to share my home or my mother with anyone else. My gut told me it wasn't good."

I vaguely remember Kitty talking about this relationship. It had been short-lived.

"My new stepfather, Gus, was a wonderful man. I'd never been so relieved to be wrong. He doted on my mother, and she glowed in his presence. Whenever they were together, they were touching. If they were in the kitchen cooking, he'd reach over and squeeze her shoulder, and she'd rest her cheek on his hand. When they walked down the aisles at the grocery store, they held hands. They were adorable and incredibly in love. I was thrilled for my mother. Gus was a godsend. After years of mourning my father and searching for love everywhere, she finally found the love she'd been looking for.

"But Gus' son, well, he was a difficult teenager. While his looks resembled his father's, his heart and soul mirrored a devil." Kitty didn't talk negatively about someone unless that person had given her good reason. My ears perked at this point in her story. "Before he graduated from middle school, he had faced multiple expulsions, burglarized a neighbor's house, and sold his deceased mother's Prozac. I feared that the bond Gus and my mother had would be tested. I don't doubt for a minute that Gus loved my mother, but I think he thought if we looked like the perfect American family, his son would fall in line as well. He hoped that by leading by example, his son would shape up. That didn't happen. The change in scenery harvested a different kind of monster."

Kitty looked devastated. I hated that she felt she had to relive this old memory, but I didn't understand what was causing her so much anguish.

"I'm sorry, Tarasue. I never wanted to tell you this, but my stepbrother, Gus's son, raped me."

Chapter 5

It took about thirty seconds for my brain to catch up to what my ears heard.

Kitty had been raped. She'd been raped by her stepbrother. What did my mother's rape as a young girl have to do with me?

Oh.

Oh, God. No.

I couldn't believe it. I didn't want to believe it. *Why tell me now?* I was twenty-three years old and managed to grow up pretty normal, considering my mother's alternative parenting style. How was I supposed to react to hearing that I was the product of a rape?

What did this information mean? I was going to be a psychologist. I was academically equipped to deal with this type of news, but first I needed to allow myself to *feel* the information. That meant shedding a lot of tears, and most likely loads of curse words. Unfortunately, my immediate response wouldn't be filled with logic or knowledge. It was coming from my gut and wounded heart.

I felt physically ill. I sank back into my chair at the kitchen table and rested my head on the tabletop. I hadn't been expecting anything like this news. I wished with all my heart that I could erase this narrative.

Is there a way to go back in time and unhear this?

"Why now? I don't understand the timing. If you've kept his identity from me this long, why change course? After all these years, why did you need to tell me now?" My forehead pressed down on my arms that were cradling my head as I lay forward on the kitchen table. My long, wavy brown hair, inherited from her, shielded me from her scrutinizing gaze. It hid all the emotions I didn't want her to see, from the tears welling in my eyes to the red-hot tips of my ears.

Kitty patted the top of my head as I dissolved into tears. "I know you think I did a terrible thing by not telling you before now, but it was all to protect you from this exact thing you're feeling. I've never regretted my decision to keep this from you, but unfortunately, you need to know. My hand was forced." She said it so quietly that I peeked out of my shield of hair.

I looked at her through my watery eyes. "I don't understand. Does he know about me?"

Quickly, she answered, "No. No. If it's up to me, he'll never know about you." She stopped playing with my hair before she said, "He was arrested recently." She let the news sink in before she added, "The authorities have discovered a lot more than they bargained for when they arrested him for soliciting a minor. The charge was just one of the many that they were pursuing against him. I guess I'm afraid they'll keep digging and come knocking on my door. I didn't want you to find out from someone else."

I sat up in my chair, wiped my tears from my face with the sleeve of my shirt, and swallowed. Not only was my beginning stained by this stranger, but he'd continued down a path of violence. A shiver ripped through my body as I understood that this man had stolen my mother's innocence and was still interested in young girls twenty-three years later. My gut told me this wasn't good.

Kitty continued to inform me of how awful the man responsible for part of my DNA was. "According to the young girl he approached, he was recruiting her to work in a brothel he planned to open in Canby. He promised her a lot of money."

"Wait! What? I read about this story." I tapped my forehead trying to make the wires connect. "Was he that preacher that used to live in Normal? Wasn't his name Pastor Tony?" Then the dots connected, and I felt bile rise in my throat. "Oh, my God. Pastor Tony Shade is my father? He was your stepbrother?"

I could tell by the pained expression on her face—her pinched lips, the deep wrinkle on her forehead, and the tears welling in her eyes—that simply saying his name and admitting his identity was hard for Kitty. However, that didn't stop me from seething with anger when the questions raced around my brain.

Her confirmation was a stiff, curt nod.

Everyone in the tri-state area knew about the scandal surrounding Pastor Tony. His notoriety was legendary. The details of the small-town sex cult were splashed on the front of every newspaper, workrooms gossiped about it, and radio DJs giggled about it during their broadcasts. Stella had called and told me. She'd been appalled that this was the same man who ran the church that she grew up in. I was not as shocked and devastated as Stella because I remembered an uncomfortable interaction with him years ago at a Bible getaway. That interaction now made my mother's news even more disgusting.

Not saying what was on my mind wasn't an option for my heart. I'd been lied to for too long, and this disquieting news was more than any human could stomach.

The bite of the delicious meatball threatened to come back up.

"He lived here in Normal for years, and you didn't consider telling me *then*?" I didn't pause long enough for her to answer. "I interacted with him. Several times. He was Stella's pastor, for God's sake. He ran Our Savior's Youth Group. I attended a Bible camp he oversaw. The fact that he raped you when you were young didn't seem like something you should warn me about? I spent time with this monster."

"You were a child. You wouldn't have been able to handle the information. You wouldn't have understood."

She had a valid point, but I was not handling it very well as an adult either. There was no guideline for the correct way to respond to this type of announcement.

"Why didn't you press charges?"

"Life was different in the 70s, Tarasue. You grew up in a different era than I did. Back then women's voices weren't strong. We were still struggling to be taken seriously. Plus, I was embarrassed and didn't want people looking at me as a rape victim. I'm not blaming my mother at all, but she begged me not to say anything. She even said she'd raise you as her own if I couldn't handle being a teenage mom. Furthermore, once you divulge that type of scandal, there is no turning back." Kitty's tone of voice sounded pained and weak, not the same one I'd grown up listening to.

"So, you kept the rape a secret from everyone? You just let people believe you were a promiscuous teenager?"

If she didn't like my line of questioning, she didn't flinch. "After my mom left Gus, we moved around a bit. We didn't lay down roots long enough for people to ask questions. Plus, I didn't care. We chose the outcome we wanted. I didn't want to stay in California and be known as a victim. I wanted more."

"What did his father, Gus, say?" Because she continued to praise Gus, I was curious how he defended his flesh and blood.

"He didn't know." Another almost whispered response.

"Wow. So, Grandma Tammy left him with no explanation? Never told him that his child raped his stepsister? Never considered telling the man she loved so much that his son was violent? She didn't feel the need to warn him to seek professional help for him?"

It was Kitty's turn for tears to pool in her eyes. "She was trying to protect me. She loved that man, but she gave up her happiness for me." She rapidly blinked, trying to stop her tears from falling.

"That's a weak excuse. You both ran because you were cowards. Rather than face the pain, you took off. Instead of doing the right thing, you chose the easy route." The words poured out of my mouth, but in my heart, I knew they weren't true.

"You think there was no pain? Do you think raising you when I was a teenager was easy? Do you think looking over my shoulder all the time was easy? Do you think leaving stability for the unknown was easy?" She was hurt by my accusation.

"Tell me differently then. Since this is the first I'm hearing about it, I'd say for years it wasn't too bad." My words were unfiltered and hurtful, but this conversation was necessary to move forward. I didn't want to revisit this topic again and again if I didn't have to.

My mom came from behind and wrapped her arms around me. I heard her whisper, "I'm so sorry, Tarasue. I love you. I know this is hard. If I could go back in time, I'd do some things differently, but I'm not sure if pressing charges and facing it head-on would've created a better result."

She was probably right, but still the news hurt.

"I can't believe this." I was talking more to myself than I was to my mother. "When I thought the other half of my biology came from an unknown man at a sperm lab, my history didn't matter. I imagined him as a college student who needed money, so he jacked off in a cup. I didn't care where he'd come from, only that his need for a couple of extra bucks had meant life for me. I was thankful. Now, when I learn that my biology came from a monster, a man who has no respect for women and thinks sex is a source of income, I'm disgusted. I don't understand how I'm supposed to digest this. I don't know how I'm supposed to react."

After I turned around and hugged her back, I stood up to pace the small kitchen again. Moving helped ignite my brain, as did vocalizing my frustrations. Kitty's gaze followed me, but her mouth remained closed.

"He's a monster. More than a monster. He started this pattern of behavior during his formative years. He preys on vulnerable girls too young to understand what is happening. They don't dare stand up for themselves. They think he's an authority figure—a pastor, for God's sake—so he knows best. And he's been like this since he was a teenager himself? He was a fucked-up kid. What is wrong with him? How did no one stop him until now? How was he not caught or charged before? Stella told me that he had a lucrative sex cult business right out of the back door of his home. For years! I don't understand. It's wrong on so many levels."

Kitty sipped her black coffee as I paced. She'd always been the calm, cool, collected one. I was the hothead. Looking back at my childhood, I now understood why her face clouded over when my temper flared. Whenever I cooled down and apologized, I used the same excuse.

"I'm sorry that I'm a hothead. I must get it from my sperm donor's genes."

My poorly timed joke earned a small smile from Kitty.

I hoped I didn't inherit anything else from him. What if his screwed-up way of thinking about sex was genetic? I stopped moving.

"I need to know what else you know about him. Does he have any family? What about your ex-stepfather? Is he normal?"

Exhaling a deep breath, Kitty said, "I know what you're thinking. Don't let your mind go there. You're nothing like him, Tarasue." When she looked up at me, she read from my expression that I needed to know even if it hurt her to give me what I needed. A moment later, she released the breath she'd been holding and said, "Unfortunately, I heard that his father, Gus, passed away. So sad. He was the kindest, most gentle man I'd ever met."

"What about his mother? You told me once that she passed away when he was younger. Does she have any family? How did she die? Was it suspicious?"

"Tony isn't a murderer, Tarasue. He is a sex addict–a violent sex addict."

"You don't know that! He could've killed someone. How did she die?" My mind was racing.

"I don't remember, and he has no other family. No siblings. I don't remember any cousins or distant relatives."

That was good. Having more skeletons and monsters in the closet would not be good.

Another question jarred my brain. "Wait. He was married when he lived here in Normal. I remember his wife. Lila or something. Did they have any kids?"

"Her name is Lisa, and no kids."

"Are you sure about that? You didn't take a moment to think about it." I fired the question.

"Yes, I know for a fact that they didn't have children." Her voice was low as if she'd been scolded.

"Okay. That's good. Maybe I'm the only one. But considering he's a sex addict, the chances that he has more offspring are high. Damn it! I don't need this right now."

"I'm sorry, honey. I wish I could tell you it wasn't true."

"You said he doesn't know about me?" With my entire being, I hoped that was true.

"He doesn't. But I don't know what is going to happen with the investigation, and like you said, you might have some half-siblings out there."

For the next fifteen minutes, I chewed on my fingernails, ripping off any excess nails while Kitty cleaned up the kitchen. This was our normal routine when we discussed heavy topics. I needed a moment to process the information while she busied herself with chores, waiting to answer any new questions my brain might create.

When I finally surrendered and decided that I needed time to process this new knowledge, I told Kitty that I couldn't spend the night and that I wanted to be alone. She understood. This wasn't easy news to stomach.

She packed my untouched meal into a Tupperware container and kissed my cheek.

"Tarasue, I wish this wasn't true, but it is. However, it doesn't need to define you. You're so much more than this."

"I know. I know that deep down, but it's still... a lot. I need to wrap my head around it to deal properly."

"I understand. You've always been like that. Very much a processor. I wish I were more like you in that regard."

"I love you, Mom."

Fresh tears glistened in her eyes. We didn't often vocalize our love for each other. It wasn't normal for us. Plus, I hardly ever called her Mom. I started calling her Kitty as a teenager after I learned her nickname. Referring to her as Mom was reserved for special occasions like Mother's Day and her birthday, but she needed to hear that I loved her and that no matter what, I'd be here. And above all else, she needed to hear the title that she earned. Mom.

Chapter 6

As I drove back to my apartment, I enjoyed the beauty of my surroundings. Iowa's landscape was a magnificent wonder that presented an entirely different personality during each of the four seasons. Summer months reminded Iowa residents why they'd chosen to live in the Midwest. The middle of the year was full of warm, sunny days and cool, peaceful evenings, with the entire state painted in shades of green. When fall arrived, every green plant celebrated the cooler temperature by changing to a beautiful burnt orange, golden yellow, or bright red color. Wildlife–deer, coyotes, pheasants, and raccoons–sprang from the cornfields. Farming equipment disturbed their hiding places. During the winter, Iowa was a stark white monster with snowdrifts reaching the rooftops. Bare tree branches glistened with frost. The tundra allowed no one to forget that Mother Nature was in charge.

When I looked out the window, I noticed signs of spring everywhere. Most of the winter snow had melted and left a wet, muddy path. The brown mess caused residents to wish away time and fast forward to warmer weather, forgetting that the higher number on the thermometer awakened the bugs that plagued the crops and tortured them. As the springtime buds beneath the soil forced their way up toward the sun, the Iowans hustled around cleaning up any traces that winter left behind. Snowblowers were replaced with lawnmowers and rakes. Long-lost neighbors ventured out of their homes to greet one another after months of hibernation. As the robins chirped, nature interpreted the arrival of spring. A renewed sense of hope filled the air.

I rolled down my window to let the fresh air calm me. I loved the smell of spring.

This stretch of the road was like any in Iowa—surrounded by flat fields. The absence of crops in the middle of March left much of the landscape dreary. Around me were acres and acres of farmland with so much future potential. I seemed to be completely alone for miles in every direction.

I inhaled a deep breath and reflected on Kitty's confession about my biological contributor. She had several valid reasons for not telling the truth. I didn't fault her for those. She wanted to erase that painful memory. Once she told the lie and everyone believed it, it was easier. Sure, she admitted that there were lots of times she wanted to tell the truth, but protecting me superseded any of them.

My mother was a strong, independent woman who'd survived more tragedy than I'd realized. My whole life I wanted to push her away and assert my independence. But in light of this news, I realized that I wanted to be more like her. Resilient. I'd learn from her example and become a better person. She was right—I wouldn't let this news define me.

Suddenly, I started to laugh so hard that my eyes watered. I pulled my car over to the side of the road about thirty miles from Normal. I laid my head back on the headrest, trying to control myself with a few measured breaths when the hiccups started, which caused me to start laughing again.

Why am I laughing? It's so inappropriate. What a mess! What a state my life, my existence, is! I should write a book! Who would buy something so messed up? I'd have to sell it as a work of fiction because no one would believe it.

Wait! I forgot all about the topic of my psychology assignment. *Could I write about this?*

A young adult learns she's a product of rape.

Technically Kitty and Tony weren't blood relatives. They were step-siblings and their parent's marriage didn't last long.

How often are intrafamilial rapes not reported? If they go unreported, how does the victim cope?

If I wrote a paper with a topic so close to home, would I be able to stay unbiased? If I researched this man, would I discover even more shocking information? Would I be able to sleep at night? Would I be better off not knowing more than I already do? Would more knowledge help me deal with this news? Was I strong enough to find out?

I didn't know. What I did know was that I wasn't a person who could take this news lying down. I was a doer. Like my mother, I never wanted to be viewed as a victim. I would seek more information until I gained a deeper understanding. I wouldn't stop until I made sure that happened. I would not allow this to define me or change the core of who I was.

If I reclaimed control, I'd learn to live with it.

As I sat in my car, I tried to recall everything I knew about Pastor Tony Shade. During the few times I attended church with Stella, his sermons were entertaining and often related to everyday life. Being the center of attention and speaking in front of a captivated audience seemed natural to him. He was a talented preacher. Perhaps he should've listened to some of his own sermons since his interpretation of the commandment, "Thou shalt not commit adultery," seemed to not apply to his own life.

I never felt like an outsider at Our Saviors. I never felt like I didn't belong, because I wasn't a member. Whenever Pastor Tony helped with the youth group, he acted like a typical, older man who simply enjoyed interacting with the younger generation. Through our discussions, he laughed, scolded, and taught us Bible lessons that we could apply to our lives. Except for one extremely awkward encounter at Bible Camp that I'd forced into the back of my memory bank, Pastor Tony's presence had never caused me any concern.

I wanted to be angry at Kitty for keeping this secret–this nightmare–from me, but I couldn't. She was dealt a shit hand, but she rose above it and was a better person because of it. I had a wonderful childhood. I never felt neglected or starved for anything. If I had part of a monster's DNA, at least the other part was from a resilient, strong, independent woman. I could rise above this.

Perhaps if I did take it on as my psychology paper, I could see it from a different perspective to help me deal with the heartache that was ripping through me. Dealing with it factually might help me wrap my brain around it.

After a glance at the road behind me, I clicked on my blinker and pulled back onto the highway. I used the rest of the drive home to sort through my ideas. I was confident that I'd be able to stay awake because I had too much to think about.

When I arrived home, my answering machine light was blinking again. It was Kitty.

"Tarasue, I love you and I've never regretted you for one second. Please understand that. You're my favorite person in the world. Well, after Oprah." She laughed. Her admiration for Oprah Winfrey was a long-standing joke in our house, because the majority of Kitty's reasoning started with the words, 'According to Oprah.' I heard her take a deep breath before saying, "I need to tell you one more thing. I'm forty years old, not fifty. I added ten years to the story to make the part about me not wanting to wait for a man to have children seem more plausible. Sorry. I hope you saved all my fifty decorations from that fabulous surprise party that you and Hank organized. We can use them again in ten years. Good night, Bug."

I smiled.

My mother was a one-of-a-kind woman who had survived so much. I couldn't even be mad at her. I continued to shake my head as I climbed the stairs to my bedroom. She loved it when people told her she looked good for her age, and now, I knew the real reason why.

Chapter 7

Summer of 1983

What happened at Our Savior's Bible Camp, where Tony was employed as the pastor, was a secret that I'd never told anyone. As a kid, I knew what had happened was wrong, but part of me believed I was to blame for putting myself in a vulnerable situation. My independent, strong mother had lectured me about the scenario so many times that I was too ashamed to admit that I'd been *that* girl, the one who knew better, the one who'd been taught not to trust every Tom, Dick, and Harry. I was ashamed that even though I assured her it would never happen to me, because I was too smart and I'd never be that weak, it did. I let it happen. I was embarrassed.

Stella's family was a member of Our Savior, so she often invited me to attend the church's youth group activities. The majority of our classmates attended them, but I was only concerned about one dark-haired boy named Tommy. During youth group gatherings, we learned Bible songs, volunteered at a local retirement home, studied passages from the Bible, and created lasting bonds. Religion wasn't a part of my upbringing, not because Kitty didn't believe in God, but because she didn't agree with organized religion. Her reasoning made sense—somehow, it always did.

"I don't need to be in a specific building to talk to God. I talk to Him all the time—when I'm cooking, going for a walk, at bedtime, and even sometimes in the bathroom. Whenever I need to, I call on Him. I'm not interested in sharing my thoughts and prayers with anyone else but Him. I don't need a sinner like me telling me that I'm not going to Heaven, because I skipped church on Sunday. No, thank you. I didn't order a side of guilt with my dinner."

Kitty and I talked about God, the Bible, and the afterlife. However, she didn't judge or push her beliefs on me. She welcomed my opinion and questions. Following youth group meetings, she enjoyed hearing about what I'd learned and discussed with the other kids. My mother and her alternative parenting style often led to great open discussions.

When Stella asked me to come along with her to Bible Camp, I begged my mom to let me go. I pulled out all the stops because I knew my crush, Tommy, was attending. "Even Lily is going."

Lily Armstrong earned a soft spot in my mother's heart when she started working at the cafe. Even though Lily grew up neglected by her parents, I was still jealous of her. Kitty thoroughly enjoyed spending time with her, and she forced a friendship on us. Lily was nothing but kind and sweet to me, and I treated her like a charity case. But I knew if Kitty heard Lily was going, she'd be more inclined to let me attend.

"Cool beans! You'll have to ask her to share a tent with you and Stella. You can do that right, Bug?"

"Of course. Does that mean I can go?"

"Yeah. Just make sure that you and Stella include Lily. Okay?"

I'd promise anything if she signed the waiver and paid the camp fee.

The Bible Camp was located in the beautiful Newton Hills. East of the Missouri River, South Dakota consisted of flat plains populated by crops planted by the hard-working farmers of the state. Over fifty percent of the fields produced corn, but soybeans, barley, and wheat could also be found growing in the adjacent fields. Perfectly aligned rows of produce formed maze-like patterns in the landscape. Beautiful shades of green and yellow dotted the land in the summer. Like the ocean on the West Coast, the green fields appeared endless. The rustle of the tall cornstalks blowing in the wind mimicked the waves crashing on sandy beaches.

Located on a one thousand-acre square piece of the state, sat a small nugget of beauty and wonder called Newton Hills. Out of nowhere, South Dakota's landscape became bumpy with lush, tall, green trees. The beautiful park-like area was named after one of its earliest residents, William Newton, who settled in the area in the 1850s along with his wife, who became an in-demand midwife.

Newton Hills was a popular destination for exploring nature, camping, fishing, and hiking. In the fall, the changing leaves brought thousands of visitors who admired the bright autumn colors. This area was known for many fall festival celebrations.

As soon as we set up our tents, Pastor Tony and his wife suggested a hike around the area to explore. We ditched our flip-flops for tennis shoes and started down one of the many trails that wound its way through the dense trees. Even though I couldn't hear all the sounds of nature surrounding us over the constant chatter of my classmates, I did notice birds fluttering from treetop to treetop causing the leaves to shuffle. The summer sun tried to penetrate through the trees, casting long sunbeams onto the trail. I wondered if any wildlife was hiding behind the bushes or tall grass, listening to our passing with a sense of relief.

As I inhaled a deep breath of the fresh air, I silently thanked God for helping convince Kitty to let me come this weekend. We'd only been here for thirty minutes, and I was already thinking this was the highlight of my summer. Just as I completed that thought, a set of long, bony fingers laced through mine. While I'd been daydreaming, Tommy had drifted to the back of the group.

"Hi," he whispered.

"Hi," I said back.

Heat rose on my neck and filled my cheeks. I was sure I looked like a radish. *Can you say, 'awkward teenager'?*

I'd been crushing on Tommy the whole year, and of course, that one-word greeting was the most I'd ever said to him.

Stella, who was walking five feet in front of us, looked back and grinned. *She told him.* I knew she'd been up to something. My best friend was known for her shenanigans, but this time I was grateful for her lack of a filter.

I smiled back.

When the group was out of earshot, Tommy asked me to be his girlfriend. After I said yes, he leaned over and squeezed my hand. The smile on his face reached up to his eyes, and I knew with one hundred percent certainty that he wanted to kiss me. Tommy explained in a whisper that there would be a full moon that night, and he suggested that we should sneak out of our tents in the middle of the night so we could see it. Along the lakeshore would be a perfect spot.

With bellies full of s'mores and Tab, the group said goodnight at 11 o'clock and crawled into our respective tents, girls in one and boys in another. For the next thirty minutes, Stella and I whispered about all the fun we were having–canoeing, fishing, hiking, making a campfire, and swimming. Even though I wanted to tell her about sneaking out to meet Tommy, I decided to keep this secret to myself. I'd tell her later. After she drifted off to sleep, I lay on my back, eyes wide open. I was too excited to sleep.

I checked my watch; it was *11:55 pm*. Like a spy slipping into enemy territory, I quietly unzipped my sleeping bag and crawled toward the tent's opening. This would be my first kiss, or at least I'd hoped he'd kiss me. The future of my kissable reputation banked on a winning escape.

I tapped my shorts pocket to make sure that my tube of chapstick and my worry bird were still secured inside. When I was eight, my mother gave me a small, stone bluebird–the size of a dime–to keep in my pocket if I ever got lonely. If I rubbed it back and forth with my fingers, she would come in spirit to me. I didn't completely believe her reasoning, but I still carried the stone with me wherever I went. She had insisted that I bring it along on my camp weekend.

The chapstick was to make sure my lips were good and ready for my first makeout session.

During the short walk to the beach, my heart fluttered and butterflies bounced around in my stomach. I'd known Tommy since first grade, but until recently I hadn't seen him as more than a goofy classmate. If I'd admitted these feelings to Kitty, she would've said it was normal and then made a lot of embarrassing references to my budding hormones. Since I was a teenager and knew everything, I kept my lips sealed and my feelings to myself.

I found a cozy spot on the beach and sat down. After the sun set, the temperature must have dropped twenty degrees. I wished I'd grabbed a sweatshirt or a blanket to wrap around my shoulders. Hopefully, Tommy's body heat would warm me up. That thought made me giggle.

The bright yellow moon hung high in the sky with a mirrored reflection on top of the lake. The water was calm, not a ripple on it. As mosquitoes bounced off the water, I noticed in the distance a couple of bats swooping in and eating the bugs. A smile formed on my lips, remembering when hours earlier Stella and I had tipped over the canoe and swallowed gallons of lake water through our laughter.

In a ceremonial gesture, I dropped the little bird onto the lakeshore and scooped up sand to make a mound over him. I wasn't a child anymore. I was a teenager. A young lady with a boyfriend. I didn't need a worry bird anymore to calm me. I patted the sand on top of him. *Goodbye, little bluebird.*

As I wiped the excess sand onto my shorts, I felt someone sit down directly behind me. I hadn't heard Tommy walk up the path. I smiled. He was so sneaky. He was taking our secret adventure very seriously.

Before I knew what was happening and was able to utter a greeting, his legs circled my body as we spooned on the beach. Both of his hands reached around and grabbed my breasts as his hot, wet lips nibbled on my earlobe.

"Oh..." I'd never been kissed before, so the idea of second base hadn't even crossed my mind. I was only thirteen. Tommy was more advanced than I'd imagined. Part of me wanted to push his hands away and explain that he was moving too fast, and another part of me wanted to enjoy this feeling and explore where his touching would lead.

I leaned my head back and moaned softly. I couldn't help myself. His nibbling on my neck ignited a tingling feeling below my waist. As my pulse raced, my blood warmed. Everywhere his lips and hands went felt good.

As he squeezed my apple-sized breasts, his sharp teeth playfully bit down on my earlobe. I felt his warm breath on my neck as he smelled me. Then a deep, throaty whisper filled my eardrum, "You smell like honey."

I jumped off the ground so startled by *his* voice that I didn't have time to digest what had happened. My body was shaking.

Pastor Tony.

What is he doing? Where is Tommy? Why is he kissing me?

Oh, my god! Pastor Tony felt me up! My first time going to second base was with an old man!

My tongue couldn't even form a sentence. There were so many things wrong with what just happened. I couldn't keep up with the questions and confusion shooting back and forth in my brain. My cheeks reddened with embarrassment, even though I wasn't sure why I should feel embarrassed.

This is wrong.

"I can see the struggle on your face. I get it. Your body reacted to my touch because you liked it. My lips created excitement in your privates, but you know that it's wrong to feel that way. Sinful even. I won't tell anyone."

I swallowed the large lump that had formed in my throat. A thousand questions fired in my brain, and worrying about my punishment for sneaking out never crossed my mind. Until now. Tears formed at the bottom of my eyes. I blinked a dozen times to stop them from falling down my cheeks.

What is going on? What just happened? Where is Tommy?

"You shouldn't have snuck out of your tent. Do you remember signing the Bible camp registration form? You agreed to follow the camp rules, and meeting someone after curfew was strictly forbidden. Tarasue, I came here, to the spot where you were supposed to meet your lover, to prove a point. You get good grades in school. You follow the rules, well, most of them. You want people to like you. But you are a sinner, and I'm here to make sure you don't do something that crosses a line that God can't forgive."

"But God forgives us for all our sins." The words exited my mouth in a whisper.

His next words were laced with fire. "So, just because the Bible teaches you that your sins are forgiven, you decide to test the theory? You planned on sinning and then simply asking for forgiveness because ours is a forgiving God? Are you testing God? I thought you were smarter than that, Tarasue." He shook his head. "I did what I did because I wanted to teach you something. Teach you that those selfish, sexual acts that you were about to perform with Tommy were sinful. Without adult supervision, you two wouldn't have been able to stop."

Pastor Tony stood up, brushing the sand off his butt as he scowled at me. "I won't tell anyone what you've done, Tarasue, but I won't forget it. I'll be watching you, and I hope for your sake God can look past your poor choice."

Tears flowed freely down my cheeks as I ran back to my tent. I felt ashamed, damned, and completely distraught. In a matter of a few minutes, my heart went from excitement and anticipation to my gut feeling sick and disgusted.

Chapter 8

My baseball teammates were typical sixth-grade boys. Instead of deep, personal conversations about weird sexual fantasies, we farted and burped a thousand times. There were dares to chug an entire can of pop after poking a hole in the bottom. Then Greg added a no-burp rule to the chugging dare. If you burped, the culprit had to pay him a dollar. Trapping large amounts of gas in your chest proved to cause terrible stomach aches, and about an hour later, loud puffs of toxic air exited your butt. The power farts lead to the next dare–lighting our farts on fire.

The smell of greasy pizza, teenage body odor, and gas caused by a poor diet filled the basement. I hoped Greg's parents planned on airing out the lower level of their house after we left. This was the kind of fun I needed after feeling so strange lately.

Unfortunately for Carson, he fell asleep around three o'clock. Instead of drawing a permanent mustache on his upper lip, a couple of boys shaved off one of his eyebrows. When he woke up the next morning, he instantly threw his baseball cap on and looked at his reflection in a mirror to check his lip for a mark. Holding back laughter, we noticed the relief on his face when he didn't see any marker lines. I bit my lip to trap my laugh inside my throat.

I wondered if this was an example of what Mr. Johnson meant when he said to regulate ourselves.

Think first. Act second.

When I returned home that weekend, I assured myself that the strange thoughts I was having were examples of what Mr. Johnson was talking about. All my friends were different, and odd in their own ways. Thankfully, my brain didn't work like Greg's. I could never come up with those strange dares and pranks, but I sure enjoyed the entertainment they provided. The boys in my class were all at different stages of this puberty thing–Greg's voice kept cracking, Kelvin had more pimples than an ant hill had ants, and Travis claimed his morning wood lasted until the bus dropped him in front of the school. Mr. Johnson was right–we were all changing. While Greg thought of the craziest pranks, my brain created somewhat violent sex scenes. I assured myself that it was a phase. So, when the dark thoughts entered my head, I wasn't appalled by them. I simply played along and had an internal conversation that no one could judge.

The following Sunday afternoon, as I watched our neighbor lady mowing her lawn, a thought formulated.

I wonder if her lipstick would stain my manhood if I made her take it in her mouth. Do you think that shade is considered red or hot pink?

When the sound of the mower cut out, I noticed Mrs. Miller staring at me. When she smiled, I saw she had lipstick on her teeth.

"Thanks for trimming my hedges last week," she yelled from behind her push mower.

"My pleasure, Mrs. Miller," I answered as I smiled back at her.

Those aren't the only hedges I can trim.

As long as these thoughts were trapped in my head, there was no harm in them. Right?

Chapter 9

March 1993

The following Monday, after returning home from Kitty's house, my alarm sounded at seven. I was going to visit Professor Doyle during her office hours, which started at eight. Technically, approval wasn't required for our paper topic, but I wanted to run my idea by her to verify I wasn't crossing any ethical lines.

I decided a walk to her office would benefit my mental health. After discovering who my biological contributor was–I refused to use the f-word or d-word when referring to him because those are earned titles–I'd been stewing. I did not want this discovery to define me, and the best way I felt that I could get ahead of the mental anguish was to immerse myself in research. After leaving Kitty's place, I spent a lot of time at the public library, where I combed through hours' worth of newspaper articles that had covered Tony Shade's trial.

I read numerous accounts from people who knew him, but each source declined to provide their names. A few church members said they had no idea what had been happening in their small town and that Tony and Lisa seemed to be respectable, lawful citizens of

Canby. One member reported, "Pastor Tony seemed well connected. After he moved to Normal, a large number of men dressed in fancy suits attended Sunday services at Our Saviors. Honestly, we thought Pastor Tony was bringing wealth to our small town. We've always been proud of our community and its values, so everyone stood a little taller and shined a little brighter whenever these strangers were in town. Innocently, most of us figured Pastor Tony was attracting the attention of influential men. No one realized that these smart suits with deep pockets were responsible for our notoriety."

A neighbor who also refused to be named said that he often noticed expensive vehicles coming and going from the Shade residence, but there was nothing to complain about. "Their gatherings were never disruptive or out of control. We had no reason for concern."

One editorial piece in a Minneapolis newspaper questioned what information was hidden.

"Residents in Normal, Iowa, are either forthcoming with their dismay or tight-lipped about being questioned. This leads me to believe if they were speaking to the press, they truly didn't know a thing about what was happening behind the closed doors of this influential, successful pastor and his obedient wife. And if they aren't talking, they may be involved. There is no way that anyone can get away with this kind of scandal without people knowing."

I couldn't wait to see what my research uncovered.

When I knocked on her office door, Professor Doyle looked up from the thick textbook she was reading. She possessed a youthful appearance, but great wisdom lay behind her eyes. Rumors claimed that she was freshly divorced after she discovered her husband sleeping with one of his co-workers. Not surprisingly, the rumors also described the scene in which Beth threatened to kill them both. Since she studied the ins and outs of criminal behavior, she knew how to do it without getting caught. The details she supplied on how she would complete the killing were too descriptive to not take her seriously. A woman scorned wasn't one to be messed with, and even though the rumor had never proved to be the truth, Professor Doyle had earned a lot of respect.

"Professor Doyle, do you have a minute?"

She set down the book on top of her desk, tucking a piece of her blonde hair behind her ear. "Yes, please come in, Miss...?"

"Tara Brady. I'm in your Abnormal Psychology class."

"Yes, I recognize you. Please come in and shut the door behind you, Miss Brady."

As soon as the door was closed, I dropped into the chair in front of her large wooden desk. Not wanting to waste her time, I said, "I know I don't need permission on the topic of my project, but I wanted to see if I could interview a subject to help prove my point."

When she leaned back, her chair squeaked due to the change in pressure points. "Of course, that would be acceptable, and I must admit I'm intrigued. How are you so sure that your subject will confirm your thesis? You haven't begun the process yet."

"Yes, but even if my research proves my hypothesis incorrect, I'd still learn something."

"Then please surge ahead." A small smile rose on her lips, and I felt like the court jester of medieval times when the jester asked permission to entertain the queen. If the jester's act or jokes pleased the queen, he would not be beheaded, and he'd live to entertain another day. "Since you have piqued my interest, can I ask what your area of study will be?"

"Nature vs. Nurture."

Her smile grew. "Ahaha, the oldest debate in history... Was I born this way? Or can I blame society? Are my mother's genes responsible for what a terrible person I am, or is it my childhood and her poor parenting skills?"

"Something like that. I plan to interview a predator that our society prefers to believe was born that way and not nurtured into a monster. It would help ease worries that there was nothing that anyone could do to stop him. It would help everyone sleep better at night."

"You as well, I assume?"

"Honestly, I don't know. I don't want to judge someone by those facts alone. I think it's a case-by-case situation." I looked down at my lap, which signaled submission or hesitation in my participation. I quickly looked back up.

"I see. You must have a personal connection with this person." Professor Doyle was observant.

I didn't answer. It was technically a question. The silence answered for me, but I held her gaze.

"My advice to you, Miss Brady, is that you keep your emotions out of your research. It is perfectly acceptable that you chose this topic because it's close to your heart, but keep your opinions out of the results. This will be a good test for what type of therapist you'll become. The best therapists can see beyond their own personal prejudice for the good of the patient's mental health."

"Yes, I'm hoping to learn a great deal from this assignment." That was the truth.

"I'm sure you will." Professor Doyle stood up to signal the end of our discussion. "Now, please be careful when you leave. I assume you've heard the news about our campus stalker? Does your roommate know where you are? Keep tabs on each other, and if you can, travel in pairs. It isn't safe to be alone."

***

Local Law Enforcement Urge Women To Stay Safe

Canby residents are asked to take necessary precautions for their safety. As soon as you enter your home, lock the door behind you. Lock your cars at night, and never travel alone. As of Saturday, five women have reported being victimized in a public area.

Police Chief Jay Nelson said at a press conference that this predator is a high-level, manipulative criminal. "He rips these women of their innocence and then makes them feel sorry for him as if he couldn't help himself. That's an intense level of manipulation." He urges the public to report anything suspicious and not trust someone you don't know. "None of the women recognized their rapist. They describe him as above-average looking, with a solid build, 5'10" to six feet tall." Police Chief Nelson confirmed that they are working on a composite sketch and will release it to the public as soon as it is complete.

Unfortunately for the authorities, this notorious man's behavior of treating his victims like he had no control over his actions has led the victims to rid themselves of physical evidence, making it hard for them to track him. One woman who didn't want to go on record said, "He cuddled me afterward, wiped away my tears, and told me that if I hadn't been so attractive and charming, he would've stayed away."

Chapter 10

Even though the rapes were the talk of the town, I wasn't worried for my safety. Maybe it was my youth and naivety that convinced me that I was safe and that no real harm would come to me. I didn't worry about him breaking into my apartment. We always kept our doors and windows locked. I wasn't actively social, but when I did go out, my roommate usually dragged me so I wasn't alone. But the fact that he didn't discriminate on age, color, or size was concerning. I needed to take the precautions more seriously.

The entire town of Canby buzzed with conversations about the rapist with a conscience. Even though he showed remorse to his victims after he attacked them, he wasn't slowing down. Reports on the Midwest University campus came in weekly. The attacks weren't limited to a specific time of day either.

Like Professor Doyle advised me, the local news and newspapers *urged all* women to stay safe, travel in pairs, and report any attacks to authorities immediately. Everyone was baffled by this predator.

Recently, the Chief of Police held a press conference to inform the public, "This man is conniving and intelligent. He isn't afraid of getting caught, because he attacks his victims in public areas in broad daylight. We aren't noticing a pattern. We need the public's help in catching this predator. If you are approached or attacked by a stranger, don't hesitate. Contact the police right away. And if you are attacked, don't shower before reporting the incident."

One woman who agreed to be interviewed as long as her face was blacked out said, "I didn't come forward immediately, because I was conflicted. He didn't hurt me. He was polite and kind, except for the rape part. He was gentle. He said he was sorry, but he couldn't help himself. His physique reminded me of Robert Redford." She shrugged her shoulders. "When it was all over, I looked at him and saw tears in his eyes."

The psychologist in me tingled with excitement at the possibility of talking with him about what drove his behavior. If he felt guilty after the act itself, was he enjoying what he was doing at all? These women didn't consent to sex, but he didn't physically harm them in another way. He didn't punch, hit, or cut them. The reports all detailed that he was gentle and kind once he gained control of his victims. Typical rape incidents include demoralizing the victim, shaming them, or blaming them for how the rapist can't control himself. A typical rapist asserts their dominance over women, because they are angry with a significant female in their life, so being considerate didn't fit the profile.

One morning before eight, the rapist grabbed a student as she walked to her first class. Behind a row of bushes, he held her at knifepoint and raped her. Before he ran away, he thanked her. Another afternoon, a woman thought she heard the mailman drop mail in the box hanging outside her condo door. As soon as she unlocked her front door to retrieve her mail, a man grabbed her, gagged her, and raped her in the front living room in broad daylight. Before leaving, he scolded her for not looking out the peephole before opening her door.

There were numerous reports of women being raped in the dark of night as well, but not one of the victim's reports helped to narrow down the suspects. He always wore a black ski mask that only showed his eyes, which were blue. One victim described his eyes as mesmerizing. "I couldn't see anything but his eyes, and they seemed conflicted with what his body was doing. I felt bad."

A rapist with manners and a conscience didn't fit the norm. Therefore, the local paper nicknamed him the Campus Rapist with a Conscience. There wasn't much known about him, because he blended in with the population. No one reported a strange man following them or lurking in a crowd. There were no reports of awkward encounters or being harassed by strange men. The descriptions collected from the victims were consistent–a tall, dark, and healthy white man with intense blue eyes had come out of nowhere, whispering that it wouldn't take long and he wouldn't hurt them if they stayed quiet. Some of the victims didn't report the attack until weeks later after the first report came out. When asked why, the answers were similar.

One woman said, "Well, he didn't *hurt* me. I've had more aggressive *consensual* sex."

According to another report, the rapist told the victim he wished he didn't have to rape her.

In the local newspaper, this week's editorial section put a sick spin on the attacks.

If you haven't heard about the man haunting Midwest University, then you live under a rock. This notorious man has made the front page of every local paper in the tri-state area. The nightly news hits the topic of his craze every night. Even the ladies at Judy's Cut and Curl hair salon are whispering about the man who preys on vulnerable women of all ages. They are intrigued and somewhat excited about this mysterious prowler.

Now, I know people are going to be skeptical of typical salon gossip, but as a seasoned news reporter, I need to confess that 99% of the time these ladies have the correct 'juice.' If I need confirmation on a source, I often check in with the regulars at Judy's Cut and Curl, because a rumor is usually backed by the truth. You just need to dig a little to find it. I have changed the names of my sources to protect their identity, but the quotes are 100% accurate.

Rose, a weekly regular at Judy's Cut and Curl, advised me that a friend of hers was attacked by the Campus

Rapist last month when leaving the salon. The ladies at the salon refer to him as Ken, like the Barbie doll.

"Audrey told Amy, who told her cousin Erin, that she'd been attacked after her hair color appointment. It was a gorgeous afternoon, so she walked to the salon. She said Ken grabbed her from behind at the edge of the park and dragged her into a grove of trees. After he had his way with her—she said it didn't last more than five minutes—Ken told her that he liked her hair better this way. She was more attractive as a blonde than a redhead."

Rose informed me that information would be important to the investigation, because Audrey had only been a redhead for one month. "She changed her mind, so she went back to her blonde roots." She raised her pointer finger at me and said, "Since he knew she was a natural blonde, he'd been watching her."

Unfortunately, not all evidence makes the news. An anonymous source told me that another victim appeared to be smitten by her attacker. She described him as attractive and well-built. Instead of fearing what would happen next, she looked at him when the rape was over and saw tears in his eyes.

How does this man convince his victims that he meant them no harm *after* he physically violated them? He forced himself literally *into* them and then made them feel bad for looking so attractive that he couldn't control himself.

Are women venturing out at night *on purpose* in the hopes of meeting this rapist with a conscience and becoming his next victim? Since when have women been so desperate for attention that they are willing to put themselves in harm's way? Are real men not giving women enough attention making them feel that this treatment is acceptable?

Chapter 11

As soon as I left Professor Doyle's office, I raced to the campus library before I changed my mind. I convinced myself that this was the last time I'd venture out alone. This couldn't wait.

To visit a prison inmate, I needed to fill out a verification form to seek the Warden's approval as well as have a background check done. The form required an explanation of why I wanted to visit, how often I planned on visiting, and my relationship with the inmate. That last question was the only one I lied about.

My name is Tara Brady. I'm a psychology student at Midwest University. For my Abnormal Psychology class, I've chosen to write a paper on what societal influences push a criminal into breaking the law. I'm seeking permission from you and inmate Anthony Shade to interview him once a week for the sole purpose of the paper's completion. If you require it, I could provide a list of questions that I'd like to discuss; however, some of the questioning will occur spontaneously depending on the inmate's answers. I'd like the freedom to do so.

I met Pastor Tony Shade when I was a child growing up in Normal, Iowa. However, I was not a member of his congregation, nor did I regularly attend his church. I doubt he will remember me. I'd prefer if we left my last name off any communication with Mr. Shade to avoid any retaliation for my findings. I'd like to begin this process as soon as possible since my assignment is due at the end of the term.

Thank you for your time and consideration.

Tara Brady

Luckily for me, forensic science recently earned great notoriety with its profile of serial criminals. Everyone was interested in discovering the 'why' behind crimes. Before profiling, most people assumed that criminals were born that way.

Through several interviews, while incarcerated, serial rapist and murderer Ed Kemper helped investigators understand the mind of a criminal. Because his answers were true and blunt, he painted a grotesque picture of the logic he created in his mind for the killings. However, not everyone wanted to hear the reasoning behind them. His explanations prompted people to question whether he would have become a killer under different circumstances.

When he was a child, Mr. Kemper killed his grandparents. When investigators asked him why he did it, his explanation was simple. He wanted to see what it felt like to take a life. After killing his grandmother, he decided to kill his grandfather because he didn't want his grandfather to know what he'd done.

During his time in an asylum, Mr. Kemper created and administered questionnaires to assist the police in discovering what type of people would commit such crimes. Even though no one wants to credit a criminal, Mr. Kemper created the questions that would forever aid the lead investigators down the right path. I wanted to use some of his ideas to probe Anthony Shade.

The concept of profiling criminals was receiving wonderful, supportive feedback. Everyone wanted to understand the minds of the deeply troubled. Including me. A local paper recently quoted the prison warden stating, "Our dependable court system defines the *how* and *when* of criminal activity, but it's the investigators, more specifically the profilers, who crack the criminal's minds and help us better understand the *why*. They're the true heroes."

I was sure that the Warden would love to be given credit for backing my findings if there were any.

Ten days later, I received a phone call that would start the ball rolling.

"Hello?"

"Hello. Is this Miss Brady?"

"Yes. This is her."

"Hi, Miss Brady. My name is Ms. Haley Gorski. I'm Warden Jespersen's secretary. He'd like to let you know that he approved your case study of Anthony Stanley Shade. He also wanted me to tell you that you're able to start the interview process on Monday. However, he'd like to explain a few ground rules before your first interview with Mr. Shade. Would you be able to meet with the Warden on Monday at one?"

My gut reaction was excitement that I was giving the green light to move ahead with my research. Interviewing an inmate would be so interesting. Then a little voice inside my head reminded me that I'd be meeting with not just any prisoner but my biological contributor. Monday was in three days. Even though I'd already created a list of questions, I still needed to mentally prepare myself for meeting him.

"Hello? Miss Brady, are you still there?"

I'd been so consumed with my internal dialogue that I forgot to speak. "Sorry. Yes, Monday at one is perfect."

Before we ended the call, Ms. Gorski explained what I was expected to wear–nothing low-cut; long pants and long sleeves were suggested, and no jewelry or belts–and where I was supposed to report to–the guard at the exterior gate would ask for my name, which she'd add to the visitor log, and three forms of identification. I wouldn't be able to enter the prison without being on a preapproved list. "Warden Jespersen takes his job very seriously." The second set of guards would also verify who I was, as well as collect any personal items that were not allowed into the building. I grabbed a notepad and pencil to write down all of her instructions.

"If you don't follow these rules for each visit, you won't be allowed in. These regulations are for your safety."

"Thank you, Ms. Gorski. I understand."

***

Over the weekend, as I prepared for the first meeting, the nerves in my stomach would not settle. Everything that I consumed caused diarrhea, and on Saturday afternoon, a pimply, stress rash developed on my neck. By Sunday night, I calculated that I'd only slept four hours all weekend. I was a wreck. I prayed that my body's response to this stress wouldn't occur before every meeting. I understood the different levels of stress that I was feeling. My collegiate career was riding on this research; however, the upset stomach, inability to sleep, and stress hives were a direct result of my meeting a relative.

For twenty-three years, all of my daydreams of meeting my biological contributor resembled a Hallmark movie, not a horror one. Even when I thought he came from a sperm bank, I never considered reaching out to find him. His contribution to my life was over. But never in any of my fantasies did I imagine that he would be in jail for even more heinous crimes. He was a monster, and I had chosen to come face-to-face with him. I questioned my sanity.

I decided not to tell Kitty about my plan. She wouldn't support my idea. Plus, she'd been shielding me from this man for my entire life out of fear. I didn't want to burden her further with unnecessary worry. I wasn't worried about my physical safety, but I figured she would be. That would be a logical response considering what she'd been through.

One of my internal voices sounded like her. The sweeter, more realistic one.

You can ace this final paper with a different topic. This is a terrible idea. No good will come from this research. What if you discover something about yourself that you don't like? What if you see yourself in him? It isn't too late to back out.

But I was stubborn. I argued with myself that I was stronger than I was giving myself credit for. I thought knowledge was power and convinced myself that it didn't matter what I learned. I was a good person. Understanding my biology would not change that.

Then I ran to the toilet and threw up.

Chapter 12

I wasn't a complete monster. I felt terrible for victimizing these women, but I couldn't help myself. Once I started, I craved the high I achieved after stalking, hunting, and then hurting them. I compared the sensation to how an alcoholic feels when he has his first drink of the day. He swishes the amber-colored liquid around in his mouth like mouthwash. A tingling sensation engulfs him. As the drink drips down the back of his dry throat, warmth fills his body. It is like water to a starving, dry plant. It's a rush. As he licks his lips, it tastes like licking a slice of heaven.

Should it taste this good? Does it taste this good for other people? Does it taste good because I know it's wrong?

Because the feeling is so intoxicating, the alcoholic wants to do it again and again, trying to duplicate that feeling when he feels larger than life. But after the third and fourth drinks, he feels nothing. He's numb. The urge to drink can't be stopped. For some reason, he can't understand that he's gone too far. None of the subsequent drinks will bring back that initial euphoria.

I empathize with the alcoholic because women are my alcohol. I crave them. I want to lick and taste them. My mouth waters just thinking about the next time I will be with one.

My eyes darted back and forth, searching for someone—a police officer or a witness—who would prevent me from having my 'fun.' This feeling reminds me of pulling out into traffic. You look left. You look right, and then back left, and right again. It's all clear. You merge into the traffic flow at the precise opening, or you'll be stuck on the side of the road for longer. Sometimes when you don't recognize the all-clear signal, you back up and decide to take a different, less dangerous route.

But it's the danger that fuels the drive. I craved danger.

Like a gambler, the first bet was the hardest. He doesn't know what he's doing. He's unsure of how to play the odds. He doesn't believe in his ability. Then he wins a hand, and confidence oozes from his pores. He tells himself that he won and that there is no need to gamble again. He's ahead of the game.

But he can't stop. He craves that feeling just before the bet is final. He wants those butterflies in his stomach again. His penis is only that hard just before it's all over. There's nothing like it.

I never thought of myself as a gambler or an addict until I thought of what I was doing, unable to stop. Following each attack, I rehashed everything that happened, wrote down the details, and basked in the glow of my achievement. And like any addict, I told myself that I wouldn't do it again. That was the last one. I had my trophies. I had fun. It was time for me to return to a normal life. Settle down and marry a woman. Have a family.

I wanted that. I wanted to be normal. I tried to be normal. I dated and courted women. I bought them flowers, opened their car doors, pulled out their seats at the dinner table, held their hands, and even participated in vanilla sex. However, I felt like an actor in a movie. I was playing a part, and it wasn't real. I yearned for one of my girlfriends to beg me to be rough, have my way with her, and tie her up. But when I introduced a little adventure into the bedroom, my suggestions were never welcomed. All that rejection made me feel like a middle school boy again. Odd. Strange. I wasn't like everyone else.

After a week of pretending to be normal, I'd feel that familiar itch to do it again and couldn't calm myself back down. My extremities tingled. Following each attack, it became increasingly difficult for me to resist the pleasure and convince myself not to indulge. Eventually, I stopped trying. I surrendered to the need. I was different. This was just what I needed.

The first woman I raped was my high school guidance counselor. It wasn't because she was mean to me. She didn't single me out or make me feel bad about myself. Honestly, it was the opposite. She was extremely kind and helpful. She told me that she saw so much potential in me that she'd help me apply for some college scholarships. I hadn't even considered going to college. My family had no money. After graduation, I planned on getting a factory job in a nearby town. The wages were higher than normal because the work was hard and the hours long.

Miss L had been the high school guidance counselor for five years. The students respected her; she was approachable and helpful. During our one-on-one visits, she'd praise me and tell me about all the things I could achieve if I believed in myself, if I applied myself, and if I tried harder. I wouldn't describe Miss L as good-looking. She truly wasn't my type at all. She was twenty years older than me, and she had at least thirty pounds on me. I can honestly admit that the main reason Miss L was my first was because she was available, and it was easy.

I'd been sexually active for years. The neighborhood college girls viewed me as a project when I was an awkward teen. In my opinion, they'd watched too many movies about being able to morph a teen boy into a full-blown hottie. They bought me clothes, tried to teach me to dance, and then took my virginity in the backseat of a station wagon. The backseat experience wasn't something I was completely proud of since both girls only needed about six minutes each to make me explode. My hormones were not prepared for such an adventure. But I credited those two with introducing me to sexual adventure and understanding that it was okay to be selfish.

By the time I decided that I was ready to take my sexual experience to the level that turned me on, I'd been having consensual sex for four years. Miss L's pep talk about how I needed to focus on things that interested me took on a meaning that she hadn't intended.

Because we met every Monday and Friday during my open period, I was soaking up information about her personal life even though she hadn't intended for that to happen. One Monday, I noticed a to-go container from a restaurant in her trash, so I commented on it.

"Weekend leftovers for lunch today?" I nodded toward her trash can.

She smiled and looked up from the papers she was shuffling on her desk. "I hope it doesn't smell like a greasy burger in here."

"I like the greasy burger smell." I winked.

"Sorry about that. I didn't finish my meal during my Friday night book club, so I saved it and finished it today. It was as good today as it was on Friday." As she motioned with the palm of her hand for me to sit down, she asked, "Did you get that college application filled out?"

Four weeks later, she had the same leftover container in her trash. I deduced that her book club meeting was once a month, which meant on those nights, she was home after dark. Furthermore, lunchroom gossip informed me that she was single and not dating anyone.

It's amazing what trivial information you can collect on someone when you aren't even trying.

Chapter 13

I chose to wear an outfit that I'd wear for a job interview. I squeezed my size eight feet into a pair of short, black pumps. A pair of black dress pants covered my legs. Under my black, professionally tailored blazer, I wore a cream button-down blouse that was securely fastened up to my neck. Normally, I'd dress up my outfit with a pearl necklace, but I'd read Lisa's testimony that her husband, Tony, had given her pearls to wear when she played her role as Madame of the Room. I did not want the sight of them triggering any old feelings, nor did I want him to visualize me in that way.

I felt confident and caffeinated after consuming five cups of coffee during the three-and-a-half-hour drive to Fort Madison from Canby, Minnesota. I practiced my introductory speech several times during the long drive.

"Hello, Mr. Shade. My name is Tara. I'm a psychology student at Midwest University. Warden Jespersen has permitted me to interview you about the crimes that brought you here to Fort Madison Correctional Facility."

My spiel sounded rehearsed, but it was the truth and professional. I didn't know what to expect from him. I imagined that he'd be slimy and cunning. He'd gotten away with so much for so long that I assumed he was a smooth talker. I tried to prepare myself for everything.

Since I preferred to be early for every appointment, I planned to arrive forty minutes before the scheduled visit. Thankfully I did because it took thirty minutes to get through security. I hadn't been prepared for that part. After that delay, only ten minutes remained for me to be nervous about meeting Warden Jespersen.

His secretary, who'd called me to schedule this meeting, was perched at a big wooden L-shaped desk outside his closed office door. She paused her typing to greet me, "Welcome, Miss Brady. I'm Ms. Gorski. Would you care for a cup of coffee or a glass of water?"

The good-looking, friendly guard who'd politely escorted me to the Warden's office, chatting the whole way about where I was from and the weather, tipped his hat at Ms. Gorski. Then he turned around, returning to his original post. I missed the opportunity to introduce myself to Ms. Gorski, but I assumed there were never surprise guests at the prison. Each guard post had confirmed my entry with the other like a well-oiled machine.

A big, bright smile filled the bottom half of her face. That grin reminded me of the Cheshire cat in Alice in Wonderland. A perfect row of straight, white teeth. Over the telephone, Haley's voice sounded rough and direct. She wasn't anything like I pictured her. Her curly, black hair that hung just below her chin was styled with one section pulled up over her right ear. Her bright red blazer matched her lipstick perfectly. I'd pictured a grumpy, old lady about to retire as the Warden's secretary, not a young, good-looking, friendly woman who was better suited for a dentist's office.

Because I took a moment too long to answer, she added, "Honestly, the water here stinks. I'm serious; it actually smells bad, like lead. The coffee is terrible too since it's made with the same water." She held up her hand to the side of her face like she was going to tell me a secret. "Capital punishment. I think they're trying to poison the prisoners slowly. I don't know why we have to suffer with them, though." She raised her hand as if she'd just come up with an idea. "Filtered water." She wrote something down on her notepad.

When my eyes widened, she laughed. "Sorry about that. I'm pulling your leg—no poison here. But I got you, didn't I? Just because I work at a prison doesn't mean I ain't got no personality."

She was right. Everyone deserves to be able to laugh no matter their occupation or workplace. "Yep, you got me. I must look pretty nervous."

She nodded her head as she looked me up and down. "I figured you could use a little joke to loosen you up." She typed a little something and then pushed her computer to the side. "Warden Jespersen isn't as bad as they make him out to be. In my opinion, he's mostly all bark, no bite. But then again, what do I know? I just run this dog and pony show. He is very curious about you, though. He loves the idea of getting inside of one of his prisoner's heads. Your request intrigued him and excited him. He'll be very interested in your findings."

"Me too. I'm trying to stay open to all possibilities so that my research isn't tainted either way."

She pointed her long, brown finger at me. "Good girl. I could tell that you're a smart cookie. You followed my advice on dressing appropriately." Her eyes traveled up and down my body as I sat cross-legged in the visitor's chair. "I've been judged by my knockers one too many times, so I keep them locked up tight. People see my size DD's and assume my brain must not have fully developed or maybe that they've sucked up all my brain activity. I let them think that and then pull the rug right out from under them." She grabbed each breast with her free hands. "These girls have done a lot for me. Can't hold their size against them."

Heat rose on my cheeks. I wasn't used to anyone being so casual with self-touching. This woman was one of a kind.

"I've got one more bit of advice for you, Hun."

"I'd love to hear it." I was exaggerating, but I knew she was going to tell me anyway.

"Let him do the talking. For a woman, it's a natural instinct to fill the silence with noise, but you can learn a lot in the quiet. He won't be able to keep his mouth shut." She winked at me.

I wasn't sure if she was talking about the Warden or Tony. It didn't seem likely that she had much contact with the prisoners, but either way, it was good advice. I nodded and smiled.

***

Ten minutes after one, Ms. Gorski said, "He's off the phone." She indicated to a red light that was no longer lit, signaling that the

Warden had disconnected his phone call. "Let's go in." She knocked politely and slowly opened the office door.

With his back to the door and looking out at the prison yard, Warden Jespersen held the phone up to his ear. *Didn't he just hang up the phone?* We entered the room as his conversation continued. "I will not tolerate disrespect. Everyone under my watch will obey the rules set by me. Tell Officer Estep to come see me. Now!" He slammed down the phone.

Was that an act?

As soon as I entered his office, I understood. This man thought very highly of himself and loved the power he had over others. The first thing I noticed when Ms. Gorski opened the door was an enormous grizzly bear head mounted on the wall that seemed to scream, 'I'm overcompensating.' I didn't know much about taxidermy, but it was clear that the angriest, killer expression had been frozen on its face. Because it was such an obvious fixture meant to intimidate guests, I wondered if he purchased the bear head or shot the bear himself. Maybe I should change the direction of my paper and study this man instead.

The Warden cleared his throat and looked up at us as if suddenly noticing us. "Sorry about that, ladies. Thank you, Ms. Gorski." He nodded to Haley as she quietly shut his office door. Walking toward me, he held out his hand. "You must be Miss Tara Brady. Nice to meet you." We shook hands. His palm was sweaty. He pulled it back almost as quickly as he offered it. "Please have a seat." He gestured to one of the office chairs that was situated directly in front of his massive desk.

When he turned to walk back to his chair behind his desk, I wiped my hand on my slacks.

"Thank you for this opportunity, Warden Jespersen. My professor is very interested in hearing about my discoveries."

"Yes, I'm sure she is. Understanding criminal behavior isn't a new concept. Scientists struggle to study the brain due to the minuscule size of its neurons. It's like a galaxy of stars. Circuit dynamics is the official term." He nodded to my briefcase. "You should write that down."

To show the respect that I'd been taught, I unzipped my bag and pulled out a notebook and pencil. I didn't want to deflate this man's ego by telling him that I probably knew more about psychology than he did. Better to let him feel he was in control.

"Profiling and understanding what makes criminals behave the way they do is a very hot political topic right now. I've often thought that rather than letting these violent offenders sponge off our tax dollars, their brains could be dissected for research."

"If the inmates were gone and dead, you'd be out of a job," I pointed out, trying to sound innocent. His idea flabbergasted me. He wanted to dissect men's brains like lab rats.

"There are plenty of other inmates who would still need the guidance and shelter I provide."

"Do you not believe in rehabilitating the prisoners?" This man's first impression was disconcerting. I was alarmed that he had the position of power that he did.

"This interview isn't about me and my belief system, Miss Brady, but when you've done this job for as long as I have, you conclude that some things are impossible." His tone of voice had a bit of edge to it. "I wanted to meet with you to discuss what you're hoping to discover and to let you know that all communication between you and Mr. Shade needs to be preapproved."

"Communications?"

"Yes. Phone calls or letters. I want copies of all communication as well as your notes following each interview. I run a tight ship here, Miss Brady, and I won't allow any illegal or immoral activity to take place under my supervision."

I didn't understand where this conversation was going, and because I've always lacked a filter, I blurted, "I'm sorry, Warden. I don't understand."

He cleared his throat as if detailing his regulations was beneath him. "I'm well aware that Mr. Shade has many adoring fans. He's made a record number of lady friends on the outside due to his lady's man reputation and devious personality, but there is a reason that he was denied bail. He is a flight risk and a threat to society. It's my job to keep him safe until his trial. You'll keep your interviews strictly professional and will not veer from them. After each visit, a guard will make a copy of your notes for me."

I blinked several times. *Did he think I was here to flirt with Tony?* I wanted to throw up.

"I understand."

"I will provide a list of additional inquiries that I'd like you to ask Mr. Shade as well." He handed me a white sheet of paper. At least twenty questions were typed on it. "I would like these questions to be your priority."

I accepted the paper from him and quickly glanced over the questions, and before I could stop them, wrinkles creased across my forehead. "Warden Jespersen, I have a thesis paper to write for my class. The deadline is in May. Some of these questions are not relevant to my research. In fact, most of them aren't. Asking them will be a waste of my time and, quite frankly, a bit disrespectful to the subject."

The Warden stood up from behind his desk. "Your *subject* is Mr. Shade, who is an inmate in *my* prison. Disrespecting a prisoner isn't a worry of mine. He is a man who has lost all of his rights because he broke the law more times than I can count. A man who raped and tortured women."

I shouldn't interrupt, but the question bubbled to the surface, "Presumed innocent until proven guilty, right?"

Warden Jespersen's eyes narrowed as he ignored my question. "Do you think I care if I dishonor a man who has no respect for others? Do you think I care if I waste your precious time? You're giving me far too much credit, Miss Brady. If I disapprove of any part of the conversations that take place between the two of you, I will forbid you from returning to this prison. Do you understand me?"

I stood up, realizing our meeting was finished. "Yes, I understand."

"My responsibility is to protect the public from threats to their safety and freedom. Don't confuse my job with a party host or a housemother at a sorority. The accusations alone make Mr. Shade a danger, and because I personally believe that this monster completed every one of the accusations, I will guard him like a hawk and toss him around like a pesky mouse if I so choose." As he peered down at me sitting in one of his office chairs, I imagined his hooked beak and sharp, curved claws that could tear into my soft, vulnerable, mouse-like skin. I felt a nervous flutter in the pit of my stomach.

Chapter 14

In hindsight, I labeled this day as the day I met two men that I wish were dead. Okay, maybe that's harsh. I don't wish them death, just hours and hours of torture until their bodies give out and they die on their own accord. I guess that's worse, but it made me feel better knowing they'd suffer a bit.

First of all, the Warden was a pompous ass. I understood that he had an important job, that he kept the worst of society locked away to keep us safe, and that his position of power gave him a huge ego. Even with all that understanding, I still detested the man, and I hated sharing copies of my interviews with him. He may know about what took place in our meeting room, but he wouldn't know the ins and outs of my brain. Warden Jespersen wanted facts. He wanted to be the first to know if I discovered anything new so that he could control the information and use it to his advantage. That was the real reason behind his excessive concern.

I was afraid of what he would do if he knew that I was biologically related to Tony. Every bone in my body told me he would use that information against me to get what he wanted. He gave me the same vibes that I'd soon feel about Tony Shade. Both men abused their power and influence when it benefited their sick desires.

After leaving the Warden's office, Haley called another guard to escort me to the conference room where pre-approved people met with the prisoners. By the time we reached that area, we'd walked through one hundred different double-locked gates, my legs were wobbly, and it was almost two o'clock. I had no idea that so much of my time would be getting from here to there.

When we reached the room and I was safely deposited in a hard, silver chair that was bolted to the floor, the guard, who stood at least seven feet tall, still hadn't spoken a word. In comparison to the guard who'd escorted me to the Warden's office earlier, this man was an angry-looking giant. I wondered if he was mute or if the warden had instructed him not to speak to me. Even though the silence felt awkward, it helped me regulate my breathing and concentrate on the significance of the next half hour of my life.

The one prayer that I repeatedly asked God to control was that Tony wouldn't recognize me from ten years ago when I attended his Bible camp. The memory of his creepy, unwelcome hands on my breast and his hot, sticky lips on my neck made me want to throw up again. If he did remember me, I planned on pretending I'd forgotten all about that weekend. I'd act like the whole thing hadn't affected me at all. I would not allow this man any satisfaction in knowing that he affected my life.

I was ninety-nine percent sure that he had no idea we were genetically related. I doubted the man even considered the consequences of his sexual assault on a woman. He wasn't a man who thought beyond the moment or beyond how anything affected him.

As far as Kitty was concerned, only she and her mother knew who impregnated her.

However, the one percent of doubt wanted to disguise my appearance as much as I could. I wore a pair of black, thick-framed glasses, and behind the fake lenses, I painted on a thick, black line of eyeliner, a coat of blue eyeshadow, and a thick layer of mascara on my lashes. My normal look was natural, which made the resemblance to my mother even more obvious, so I wanted to avoid that. When I was a kid, I never took the time to tame my wild, frizzy hair. Now, I wore it pulled tightly into a bun, but my natural waves still kinked my scalp.

When I was seated in the small, very gray conference room—gray walls, gray chairs, gray table—I took deep breaths begging my body to relax. After completing a long list of requirements to be able to sit in the same room as the convict, I was relieved to finally be sitting here. One hurdle jumped—more like four hundred yards of hurdles had been completed—now, it was time for the main event. The reason I was here. My stomach was tied in a tight ball of nerves. For the three days leading up to the meeting, my stomach didn't allow anything I consumed to stay in my stomach long enough to be digested. A constant headache throbbed in my temples. Even though I hadn't consumed a drop of alcohol in over a week, my body felt hungover. I was dehydrated from throwing up, and my head begged me to lie down and sleep.

I was rung out before this meeting even started.

While I waited for Tony to be escorted to the room, I reviewed my notes about him and the questions that I'd prepared to ask him. Everything I'd been taught had advised me to open with easy questions to help the subject warm up. With the words flowing, the patient would relax and be willing to divulge information in a calm, open environment. A wonderful listener would not react to the answers. *Simply receive input.* I needed to view this interview as a simple fact-finding mission.

I scoured the reports, newspaper clippings, and investigation. Several women have already come forward, claiming that he repeatedly forced them to have sex, sometimes with several other men. Some of his victims received money for the sexual acts. Supposedly, his wife Lisa had proof of a paper trail that Tony had instructed her to keep as their insurance policy.

There was no doubt in public opinion that he was guilty. He owned and operated a brothel, but I was curious as to why. Why did he disrespect women so much? Had he been abused? Did his mother abandon him? Those were the most likely reasons for his total lack of respect for the opposite sex. I hoped throughout our conversations he'd open up and disclose the root of those feelings.

From the pictures I found of him, he was easy on the eyes. He looked like the boy-next-door, which helped him gain the trust of his victims. Before criminal profiling and Ted Bundy, people imagined all monsters to be ugly and demonlike. However, Tony was the perfect image of an American man–sandy brown hair, bright blue eyes, a big friendly smile, and a healthy physique.

When I heard the sound of a metal gate shutting down the hallway beyond this room, I jumped slightly. For a brief moment, I'd forgotten where I was and became engrossed in my project. I straightened in my chair and stared at the door.

Take a deep breath. You're just talking. He can't hurt you unless you let him, whispered my rational voice.

Physically, no, but mentally is another story, spoke the Truth.

When the door opened, the uniformed guard entered first, held it, and gestured for Tony to enter. Because his feet were chained together, he awkwardly shuffled through the entryway, stepping sideways to get through. On his feet, he wore a pair of beat-up, black tennis shoes with no laces, just velcro straps. Because his bright orange suit hung over his ankles, I could hear, but not see, the chains that were secured to his ankles. As my eyes traveled up, I noticed his inmate number stenciled on his shirt pocket, JR3861027515. Compared to his mug shot and the newspaper clippings I'd collected, it was obvious by his sunken cheeks and deep, dark pockets under his eyes that he'd lost some sudden weight. His stubble partially covered his chiseled jawline, softening his angles. The white speckles in his whiskers made his teeth seem whiter, yet the whites of his eyes appeared duller in comparison. I wondered what that meant about his health.

As soon as his eyes met mine, the grin on his face grew. He probably thought I was fresh meat. How long had it been since he last saw a woman? Did that smile always win them over? I didn't want to know.

I swallowed the bile that had risen in my throat. He molested me with his eyes.

This convict, criminal, pedophile, and monster was my biological contributor. I wished it wasn't true. In my Hallmark daydreams, I imagined looking at him and noticing similarities. Maybe we'd share mannerisms or the same laugh. Perhaps, we'd have the same oval-shaped eyes or peak at the end of our noses. It would be comical, and the shared chemistry would bring us closer together. We'd build a relationship, and it would feel like he was always a part of my life.

I never imagined this nightmare—me sitting across from this man, the man who felt me up in eighth grade, the man who raped my mother, his stepsister. He was the monster who was convicted of raping at least fifty women. This was not part of my fantasy.

As the guard locked his handcuffs onto the table and secured his ankle cuff to the floor, I stared in fascination. The situation felt surreal. Part of me wanted to throw up, another part wanted to run, but another part wanted to dissect his brain until I discovered what made him commit these awful crimes.

"Sorry for all the fuss." Tony opened up the palms of his hands to indicate that the ridiculous fuss was the cuffs and security detail. "Normally, on a first date, I like to hold my girl's hand and whisper sweet nothings in her ear." He laughed at his joke. "But I have to admit that this is a first."

"This isn't a date." I blurted.

His grin widened more. "No, of course not. You're here because you're working on a paper for a college course. I remember now.

Sorry; I was just making a joke, but I guess it isn't that funny considering why I'm in here."

He directed his gaze toward the guard who was still standing in the corner, just off his right shoulder. A small smirk rose on his lips before disappearing quickly, making me wonder if it had happened at all.

Our first meeting had just started, and I'd already lost the upper hand. This was going to be more difficult than I'd imagined.

Chapter 15

I repeated to myself, *He is nothing more than a case study. He is nothing more than a resource for your paper.*

"Thank you for agreeing to meet with me, Mr. Shade– "

"Call me Tony."

"I'd prefer to keep this professional, so I will be addressing you as Mr. Shade if it's all the same to you." I could hear the shaking in my voice, but I silently prayed that he wouldn't notice.

"It is not."

"It is not, what?"

"It is not all the same to me, or whatever that means. Mr. Shade was my grandfather, and he was an angry, mean, old bastard who whipped me with a belt whenever he had a bad day. He had a lot of bad days." Tony stared straight at me. The smile disappeared. "Aren't you going to write that down? I was physically abused by my grandfather when I was a kid. That's probably what made me so evil. You can research the effects of abuse on sensitive, young men by their grandparents." He nodded toward the pad of paper and pen lying in front of me.

"No."

"Why not?" A small little smirk played on his lips as he waited for my response.

I eyed him back, narrowing my eyes. I counted to six before answering. "Both of your grandfathers died before you were born." That had been a test. I failed the first one when he rattled me with the date reference, but I did not take the bait on the grandfather.

The smirk rose, and he clapped his cuffed hands. He glanced back at the guard. "You brought me a live one this time, Officer Estep. And she's smart. She did her homework." Again, he laughed at his joke. "Please, Miss Tara, let's get started with your assignment."

I asked him a few basic questions about his personal history, some of which I already knew the answers to, but it was still part of the process. Even this part of our interview helped me relax. For his part, he answered them to the best of his knowledge. He wasn't sure if his mother was part German or Norwegian. He couldn't remember his father's middle name. If I hadn't known any better, I would've considered him a normal, considerate man. He was a wonderful actor.

"Part of my assignment is to understand my subject–"

"–Which is me. I'm the subject."

"Correct. I wondered if you'd start journaling." I assumed my request wouldn't be seriously considered. Most men didn't enjoy discussing their feelings, and writing about them would've been an even more strenuous task. However, I hoped he'd learn to trust me and wanted to tell his side of the story. In many of our criminology courses, we learned that criminals yearn to confess the details of their crimes. The side of the story they provided was a sick, twisted version of the truth that only their minds could comprehend, but it spiked my curiosity even more.

Tony wasn't simple-minded enough to fall for a ploy that would involve him admitting to any wrongdoing. He still claimed he was innocent and that he was only doing what he was asked to do. I prayed that in a thousand-word jumble of a journal entry, I might get a hint of what I was seeking, what everyone wanted to know. Why? How did you become this monster? But obviously, I had to go about it in a less apparent way. I needed to get him to think that his journaling would benefit him, not anyone else.

"I do not."

"You do not, what?"

"I do not want to start journaling. If you want to come here and ask me your random, time-sucking questions, I'm fine with that. It isn't often that I get to spend time with a pretty young thing like yourself. *That* I don't mind. However, if you want to discover my deepest, darkest secrets, you need to do the work yourself. I don't plan on pouring my heart out onto a piece of paper that you could use in court or hand over to the Warden. No thanks. Sorry, not that dumb, Tara. Try harder. Think outside the box."

Another point for Tony Shade. It was a long shot, and I doubted he'd go for it; however, the Warden had asked me to try. And Tony was correct—the Warden would've used every word of that journal against Tony.

"Totally understand. I had to ask. Some people find journaling therapeutic and helpful to put their feelings on paper. You can throw it away afterward or save it, but you shouldn't knock it until you try it." I pushed the legal pad toward him in case he changed his mind. I'd bought a spiral notebook that I hadn't used yet to give to Tony, but the guards took it away because the spiral wiring could be used as a weapon. I hadn't even thought about that. Luckily, they found a legal pad that I could give to him.

As he stood up, he picked up the legal pad and signaled to the guard known as Officer Estep that the meeting was over.

"We have fifteen minutes left." I yearned to ask him more questions and find out more about who he was, but I also knew that I needed to be patient. In order to form some kind of a patient-client bond, I needed his trust.

"I've reached my patience level in answering your probing questions." He wiped an imaginary ring of sweat off his forehead. "Let's call it a day. I do have *that* right still, correct?"

"Of course. We can pick up next week where we left off today. Mr. Shade, I appreciate your time and patience with this process." It took every ounce of strength to remain professional. Even as a prisoner, he acted so arrogant and superior. In real life, I wouldn't have given him the time of day.

"Oh, I can't wait." He chuckled at his sarcasm. "Thanks for the journal, Pretty Young Thing." The nickname he'd given me made my blood boil, and a shiver ran up and down my spine. That was part of his plan. He preferred me to be uncomfortable. It made him feel in control. "I'll think long and *hard* about what thoughts and feelings I have if I have any at all."

***

DATE: March 15, 1993

A guard escorted me to the Warden's office while I patiently waited for our one o'clock interview to start. The Warden was available at 1:11 pm.

After discussing the regulations of my visit, another guard showed me to the conference area of the prison. By the time we reached our destination, it was two o'clock. I waited ten minutes for Mr. Shade to arrive.

Here are the answers to the first set of questions I asked:

1. What were your parents' names? *Gus and Amelia Shade*

2. How did they meet? *According to my dad, they met at a drive-in movie theater. Something happened with the projector, and the movie stopped playing. While it was being fixed, all the teenagers hopped out of their cars and started mingling. Dad said it was love at first sight. My mom simply confirmed my dad's version of the story.*

3. What year did they get married? *I'm not sure.*

4. Where were they originally from? *I think my mother's family moved to the United States from Germany or Norway; I can't remember. My dad's family moved around often, so he didn't claim any town as home.*

5. What was your father's middle name? *I don't remember.*

6. Did your parents have a happy marriage? *I have no idea. People define happiness in many different ways.*

7. Did they argue or fight a lot? *No.*

8. What was your mother's middle and maiden name? *What is the point of these questions? Are you trying to find a rotten branch in my family tree? Find the crooked limb, and discover the reasoning for why I did what I did?*

9. What did you do? *Good follow-up question. Quick. I like you, Tara.*

Questions from Warden Jespersen that were not complete because Mr. Shade ended the interview before our time was up:

10. Do you remember a girl named Lucy Kolbeck?

11. Do you remember her mother, Molly?

Chapter 16

O n the Friday that I decided to take my desires to the next level, I felt more excited than a kid in a candy store. Adrenaline pulsed through my veins, causing me to be jumpy and restless. Every one of my senses was on high alert. The hairs on my arms prickled. Colors were brighter. I could hear our chemistry teacher pass gas when he bent over the desk of a student next to me, but luckily, I couldn't smell it.

During class, my lab partner commented on my uncontained happiness while we were working on our experiment.

"Dude, what are you grinning about? Your smile is ridiculous considering what we are doing." Josh jabbed my forearm with the eraser of his pencil.

I shook my head, but the grin did not dissipate. "Sorry. Is it that obvious?"

"Umm, yeah, to anyone with vision. You're either high or just got laid." As he pushed the microscope toward me, he added, "Prophase."

I pulled the microscope toward me and adjusted the lens. The round, dark blob between the glass sheets resembled an alien with tentacles. I'd been so preoccupied with my evening plans that I had barely paid attention during the lecture portion of the class. Josh was dependable and studious. I trusted him.

"Prophase."

***

When the sun had set and the shadows of the night settled on everything, I dressed in all black and walked to Miss L's house. Because it was a small town, her address was listed in the phone book and was located only five blocks from my house. As I snuck through the back alleys, I breathed in the fresh air. The rain subsided and left everything in its path with a shiny, wet glow. With each step bringing me closer to my destination, I breathed deeper to calm my jittery nerves. The anticipation and excitement caused an erection to grow. I adjusted myself and continued my deep breathing.

Focus.

I didn't have a detailed plan of what I was going to do once I overtook her. As soon as I successfully broke into her house and trapped her, I wanted the rest to come naturally. I wanted to follow my instincts. I wanted it to be spontaneous and wild.

When I arrived at her little house on the corner of a very quiet, dark street, I crept up to a window and peeked in. During my pre-sex days, I was an active Peeping Tom. I looked in windows, dressing rooms, bathroom stalls, and even into cars parked at the drive-in movies. Fortunately, my youthful appearance led people to overlook my actions when they caught me.

"Boys are naturally curious."

"He doesn't even know what he's looking at."

"Puberty is a confusing time for young boys nowadays."

Sometimes, the couple I was spying on would ruffle my hair and send me on my way. My lack of height was a benefit in this situation. People thought I was younger than I was. At the drive-in movie theater, car windows that were steamed over were a dead indicator that some heavy panting was taking place inside. One night, I noticed a brown four-door Buick slightly rocking. I crept up to the window and tried to peer in. The male inside the car noticed me looking in, and rather than appearing shocked and appalled, he smiled at me as he shoved harder into his date. He even rubbed away some of the steam so I could get a better view. He enjoyed having an audience.

I wanted to be that man in the car, the one having sex, but I had no idea how to approach a girl. So, I studied the teenagers before they climbed in the steamy cars, while they were holding hands, and when they were kissing. I watched their dating rituals. To my delight a few months later, some eager girls were willing to teach me.

As soon as I lost my virginity, spying and watching others lost its appeal. Being a Peeping Tom didn't excite me anymore. I wanted only to be participating. Unfortunately, all too soon, I grew bored of sex too. Consensual sex was losing its excitement just like my Peeping Tom adventures did. I yearned for something more, which led me to stalking Miss L.

Confirming that her car was not in the carport of the driveway, I reasoned Miss L wasn't home yet. There was a small lamp sitting on an end table lit so that she wouldn't trip on anything when she came home. If she'd been home, the TV would've been on, an empty TV dinner discarded and Miss L sleeping on the couch. Usually, a little drool hung from her open mouth. Every Friday night for the past month, this was my routine. I'd eat supper, excuse myself to my room to read, and then I'd sneak out of the house to check on Miss L.

And just like I figured, Miss L was attending her monthly book club meeting at the local restaurant. This much I'd planned because I studied her routine. Her cozy, little, two-bedroom house was empty. Miss L was a woman of routine. She'd order the bacon cheeseburger with french fries and only eat half of it. She'd request a to-go box so she could eat the other half of her burger for Monday's lunch.

Calculating her return home within the next fifteen minutes, I plucked the spare key from under the potted plant that she had sitting on the little table and chair set on her back porch. The week before, I'd unscrewed the light bulb from the light, and now noticed that she still hadn't checked or changed it. I figured as much. She was a busy lady and wasn't usually up much past ten. She probably didn't even notice that the light was out.

When I heard the deadbolt click open, I placed the key back under the pot and slipped inside. The door led into the small kitchen. I took a deep breath, willing myself to remember everything about this moment. This was a first.

Even though I didn't see any fresh, blooming lilacs, the entire kitchen smelled like them. A small night light in the corner of the room helped me see my way around. Stationed next to the back door stood the tall, white refrigerator humming its usual greeting. Underneath the small kitchen window, the sink contained only a coffee cup and a small plate.

Probably a quick breakfast before school. On the counter, a toaster and coffee pot sat. The kitchen was spotless and felt very homey with a small white kitchen table inviting its guests to sit.

I wiped my feet off on the small rug. I didn't want to track into her house for a couple of reasons. I didn't want to make a mess that Miss L would have to clean up. I also didn't want any visual footprints to indicate someone was in the house. Even though I'd refused to plan the sex, I did know that I wanted the element of surprise to be on my side. That part excited me.

As I exited the linoleum of Miss L's kitchen, I stepped onto the plush, cream carpet in her living room. Her decorating style was simple and cozy. She arranged two dark brown loveseats in an L shape in the room, facing the small TV in her entertainment center. On the built-in shelves along the wall, located between the two rooms, were approximately twenty candles, twenty novels, and a plant that needed some TLC.

The front entryway had been built on the opposite side of the living room. It was located just below the stairs that led up to the two bedrooms and bathroom. The house was small but perfect for a single woman, I assumed. Even though I was the only one in the home, I tiptoed up the stairs in search of the master bedroom where I planned on watching Miss L get undressed before I pounced on her.

Discovering which one was her bedroom was easy. The guest room didn't have anything but boxes. Miss L's bedroom had a big queen-sized bed in the center of it. She'd decorated it with a rose-embossed pink comforter and about ten throw pillows. On each side *of the bed was a nightstand with a lamp. She must sleep on the left side of the bed since that was the side that had a box of tissues, an empty glass of water, and a novel with a bookmark in it. I picked up the book to see the front cover.*

Miss L likes spicy romance novels. Interesting.

The entry to the bathroom was only available from the hallway. Unfortunately for me, I wouldn't be able to watch Miss L's nightly bedtime routine from the closet I planned on hiding in. Her closet was long with accordion-style doors. They reminded me of the closet ET hid in when Elliot didn't want his mom to discover his new, strange, alien friend.

The faint smell of her perfume still lingered in the air. It probably stained the walls. Before I hid, I lay down on her bed. Her bed was significantly softer than my hard, cheap mattress that was as flat as a board. When I looked up at the ceiling, I saw a dusty, ornamental ceiling fan hanging at the center of her bed. This was what she would see as I thrust into her. A small smile rose on my lips as I felt myself grow hard.

Suddenly, I heard the front door slamming shut on the floor beneath me. She was home early from her book club. I quickly rose from her bed and smoothed out the comforter, removing my imprint. As softly as I could, I tiptoed to the closet and slowly opened the doors, praying that they would not squeak. Cautiously, I moved inside and pulled the door closed behind me.

Calm down, slick, or you'll explode before you even touch her.

My breathing was becoming labored as I anticipated her arrival.
I pulled down my ski mask and peeked through the crack in the door
opening. I couldn't hear any more noises from below. I imagined her
placing her half-eaten burger in the refrigerator and perhaps opening
some mail. From my Peeping Tom escapades, I'd learned that she
wasn't much of a night owl.

What if she decides to watch TV? Then she might fall asleep on the
couch. How long do I wait up here?

Nerves bounced around in my stomach. Studies show that over 75%
of the reported rapes were committed by someone they knew. If Miss
L reported her rape to the police, I wanted her to think her attack was
committed by a stranger. I decided that in order for that to happen, I
would not allow myself to talk for fear she would recognize my voice or
I would say something that only one of her students would know. Miss
L was a nice lady, and I figured if she thought she was being stalked by
someone she knew, it would be worse than a stranger or an unprovoked
attack.

How long has it been since she came in the front door? Fifteen
minutes? What is she doing?

I wasn't sure but remained steady. Holding my position in the closet,
I finally heard her feet pounding up the stairs. My pulse started to
quicken as my breathing intensified.

This is it.

The flick of the light switch announced her arrival in her bedroom.
She kicked off her shoes and sat down on the edge of her bed to pull
off her socks. She rolled them into a small ball, lifted her arms above

her head, and tossed one of the socks into her cloth hamper, which was positioned in the corner of her bedroom, just two feet from the closet doors.

"She shoots, she aims, and she scores!" She leaped off her bed and did a little victory dance. "Lainey Leekster has tied the game, folks. Will she be able to pull off the win for the home team? One more shot, and we will see." Miss L imitated a basketball announcer. She drew back her form and aimed her sock. I watched her throw her balled-up sock into her hamper; she missed. Her black sock unfolded itself after impact, and Miss L flopped down on her bed. "Fans, this may be the worst night in Lainey's life."

Chapter 17

"These questions bore me." He pushed his chair back from the table and crossed his arms over his chest. He mimicked my voice. "*Did you have a pet?* What kind of question is that?"

"If we don't stick to the script, Warden Jespersen won't allow me to keep coming here." I sighed. I wasn't getting far with my standard questions, and I hadn't discovered anything significant yet.

"Fine by me. Good riddance. This is a waste of my time anyway."

I was done playing nice. Each week I drove three and a half hours for a half-hour meeting that I spent preparing for all week. This was our fourth interview, and I hadn't gotten much useful information from him yet. Tony only shared if he felt he was in control and benefitting from what he shared. After our second interview, I recognized that Tony pouted like a child when he wasn't entertained. I set my clipboard on my lap and looked at him, challenging who wanted to be where. "You don't have anything better to do."

"Not true. The lively bingo game is occurring right now in the main area. The winning prize is a KitKat. You don't know how far I'd go to wrap my hands and then my lips around a KitKat."

"If you don't want to answer my questions, we can be done here." I challenged him. "But I wonder how long it'll be until your next visitor. Your only regular visitors are me and your lawyer—who, in my opinion, wishes you'd get shanked because representing a pedophile pastor isn't great for his reputation. Your so-called friends from Normal only come to ensure that you aren't ratting them out and that their secret is still safe with you. They don't give a rat's ass if you are healthy or happy. In fact, like your lawyer, they think you'd be better off dead, which makes me curious as to why you're still here. Everyone would rather see you get sliced and diced. How does that make you feel? That no one enjoys your company?"

As I watched him take in my words, I studied him for a shift in his conscience, maybe a flicker of guilt, or heaven forbid, remorse, but I didn't detect any. The words rolled off my tongue as sound waves entered his ears, but there was no proof that he comprehended a word I said. He was stone.

In the corner of my eye, I saw Officer Estep's eyebrow raise.

I waited patiently for his response. When no words are spoken, psychologists are taught to watch for nonverbal cues like changes in pupil dilation, which could indicate emotional processing, or arms that are suddenly folded across the chest to indicate defiance. I watched his lips to look for signs of stress. If he bit the side of his lip, it could indicate that he was anxious, and pressed lips would show disapproval or distrust.

However, Tony built a wall. His expression and posture didn't change in the slightest. I watched him to see if he was even breathing or blinking. He reminded me of a statue. Initially, his steady gaze proved that he was engaged and interested in our conversation. Now silent, he contemplated his next move. His unwavering stare was threatening as he asserted his power without saying a word.

After what seemed like thirty minutes but was only four minutes, I ripped my gaze from his and started to pack up my belongings. I'd truly hoped for more from him. I'd hoped that he was so filled with guilt that he would want to explain everything he did and why. I hadn't imagined it would be like pulling teeth, and he wouldn't want to brag about all the crazy shit he did. I assumed that with my constant badgering, we would have an *A Few Good Men* moment–'You can't handle the truth!'

Tony wasn't interested in revealing anything about what led him to commit these horrendous crimes against women. I studied his nonverbal responses, the unspoken words, and his acts of defiance. But I needed something that would create a strong reaction. I needed to come up with something that would interest him. Motivate him to tell his side.

As these thoughts bounced around in my brain, I heard Tony's husky voice. "Ask what you *really* want to know. You can't truly be interested in what my first pet's name was." He sat up, his chest touching the table. With a smirk on his lips and a dark twinkle in his eye, he said, "Or perhaps you're as hollow as you appear. Just an ornament with no real substance inside. Ask me what is keeping you awake at night. I dare you, Pretty Young Thing. I double-dog dare you."

The disgust and hatred that boiled under my skin for this man bubbled to the surface.

Never one to back down from a legit dare, I spewed out, "When did your sexual frustrations peak? When did you know your sexual taste wasn't like other normal men? How old were you when you first took advantage of a woman? Is there a pivotal event from your childhood that fueled the monster within you?"

A large smile grew on his face. It reminded me of a killer clown smile, full of insane satisfaction. "Well, that didn't take much probing. I knew you had it in you. You look like the type who'd fight to the death. Claw your way about a grave if buried alive. Maybe even bite an attacker." When he muttered his last comment, he licked his lips.

I shivered despite myself. I couldn't control it. He disgusted me, and a small part of me was afraid of him. Imagining him touching me and exploring my body without my consent caused another shiver to envelop my body. Tony noticed.

Stop! Don't react to him.

This was what he wanted. Tony wanted me to show my vulnerability. It was what he craved. After being locked up, he'd been denied the thing he craved the most—dominating a woman. I would allow him to do it with his words because I could shake it off. I was getting what I wanted as well—a glimpse into the real person he was.

Be strong, Tara. It is just words. What hurts you makes you stronger.

"To answer your questions, while growing up, I did not have a pet. So, you can rule out animal bestiality. Sorry." He winked at me, and it took every fiber in my being not to react to his gesture. He sat back in his chair and looked up to the ceiling for his answers. "Puberty for me, like for every teenager, was difficult. My body reacted to stimuli that it normally hadn't before. But if you must know, I'm not a monster, Tara. I know that would change the direction of your paper, but you won't discover a revelation that suddenly made me appreciate women's bodies and what they could do for me more than any other man. All men are like me. All men have perverse thoughts like I do. The difference is that I acted on them. I did what was natural. I enjoyed everything that a woman's body had to offer. I–"

"Offer? Are you kidding me with your choice of words? Most of these women did not *offer* themselves to you. You used them. You used their bodies for your own sick pleasure." Everything I'd learned up to this point advised me not to interrupt, even if the patient was outright lying, as Tony was. I was struggling to remain professional when I was appalled.

"Pretty Young Thing, I wish you'd get your facts straight. Not everything you read about me in the papers is true. These women offered their bodies in service and were paid handsomely for that. Did some of them regret what happened? I'm sure, but they were not raped. They weren't forced into doing things they didn't want to do."

"Wow. Has your lawyer not informed you of how many women are coming forward and supplying details of their rapes?" I shook my head. I studied pathological liars during my classes, but I'd never seen one in action. "At least twelve women claim that you tied them up for hours at a time, and you locked them in a room with several different naked men for the sole purpose of abusing them. You seduced young girls right off the street. Are you implying that all those allegations are false?"

"They came willingly. They signed a release form. They received money for their services. Like I said, many may regret agreeing to it, but that doesn't make me a monster. You make it seem like a horror movie."

"Exactly." The red-hot blood pulsed through my veins, making my disgust and anger bubble to the surface. I couldn't stop myself. He pushed my buttons. If I'd been a naturally violent person, I would've reached across the table and scratched at his face. His good-looking, chiseled face. The one that charmed and seduced hundreds of women. I hated him. My nostrils flared as I tried to hold back my temper. I could hardly believe this man and I shared the same DNA.

Hot, heavy tears threatened to pool in my eyes. I blinked rapidly for several seconds.

Do not show weakness. He is research.

Through clenched teeth, I said. "The women were unable to leave. You'd locked them in a room. You demanded that they take off their clothing and then proceeded to tie their legs and arms to the furniture. They were prisoners. Sex slaves." I tried to make my words sound unemotional, but I was failing.

"Well, I was hoping to change your opinion of me, but it's taking longer than I thought. We only have, what? Four more sessions and then you've reached your invitation limits. I wonder if you have enough already to warrant Warden Jespersen's approval. Maybe he'll allow you to come this summer just for entertainment purposes."

He pushed his chair away from the table and stood up. His hands were cuffed together with about six inches of room while his feet were cuffed with about ten inches to shuffle. After he nodded to the guard standing in the corner of the room that he was finished with our meeting, he looked back at me and smiled. "Thank you for your time today, Pretty Young Thing. I look forward to more thought-provoking questions next week."

***

DATE: April 12, 1993

I arrived for my weekly, preapproved interview with Mr. Anthony Shade (inmate #JR3861027515). I waited ten minutes for Mr. Shade to arrive.

Summary of our discussion:

12.   Were you physically abused as a child? *I guess my answer depends on what you think is physical abuse. I received several spankings and a few slaps as a child. And no, I didn't enjoy them, but they were quite effective forms of punishment. It's not like it is now; every time someone touches you, you need to evaluate how you feel about it. People are too damn sensitive. Getting the belt and a quick slam across the cheek worked.*

13.   What did you get spanked for? *I grew up like any normal American child. I was spanked because I sassed my father, lied about doing my chores, cheated on a spelling test, or spit my dinner out.*

14. Why did you spit out your food? *I told my mother that it tasted like ass and I couldn't swallow it for fear it would kill me from the inside out. I may have added that a homeless, two-bit whore could cook better than her.*

15.   I bet that hurt her feelings. *Yep. There were tears.*

16.   How old were you when your mother died? What was her cause of death? *Why are you asking me questions about my childhood? How is that relevant? My mother never abused me, never harmed me in any way, and no, I didn't feel abandoned when she died. She had cancer. These things happen.*

17.   Were you ever diagnosed with any mental illnesses? *Do you think I'm mentally ill? This is hilarious. Next question.*

18.   Did you have a pet growing up? *I never had a pet.*

Questions from Warden Jespersen that were not complete because Mr. Shade ended the interview before our time was up:

19.   Do you consider yourself a pedophile or sex addict?

20.   Did you keep trophies from all your conquests? If so, where are they now?

Chapter 18

Quickly, I discovered writing this paper while collecting extremely sensitive information would not be easy. I'd overestimated my ability to desensitize myself. The things he was revealing to me actually happened. These were real women, and what had happened in Normal, Iowa, was horrific. As I was beginning to understand Tony's nonverbal cues, I realized that some of the original answers might not have been completely true. I just wasn't sure what parts.

Even though it was difficult to admit, I looked forward to our weekly interviews. Each visit was like opening a gift, but only being able to peel one piece of tape off each time. The anticipation was intense, and my imagination was working overtime wondering what I'd discover next.

Unfortunately, the logical part of my brain reminded me that I might never truly be able to disclose everything inside the 'gift.' The optimistic part of me excitedly responded that Tony was an onion. Each layer was as ripe and stinky as the last, but after each visit, I understood a little bit more about the mystery that was Tony Shade. I felt like a true therapist, but I didn't know if I was helping my 'patient' or fulfilling my own sick interest.

Last week, I received a phone call from Haley Gorski, the Warden's secretary, to inform me that her boss wasn't pleased that I hadn't asked Tony any of the questions he provided.

"Hun, my advice is to provide the Warden a little drop to satisfy his thirst. Women are the neck, so we have the power to turn a man's head."

"Um Okay. Ms. Gorski, do you always speak in riddles?"

She giggled. "Hun, you're young. Give it some time, and you'll see I'm right."

"Thank you for calling, Ms. Gorski. I'll take that under advisement."

"I've seen a copy of your notes. You're doing great, and the Warden's questions are off-color, but what if Tony truthfully answered one? Wouldn't that be something?"

Even though the Warden's questions were harsh and frowned upon, if I wanted to get him to open up to me, I decided to try that route at least once.

***

"According to the Lutheran Synod, your pastoral license has been revoked. You've been stripped of your professional title. They issued a statement that was printed in several of the towns where you'd lived." I read an article out loud.

The Lutheran congregation of Our Savior's was deeply saddened by the news of the immorality and sinfulness of a previous head pastor, Mr. Anthony Shade. One of the congregation members who regularly volunteered at Our Savior's was appalled by the news of his arrest. Karen Henry told us, "The church attendance increased immediately when he arrived. At first, it was due to morbid curiosity–people were comparing him to a young Paul Newman. But then his sermons were so interesting and inspiring. He had a true gift to engage people. But I had no idea what was happening behind the closed doors in his home. Just appalling."

I set down my copy of the newspaper clipping and looked up at Tony.

"Wow. Good afternoon to you, too. It must be your moon cycle, Pretty Young Thing." Tony threw his head back and laughed. "So, we're jumping right in today. No small talk, no wasted time." He glanced back at Officer Estep, who showed no reaction to my bluntness. "I have to respect that."

"How do you feel hearing that? Are you disappointed that your title was revoked?" I powered forward.

"You make it sound like I was royalty. I wasn't a prince or a duke, but it tickles me that you think of me like that."

I ignored his flirtatious comment. "You enjoyed your job as a pastor, right?"

"Yes."

"How does it make you feel that you aren't allowed to do it anymore?"

"I'm in jail. It doesn't bother me."

"When you get out–if you get out–you won't be able to serve any Lutheran church, and that doesn't bother you?"

"No, not really. I'm sure I'll find something to occupy my time. Are you worried about me, Pretty Young Thing? I'm flattered."

"Tara." I corrected him, even though I wasn't sure why I had wasted my time in correcting him. "How does it make you feel to hear Karen Henry once called you a great preacher?"

"Her opinion means nothing to me. Karen was a nosy, gossipy old biddy who volunteered at the church because she wanted to boss people around. She didn't care if she was helping people. She just wanted to be in charge of something since no one at home gave a lick about her. And no, I'm not surprised to hear that she enjoyed my sermons. I'm a great storyteller, and the majority of those people who sat for hours in those hard pews are lonely and pathetic. They're sponges, yearning for an answer to their miserable prayers. I'm used to being an answer to a prayer." A small chuckle echoed in the conference room.

"So, you describe yourself as a storyteller, not a pastor; a man of God?"

"Now, we're getting somewhere. Did the hairs on your arms spike when you came to that realization?" He laughed again.

Damn it. I hated how perceptive he was, always one step ahead of my questioning. I subconsciously rubbed down the hair on my arms. If allowing him to feel like he was in control of this interview helped me get the answers I wanted, I'd be willing to relinquish control.

"I find it truly sad and completely unholy that your influence on several congregations was merely a source of income and not a vessel to inform others of the teachings of the Bible. Most people choose a career based on their passion. Don't people in your profession consider it a calling, inspired by God to serve the greater good?"

"Tara, is that what you want me to call you?" I raised my eyebrows in response. He knew the answer to that question. "Tara, I'm a simple man. While I was in college, I was required to declare a major. My advisor had me fill out a questionnaire, a lot like the boring questions you're asking me, to find out my strengths and interests. Lo and behold, I'd make a wonderful speaker. When I talked, people listened. There was a power of persuasion in my words."

"You're implying that it wasn't until this college questionnaire that you became interested in being a pastor?"

"Correct." His condescending tone made me excited to ask my next question.

"That's interesting because according to someone who knew you when you were a teenager, you had an unhealthy obsession with a pastor *before* college."

His small, relaxed smile froze on his face. In his eyes, I noticed his pupils dilate. I returned his stare, but from the corner of my eye,

I noticed Officer Estep's stance shift slightly. I'd earned both men's attention.

"Someone from my teenage years? Have you been snooping around in my past?" He didn't seem too pleased.

I ignored his questions and surged ahead. "Is it true that you became obsessed with religion and that the church officials at your hometown church requested that you not attend any church services alone? That you must be accompanied by an adult even though you were only fourteen? Why was that? What happened that a *church* would be forced to establish such a strange guideline for a teenager?"

I was asking questions that I knew the answers to, to gauge if he was telling the truth or not. This was one of those times. "Does this have anything to do with your sealed police record?"

The frozen smile faded quickly as his eyes narrowed. Normally, this was the point in our discussion that he'd excuse himself because he didn't want to answer my questions.

"Miss Brady, you're surprising me today. I'm not sure if I like it or not, but I'll admit that I'm intrigued. Who told you about the ridiculous allegations from that church?"

"I'm sorry, but I'm not allowed to reveal my source."

"Of course, she requested that. She always liked to quietly stir up drama and then innocently back away." Under his breath, he added, "Or run away." His gaze moved to the ceiling as he reflected on his memory. "I guess you could describe it as an unhealthy interest in a pastor. Every Sunday during his sermon, I noticed that every word flowing out of his mouth mesmerized the congregation. His words calmed the crowd. No one spoke. His teaching filled a space in their souls. I remember looking around the church in awe as the people hung on his every word. Everyone believed this man. Everyone trusted him. This man interpreted a book that was centuries old, and no one questioned a damn thing he said." He paused and returned his attention to me. "Except me. I didn't believe him. I didn't trust him. I questioned what he said, and he didn't appreciate my doubt. He banned me from attending without my father sitting next to me because he worried that my questions deflated his flock's trust."

If a blood pressure cuff could measure the temperature of someone's blood, Tony's would be boiling at 212 F. His nostrils flared as the words poured out of his mouth without his usual filter. I decided that I had nothing to lose.

"What did you do to him? You must've done something more than question his authority. It doesn't make sense."

"I did nothing to that weak, pitiful man. He couldn't handle anyone questioning his authority or his interpretation of the Bible. I was new to the church. What did I know? I was merely a boy, and he was supposedly an educated, intelligent adult. According to him, I had no right to question him in front of his congregation, his flock, or his people. He liked his followers to be obedient and unquestioning. The man's ego was overinflated."

"You must have done *something* that required an escort to a church service. That isn't a normal practice for a church."

He glared at me. "You know what, Tara? I feel like teaching you a lesson. Don't ask a question if you aren't willing to hear the answer.

Don't assume that since you know partial facts, you can put the pieces together. You don't. You can't. This time, your assumptions about me are incorrect.

"I was a fourteen-year-old sponge. I wanted to learn. I wanted to understand." The words—his confession—tumbled out. "And that filthy, old bastard assumed that my questions demeaned *him*. He called me out during one of his Sunday sermons in front of everyone! Stared right at me when he preached: 'Do you remember Judas, the man who betrayed Jesus? Judas, the man responsible for leading to the downfall of his reign? He questioned Jesus and his generosity. He thought he was better than Jesus. He believed he had a better understanding of how to handle the bounty. But he didn't. He was a sinner—an inexperienced sinner who should've trusted Jesus and his teachings rather than publicly defy him.' Everyone knew he was speaking directly to me. That day during the service, every single person in that room stared at me, turned to their family, and whispered about how I must've been spawned from the Devil. The man who was supposed to guide others toward a righteous life compared me to a thief. He compared me to the most hated man in the Bible."

Tony abruptly shifted in his chair, causing his chains to rattle. I jumped.

"How do you think that made me feel? I was only fourteen and looking for guidance. My mother had just died, and I was trying to understand. I idolized that man, and he demoralized me. Out of pure jealousy and fear, he made me look like a freak to protect himself and his precious reputation. How do you think everyone looked at me after that?" He paused as if waiting for my reply. I could smell the coffee on his breath. "With full-blown pity and mistrust. Even my own father wondered what evil lay under my skin. I was never the same after that, and rightfully so." He dropped back into his relaxed position.

The silence in the room was thick. I wasn't sure what to say. I hesitated to speak, fearing Tony might have more to say. As I quickly glanced at Officer Estep, I noticed that his eyes widened as he attempted to gauge Tony's mood.

When he spoke again a minute later, his voice was void of the anger that had caused the weighted silence. Tony had regained control. "Pastor Gerald might have gotten the last word that Sunday in front of the whole town, but I believe I left my mark on him, his wife, his sister, and his daughter. He regretted what he did to me. I know it.

"And even though he predicted I was Judas, I didn't hang myself like Judas did. *He* did a few years later. The poor old man thought suicide would be an escape. I wonder how Hell is treating him."

The smirk on his lips caused the goosebumps on my arms to rise again.

***

DATE: April 19, 1993

Check-in went smoothly this afternoon. I waited the usual ten minutes for Mr. Shade to arrive.

Topics discussed today:

21. Why did you choose to become a pastor? *In college, I answered a questionnaire that suggested I pursue a public service job that involved speaking and gaining influence and power. I've always been very interested in the Bible and its teachings. It seemed like the perfect fit.*

22. The Lutheran Church has declared you unfit to be a pastor. Your earned diploma has been revoked. How does that make you feel? *Like I wasted a lot of time and money on a college education. (He laughed) It doesn't bother me. I'm in jail. I've been stripped of my rights.*

Questions supplied by Warden Jespersen:

23. There is a sealed record from the state of Iowa. Tony was fourteen at the time. What is in that record? *(In a roundabout way, I discovered that his sealed record was from an incident at his hometown church when Tony was fourteen. It might have had something to do with the residing pastor, Gerald, who ultimately committed suicide.)*

24. Have you ever been sexually abused? *I know what you are getting at. You think the closed record is a sexual allegation. Pastor Gerald did not molest me. I don't even think the old, wrinkly man could get it up.*

Questions that were not completed because our time was up:

25. Do you feel guilty for harming the women who charged you with raping them?

Chapter 19

Two days after I turned eighteen, my parents informed me that we were having a family meeting after dinner. All day at school I fantasized about what the big news would be.

We inherited a small fortune from an old relative who we hardly knew. In his will, he left us his mansion with an outdoor pool. We're moving!

We won the lottery and are moving to a remote island off the Florida Keys. Pack your bags.

Your dad landed a new job, so he bought a yacht. Pack only shorts and summer apparel. Do you have sunscreen?

Every scenario involved swimsuits, moving away, and receiving piles of cash. That wasn't an odd fantasy since we'd been strapped for money after my dad lost his job. Daydreaming about some financial gain for them was a natural response to the financial stress my parents were feeling.

After the last dirty dish was loaded into the dishwasher, my dad cleared his throat to signal the start of our family meeting. "Son, I know this news may come as a bit of a shock, but biologically, I'm not your father. In my heart, you'll always be mine, so biology won't change that.

However, you're an adult now, so we thought it was a good time to tell you the truth."

"I don't understand."

It was Mom's turn to explain. "Honey, I'm not proud of this, but I had..." She looked to the ceiling for the correct word. "... relations with another man a few weeks before I met your dad. It hadn't meant anything, and I never saw the man again. I didn't know I was pregnant with you when I started seeing your dad. In fact, it wasn't until you gave blood during Easter break that we discovered your dad wasn't your biological father. Remember how you got all squeamish when you saw the needle?"

I repeated myself. "I don't understand." This wasn't even on my radar.

Because the conversation was too stressful for my delicate mom—who disliked yelling, being questioned, or physical aggression—my dad responded. "We signed up to donate blood that day during Easter break because there was a shortage of type O blood. Your mom and I knew we were both type O and genetically speaking, our offspring would inherit the same blood type. O is dominant. Anyway, we were told you were not type O. That was the first time we'd ever questioned if you were my son." Dad paused to let the news sink in. He took a large sip from his whiskey neat. "Of course, we sought a second opinion just to be sure."

Sarcastically, my brain fired back a response that my mouth knew better than to vocalize. Like a second opinion, which probably was just a second blood test, would make it all better. Before I could respond, I studied my dad's exterior. We were the same height, different builds—I was more filled out–muscular–and my dad was more lanky, but I'd assumed that was because I was an active teenager and he was older. My features were soft like my mother's–same big, cheesy smile, same pudgy nose, same oval-shaped eyes. Despite both of my parents having brown eyes, my eyes were blue, which was not particularly unusual.

"Who is my father?" I finally asked. I wasn't interested in the story behind how they figured it out. I wanted facts–details. I wanted answers.

My mother's cheeks burned bright red. She looked down at her lap and fiddled with the seams on her dress pants. Even though it was the next logical question, the four words pained her. As soon as my dad noticed her reaction, he nodded to me and stood up. "Let's you and I go outside and talk. Man to man."

I followed him to the kitchen, where he mixed another whiskey neat, and we walked out onto the back deck. As soon as the glass sliding door was shut, I asked again, "Who is my father?"

Given the news I'd just received, my question seemed reasonable.

"Sit down a minute." My dad gestured to one of the deck chairs. I plopped down in it and impatiently waited for what I was sure was going to be a long answer since my dad was known for his long-windedness. "First of all, you need to understand that your mother was devastated by this discovery–"

"She's the one who had sex with someone else. Why is that such a shocker?"

"Be kind, Son. Your mother isn't proud of that fact. Never once, not even for a second, did we consider anything different until that blood *test came back. At first, my brain assumed you must've been switched in the hospital. Imagine that? You were supposed to be Crazy Carolyn and Smilin' Sam's kid."* Dad was referring to our overly friendly neighbors who had earned their reputations because everyone thought they had a screw or two loose.

"That would mean Hoodie Harold is your kid. Remember we share the same birthday?" Every nickname earned by a neighbor helped us to remember their names. Of course, outside of our house, we didn't add the adjective.

If I played along with Dad's story, he might have opened up more as he relaxed and kept sipping his drink. Inwardly, I prayed for patience that I wasn't sure I had.

He laughed at the idea of the neighbor kid and me being switched in the hospital. Hoodie Harold wore a big, black hoodie every day, no matter the weather, and always had it pulled up tightly around his head so that only his eyes were visible. The neighborhood consensus was that Harold would grow up to be a serial killer. I wondered if anyone nicknamed me.

"That's right. I forgot that." My parents loved to tell the story of meeting Carolyn and Sam in the hospital. Both sets of new parents had been cooing at their baby boys, who were sleeping peacefully in the hospital nursery side by side. *"Your mother's delicate nature could not have handled it if her only son acted the way Harold does."* He shook his head. He was referring to a recent incident when Harold had screamed obscenities at his parents on the front lawn. Harold's obvious disrespect

and large vocabulary of swear words were shocking and burned my mom's eardrums.

After witnessing the scene next door, my mom cried and retreated to her bedroom for the rest of the day, claiming she had a terrible headache. My dad and I knew what she'd simply witnessed had upset her, so we let her have her time.

"Son, this discovery broke her heart. Sure, she'd had sex with another man, but she loved and married me. We made a family together."

"What about you, Dad? Discovering the son you raised for the last eighteen years isn't related to you couldn't have been easy."

"Yes. It was a shock, but it didn't change how I felt about you. I love you, Son. For me, it isn't about biology. Some people label families as people who share the same heritage, but in my experience, a family is more about people who love and care for each other no matter what. It doesn't matter if you don't have my DNA. I love you for who you are. I love your mother for who she is, regardless of her family lineage."

"So, who is my father? You still haven't answered that question, Dad."

"I know. Sorry about that. You know me. I'm a talker. And unfortunately, I don't have a name for you. Your mom only gave me a brief description of the other man. I don't think she knows much about him, but I do know she has taken great pains to forget him and move on with her life. Your mom's history—before me—haunts her, and I think this is part of her nightmare."

As he sipped his whiskey, we both looked out into the backyard and watched the tree branches wave in the light breeze. Nature provided a *perfect evening, but karma poured a bucket of maggots on top of a fresh pile of meat. I leaned my head against the back of the chair and closed my eyes.*

Neighbor kids played a lively game of horse next door. Echos of cars driving on the highway a few blocks away provided an even rhythmic hum. Across the yard, I heard a dog barking to earn someone's attention. The melting ice in my dad's highball glass clanged against the side.

Everything around me screamed, normal, average, ordinary, but voices in my head teased and taunted, oddity, unwanted, accident.

Well, this makes more sense. Your biological father is probably a perverted psycho. That's where you get your perverse sexual desires. I wonder if he is locked up.

My dad only knew surface-level information, but he was the only one who could pry more information from my mom. Showing her I was interested in knowing more might throw her over the edge of sanity. My dad and I described her as a delicate flower, and that description was proving to be quite accurate. I tread lightly with my next line of questioning, taking a cue from his calm demeanor.

"*There are so many reasons why I should know who he is. What about hereditary illnesses that could affect me? Shouldn't I know about them so I can be better informed about my health? Or what if my biological father is a millionaire and he wants to leave me—us—an inheritance?*"

"*Nice dream, Son. Let me try to get more information from her, and I'll keep you posted. I think it would be best if you acted like you weren't concerned. It would help her heart from breaking and ease her conscience. This was all very hard on her. Remember that week in middle school when she went to visit Aunt Jackie for two weeks?"*

I nodded. It had been the summer after I'd given blood, the summer when the abnormal sexual thoughts consumed my body and mind. In her absence and without her watchful eye, I explored some of my desires, so yes, I remembered that summer.

"She wasn't with Aunt Jackie. She'd checked herself into a mental health facility for some intense therapy and much-needed rest."

"Oh..."

"Yeah, after the second blood test and talking to a genetics doctor, your mom wasn't accepting the news very well. And believe it or not, I didn't either." A small, uncomfortable laugh escaped his mouth. "I'm not proud of my dramatic reaction, but I had no idea. After I got over my initial selfish response, I noticed how your mother was handling it all. It wasn't good. Her reaction mirrored an abuse victim or something of that nature. She opened up a bit. I'm not comfortable right now sharing everything she told me. I will let her do that when she is ready. But I want to tell you that the relationship with the XY chromosome wasn't a positive one." I heard him exhale a deep breath. "The moral of the story, Son, is that you are loved and will always be loved no matter your conception."

"Knock-Knock. Knickety-Knock," my mom said as she slid the sliding doors open. "Can a sweet, old lady join you boys?"

We both turned toward her voice. She'd been crying, and by the looks of her quivering lip, it wouldn't take much for her to break down again. I smiled at her.

"Who is here? Is there a sweet, old lady inside the house? I only see you, Mom. And you aren't old." I winked and motioned for her to join us on the empty chair. Teasingly, I added, "... or sweet."

She grinned at me. I didn't want her to feel bad for something that happened eighteen years ago. I loved her, and watching her internally struggle was more than I could handle. Furthermore, my patience would benefit me if I wanted to know more.

That evening when I crawled into bed, I wasn't angry or confused by the entire conversation. Relief flooded my heart. There was a reason I was the way I was. I didn't have these crazy sexual urges because something was wrong with me. I had inherited them. It wasn't my fault that I was a monster.

Chapter 20

After my last interview with Tony, I concluded that being polite and reserved wasn't the appropriate method for interviewing him. I was interviewing him for research purposes, not providing him with therapy. If I wanted to get somewhere, I needed to be bold and pushy. We didn't have much time left.

When I arrived at Fort Madison Prison, a noticeable spring influenced my step. I was determined to peel back a thick layer today, get him to admit his guilt, and focus on rehabilitation. His trial was about to start, and I was hoping that his nerves would be shot, making him more vulnerable.

"Hi, Oscar." I greeted the guard who normally collected my personal effects before I was shown into the rest of the prison. "Looks like you got some sun this weekend. Were you doing yard work, or did you go fishing?" As a frequent visitor, I naturally forged friendships with several guards. Oscar was one of my favorites. Pushing seventy, Oscar disclosed that he wasn't ready to retire because his wife would give him a million and one honey-do tasks if he was home every day. He preferred his cushy job at the front desk of the prison or fishing.

Oscar's wrinkly brown skin creased in all the worn places as a smile rose on his face. "Good afternoon, Miss Brady. The wife was a battle axe this weekend, and I was more than happy to come back to work, where I could at least sit my old, wrinkly butt down."

We shared a smile. I bet his wife wasn't that bad.

Suddenly, Oscar's smile disappeared. "Sorry, you drove all the way here for me to have to tell you this, but you ain't allowed to see Prisoner Shade anymore."

His announcement caught me off guard.

"His lawyer done found out. He said while the trial was going on, Tony ain't allowed to talk to anyone but him and his family. Especially no interviews. Sorry." Oscar gave me a half grin. "Somebody should've called you."

"No worries, Oscar. It isn't your fault. At least this trip gives me a chance to say goodbye to you."

"Yeah, you're a good one, Miss Brady. And hey, I love the Chris Poore book you gave me last month, *Bicentennial Summer*. Can't put it down. Brings back lots of good ole memories from the 60s."

"Glad you like it. You take care of yourself, Oscar, and if you ever visit Canby, look me up."

"I'll do that." He flashed me one of his big smiles that made his dimples appear. "Stay out of trouble."

***

One month later, at the end of Professor Doyle's lecture, my ears perked up. "Thank you all for your attention today. On Friday, we will be wrapping up our discussion about obsessive-compulsive disorders." As she scanned the lecture hall, her eyes found mine, and she said, "Miss Brady, can I talk to you for a minute before you leave?"

My stomach dropped into the pit of my stomach. I'd never been asked to stay after class before. Ever. I turned in my Nature vs. Nurture paper a week ago, and my grade wouldn't suffer when my visits to the prison had stopped.

Even though I was hyper-aware of everything around me, I subconsciously packed up my books and notebooks as I listened to the hum of the rest of the class. After the majority of the class had filed out of the room, I climbed down the steps toward the lecture stage.

Professor Doyle was jotting down something in her calendar and looked up as I approached. As soon as she shut the calendar and placed it in her briefcase, she looked up at me and smiled.

Oh, thank god.

"Thanks, Tara, for staying after class to talk with me." She glanced around the room to make sure we were the only two left in the lecture hall.

"Sure." I was at a loss for words, which normally wasn't the case.

"First of all, let me start by saying your paper on nature vs. nurture surprised me. It's an old theory that dates back to the 1800s, but you gave it a fresh approach and a new life. While I was reading it, I was sitting on the edge of my seat wondering what you'd tell me next. That's pure talent."

"Thank you."

"With that being said, I wanted to let you know that I submitted your paper to *Psychology Today*."

"Wow. Thank you."

"And I just found out this morning that they've already decided to publish it."

"Oh wow." I didn't know what to say.

"It all happened pretty fast, but I believe you deserve every ounce of the attention you're about to receive."

I wasn't completely naive. I was aware that Tony's case gained national attention due to its high profile. Understanding criminals and how their minds work was hot gossip at that moment. Everyone wanted to understand the reason behind such violent crimes. *Actually, let me rephrase that.* Society wanted an answer that would help them sleep better at night.

Chapter 21

1994

"**G**irl, you're lookin' fly!"

Stella and I hadn't seen each other since Christmas break when we both returned to Normal to visit our parents for the holiday. While I was up to my eyeballs in earning my master's degree in psychology, Stella decided to take a year off to travel and, according to her, expand her horizons. Before she headed out on another soul-searching adventure, Stella detoured to Canby. Because I hadn't inherited my mother's talent for cooking, I chose to treat Stella to breakfast at my favorite diner, creatively named Canby Diner.

I looked down at what I was wearing—a white T-shirt and a pair of cut-off jeans shorts. I was glad my fashion-conscious friend approved because they were the only articles of clothing that were clean.

"Thanks."

Stella and I were sitting in a booth near the front door where the sun was shining through. Stella's back was to the door, claiming it proved to be the best lighting for her, and apparently, my squinting into the sunshine flattered me.

"Your boobs are perky, your skin is freakin' glowing, and your legs look amazing in those shorts." Suddenly, her smile disappeared, and she squinted at me. "What aren't you telling me? Are you having sex?"

I choked on the sip of coffee I'd just taken. Stella's lack of a filter and the fact that she knew me so well was a welcomed interruption. "Ahh... no. Maybe you missed me so much that I look more appealing than usual. I haven't changed at all." I put my hand on my forehead and squinted at her. "Perhaps your recent activities have impacted your eyesight. Are *you* having sex?"

"As often as possible, wherever I can, and with whoever is willing." She laughed at her joke, which I knew wasn't a joke. Stella and I viewed sex differently. "Sex is like math. You add the bed, subtract the clothes, divide the legs, and pray you don't multiply. I've always been good with numbers."

"You've heard of STDs, right?" I lectured.

"Studly, tall, and dark? Yes, I've been well-versed with him." She raised her eyebrows up and down, indicating that she didn't take my warning seriously. "Plus, I learned my lesson. I take all the necessary precautions."

I shook my head. Stella and I have been friends my whole life. I don't have many core memories without her in them, and I wouldn't have it any other way. People were drawn to Stella. Kitty claimed that Stella had a magnetic personality and that her aura inspired anyone that she came in contact with to let their guard down. "But that can be a bad thing, too. She can influence people to do things that aren't always in their best interest."

My mother was skeptical of Stella, and I assumed it was because she was jealous. Kitty was free-spirited like Stella, but my mother needed to provide a stable home for a baby, so she retired from her adventures and settled down. Even though that was what I believed, she never made me feel like a burden. I think my mother embraced motherhood and kept a positive outlook on her new situation.

Despite having similar personalities, Stella and Kitty did not share the same physical appearance. As her personality reflected, Stella's hair was a gorgeous, fiery orange with natural blonde streaks that turned heads wherever she went. Stella's stunning emerald green eyes perfectly complemented her Irish heritage. For the grade school's *Annie* play, she was immediately cast as Little Orphan Annie. Just like the fictional movie character, Stella and her perfectly curled, orange locks stole the show. Plus, she could sing like an angel. As Stella matured, her thin, flat-as-a-board body curved and filled out in the most desirable places. She was a captivating, charming bombshell without having to try.

"What's your birth-giver been up to? Has she admitted to shagging Hank yet? I bet he's domineering in bed, shouting, 'Order up' just before he cums."

"Stella! Gross." I immediately responded, but I still grinned even though I cringed at the thought of Kitty and Hank having sex. Stella had the unique ability to make any conversation entertaining. "No. As far as I know, Hank and Kitty's friendship is purely platonic, and Kitty is doing well. Nothing new there."

"Kitty is good shit. I wish my mother was half as cool as Kitty. Mine is only into her crochet needle. My poor dad sits next to her in his matching, beat-up old recliner, praying that she'll play with *his* long, pointed needle. Poor, old, horny bugger." Stella exaggerated. Her mother crocheted a lot, but her parents had a healthy, steady relationship; however, to Stella, 'steady' meant boring. Numerous times during sleepovers, we overheard their lovemaking from Stella's room.

After she laid down the menu, Stella sat back in her seat, circled her legs up under her, and asked, "Have you been keeping up with all the gossip surrounding Pastor Perv's trial? Such a freakin' scandal. Totally proves that you don't know what is happening behind the closed doors of someone's home. And what a crazy coincidence that he ends up in the same town you're living in. Creepy. When I was a kid and he was preaching, I thought he was hot. "

Besides the Campus Rapist, it was all the town was talking about. Since finishing my paper on the psyche of Tony, I tried hard not to think about him, or at least told myself not to. He'd already taken enough space in my brain.

After Kitty revealed her news, I chose to keep the information about my biology from Stella and everyone. For starters, I wasn't sure how I felt about the situation, and until I figured out how I felt, I didn't need anyone else's opinion. If only I could rip that part of my DNA out of my body and replace it with some other man's. Any other man's. Secondly, I didn't want anyone to look at me differently like I knew they would. As soon as someone heard who my father was, they'd inspect me for similarities. Do I have his eyes? His nose? Tony enjoyed watching football; did I, too? The comparisons would never stop. So, I decided to never let them start. I knew Stella would be heartbroken that I didn't share it with her right away, but as my best friend, I also knew that she'd understand. Plus, it was a twenty-three-year-old secret. What would be the harm in keeping it that way a little longer?

Stella didn't wait for me to respond. "Rumor has it that Lily Armstrong was in town and caused quite a stir in the courtroom. Dyed her hair platinum blonde, squeezed her ass into a short, tight leather shirt and a pair of sky-high, poke-out-your-eyes heels, and paraded into court as her mother's ghost. Can you freakin' believe it? I bet Pastor Perv got hard, or maybe he went limp out of pure fright."

"That ain't no rumor, darlin'." Our waitress suddenly appeared at our table, topping off our coffee cups. "I was in the courtroom that day. When she strutted into court, Pastor Tony nearly had a heart attack. Not sure how his wanker reacted, but the scene was amazin' all the same. Hopefully, the shock of seein' her ghost ripped years off that man's life. The man deserves all that Hell is goin' to give him."

I flashed a courtesy smile at this woman whose name tag read, Flo, but I didn't offer any additional comment. In one hand, she held the coffee carafe while her other hand rested on her hip, indicating that she had nowhere else to be. I wasn't sure how she'd snuck up on our table when the woman and her boisterous personality were hard to miss. Her bright red hair that was pinned into 1950s waves reminded me of Marilyn Monroe's classic look. Matching red lipstick coated her lips, and her hourglass figure that was squeezed into her baby blue waitress uniform shouted, 'Look at me.' Flo was no wallflower. She stood out.

Before I could dismiss her by placing our food order, Stella, who could befriend a rock, leaned forward and responded, "What a small freakin' world. We graduated high school with Lily back in Normal. How do you know Lily, Flo?"

"Well, bee's knees. She was sittin' at this here table just a month ago." Flo tapped the tabletop. "But I first met dear, sweet Lily years ago when she frequented this dump." She looked around and then lowered her voice. "I mean 'restaurant.' We started talkin' and the rest is history. I love that kid!" Flo's face glowed when she mentioned Lily. "Do you girls live here in Canby?"

Stella answered before I formulated a lie that would dismiss Flo. "She does." Stella gestured her thumb in my direction. "But she doesn't get out much." Stella flashed me a wink.

Flo chomped her gum as she looked me up and down. "You, darlin', are too pretty and innocent for Canby. I hope you're stayin' safe." I nodded to Flo, assuming she was referring to the Campus Rapist. "Canby seems to be a magnet for sexual deviants. I always pack heat." She patted something in the middle of her breasts.

Stella yelped her approval.

As much as I wanted to get rid of Flo so that I could enjoy my visit with my best friend, I knew whatever this flamboyant woman was about to say would stick with me for a long time.

She leaned closer to our table, put the back side of her hand up next to her lips, and whispered, "See that woman sittin' over there alone, starin' off into her coffee as if the coffee itself will answer her burnin' questions or heal her pain? That's Lainey." Flo gestured to a female customer about forty feet away.

Even though Stella and I had both been taught not to stare, we couldn't help ourselves. We both whipped our heads around and took a long, hard look at who Flo was referring to. Lainey sat hunched over a table alone and blankly stared down at the tabletop. With her fingers, she combed her long, brown hair around her face. As her fingers reached for another strand, I noticed her hot pink chipped nail polish on her chewed fingernails. Her stick-straight hair needed a wash and a good trim. She was dressed from head to toe in black. Even though the day was predicted to be near eighty degrees, she wore a black turtleneck, baggy black sweatpants, and a pair of dirty black tennis shoes. She looked completely uncomfortable in her skin—like she wished she could just disappear. Before Flo said another word, it was obvious that Lainey was depressed and unhappy. Kitty would've announced her aura as a cloud of black.

"She was raped a few years ago, and she ain't never been the same. The 'before Lainey' was friendly and upbeat, full of life. One night after our book club meetin', a man waited inside her house, attacked her, and forced himself on her. Unfortunately, by the time she reported it to the police, days had passed and the evidence was gone. In her report, she claimed that he cuddled her after he had his way with her and whispered to her that he was sorry."

"That sounds oddly familiar." I glanced at Stella and briefed her about what the papers were saying about the Campus Rapist.

"Poor girl. The whole town doubted her. The police weren't very sympathetic. They believed she had sex with her date and days later changed her mind, claimin' rape. Around town, the rumors ranged from her trying to get attention to claims from parents that she was a little too friendly with their teenage sons. But I've been around the block a few times; I watch people. Those jerks were wrong." Flo took a deep breath and straightened her back. "She still comes to our book club, and some nights I think she's afraid to go home because she thinks he'll be waitin' for her again. One night, I felt so bad for her that I walked her home. As her legs moved, so did her lips. She said she knew who her attacker was. A student. He graduated a few years ago." Flo looked over her shoulder at Lainey again. "I asked her for a name and told her I'd take the kid down myself, but she wouldn't tell me. She said it was too late. No one believed her years ago, and no one would believe her now."

"You should try again, Flo. He sounds very similar to the Campus Rapist, at least in that part where he apologized afterward. She might know the identity of this rapist." Stella offered her advice.

"Yeah, I tried. She hardly speaks anymore. After she quit her job at the high school, she took a job doing payroll for a small company. Supposedly, as soon as she enters her office, she locks her office door behind her. Whoever the kid is, he did a number on poor Miss L."

***

Two hours later and way too soon, Stella and I said our goodbyes on Main Street. She was heading to Canada to meet up with some people she'd met when she dabbled in pursuing an undergraduate degree a few years ago. She planned on living the next six months in a camper with them as they attempted to live off the land. Her zeal for life and love for adventure reminded me of Kitty. It was a wonder the two of them didn't get along better.

She pulled me into a huge bear hug before she waved goodbye and turned in the opposite direction. I smiled. Stella was a bucket filler. Because she didn't have a mean bone in her body, her positivity and love for life always radiated onto me whenever I was with her. I wished I could've bottled her up and taken her everywhere.

As I stood on the curb waiting for a pause in the traffic, Stella called out one last goodbye, "Tell your birth giver that I'm living her dream. Ciao!"

"Ciao?" I giggled at my friend. She never ceased to amaze me with her boundless amount of energy, willingness to experiment, and zest for learning new terminology.

With a flick of her wrist, Stella turned the corner and was gone.

Before returning to my apartment, I decided to explore some of the cute shops that lined Canby's Main Street. As I crossed the street, a sudden shiver ran up my spine. Because Kitty was extremely attuned to nature and its energies, she taught me not to ignore these signs and my intuition. I glanced both ways, searching for the cause of my unease. The traffic was light, and the people crossing the street with me were dressed in their business attire. None of them were paying me any attention. When I reached the other side of the street, I noticed a door shutting to one of the boutiques, but otherwise, there was no activity. I shook my head to scatter the bad feelings away. Kitty would love to hear that I used one of her perceptive skills.

Chapter 22

When I saw her *standing across the street looking both ways for traffic, it was the first time I felt truly guilty for the ugly thoughts that entered my head. She was stunning, possessing a beauty she was unaware of, and perhaps even more so because she didn't realize it. She stood on the edge of the road, balancing on the curb to ensure no cars were approaching before jogging across to the side of the road I was on. Staring at her. Frozen in place. An idiot without a brain. I had literally stopped walking, stopped drinking my coffee, and just stood there with my mouth gaping open.*

"Ciao!"

As the wind blew her long, wavy brown hair in her face, she flipped it out of her face and tucked a few loose strands behind her ear before she waved to her friend, who had called out to her as she walked away. A tight white T-shirt covered her perky breasts and accented her small waist and curvy behind. I'd had my share of women, and I wasn't sure why this woman drew so much of my attention. Yes, she was gorgeous, but so were a lot of the others.

Is this love at first sight? Do I believe in love at first sight?

Love? Are you kidding me right now? You see a hot woman one time and think it's love. Are you even capable of love?

I don't know. I don't have the urge to rip her clothes off and force her to do things. So, it feels different.

Getting soft on me.

I shook my head to shift common sense to my frontal lobe. I could feel an erection growing in my jeans. As she started to narrow the distance between us, I looked right and left for an escape route. I wasn't sure why I suddenly felt so shy and awkward. Normally, if a good-looking woman crossed my path, I regarded it as a sign. A sign that I used to my advantage. I puffed up my chest, flashed her a killer smile, and laid out all my charm. My confidence oozed out of every pore. I was a magnet.

But this time it felt different. I didn't know why, but I didn't want her to see me. At least, not yet. I didn't want her to scrutinize me intensely, lustfully, as most women her age tended to do. Honestly, it wasn't hard to do the things I did to them. It was like they were asking for it. Alone. Vulnerable. Dependent.

My reaction to this woman was different. I didn't want to hurt her. I was attracted to her, but I didn't want to perform perverted acts like normally I would. Until I could figure out what was happening, I decided to avoid her.

She was only about forty feet from me, and like a coward, I ducked into the nearest boutique. As the bells chimed above me, I pushed the door closed behind me and looked around at my surroundings. I was in a lingerie shop. This was karma getting back at me. I closed my eyes and took a deep breath.

After I popped a mint in my mouth to help with the coffee breath that I was sure plagued my mouth, I heard a seasoned voice greet me. "Good morning, Sonny. What brings you to Amy's Secrets?"

I peeled my eyes open to find a wrinkly, lilac-colored-haired woman walking toward me from the back of the store. I glanced over my shoulder to the sidewalk just feet from me and watched her walk by the glass door. She didn't look in. I exhaled a large breath that I hadn't realized I'd been holding in.

As I turned my attention to the little old lady who was probably pushing seventy, I was already preoccupied with a new train of thought. For the moment, I forgot about the sexy stranger as an odd desire overtook me. Dressed in a baggy, overly embroidered purple shirt, the woman was at least a foot shorter than me. I loomed over her. This would be easy.

I flashed her my biggest, most seductive smile. Every white tooth in my mouth sparkled as I tried to gain her trust.

"Well, hi, Amy. Are you the owner of this fine establishment?" In one swift glance, I made two assumptions. Her name tag told me her name was Amy. Therefore, she must be the owner.

Recovering slightly from my undivided attention and already smitten, she giggled when she looked down at the name tag pinned to her shirt. "Nah, Amy isn't here today. I'm covering for her and just grabbed the first nametag I saw. I forgot my glasses at home today, and I'm as blind as a bat without them."

I decided to test that theory. I held up my right hand. "How many fingers am I holding up?"

She giggled again. "Sonny, I can't tell. I have a terrible case of double vision. So, my honest guess is eight."

We both laughed at her joke.

"Amy is my daughter-in-law. She's pregnant and had a doctor's appointment today, so I volunteered to help here at the store. As long as no one asks my opinion on if they look good or not in a lacy number, I'll be fine." She cleared her throat. "Now, how can I help you? Go easy on me." She laughed again. "Looking for a gift?"

"What did you say your name was?"

"I didn't. It's Gertrude." Even though this woman was considered elderly by most of the public, I noticed that she still had a great figure under her bright purple tracksuit. Personally, I wasn't a fan of the dye job, but I could look past it for what I had in mind. Gertrude would be my first in her age bracket. It might prove to be interesting.

My smile widened as I stuck out my hand to shake hers. "Nice to meet you. Can I call you Gertie?"

It turned out that she didn't like me calling her Gertie because her ex-husband nicknamed her that. So, instead, I called her Amy as I trapped her in a dressing room and tied her arms and legs with zip ties I always carried in my pocket, just in case an opportunity like this presented itself.

With her hands tied behind her back and a pair of pantyhose stuck in her mouth, I left her crying on the floor. I turned the deadbolt to the store and flipped over the open sign to close. Why hadn't I thought of this scenario before? If she's blind, I don't need to wear my ski mask.

Chapter 23

To start my Sunday routine, I retrieved the newspaper from my front step. The Sunday edition was always the thickest, filled with the business' weekly ads. Kitty taught me to be a coupon cutter just like her. We saved money by planning meals around the grocer's specials. At the cafe, she only made fresh fruit desserts when the fruit was in season. Strawberry pie in December was forbidden, but in the middle of July, the local farmers produced strawberries like weeds.

Under my mom's roof, the living room television would be blaring loudly as she watched mindless game shows, while I preferred to listen to country music at a respectable volume. Kitty would be wearing a freshly washed pair of bell-bottom jeans and a flowy top, while I preferred my worn-out slippers, a baggy pair of gray sweatpants, and a T-shirt stolen from my ex-boyfriend, Brian. He didn't even know who Johnny Cash was. So when I boxed up the stuff that he left at my apartment, I purposely kept the 'Johnny Cash, Man in Black' T-shirt, as a token from our relationship. I knew he wouldn't miss it. Plus, it became my Sunday wardrobe. Wearing it every Sunday had nothing to do with missing Brian—I could care less about him—and more about honoring Mr. Cash.

I shuffled back into my apartment and grabbed scissors to start my Sunday morning process of coupon cutting. I dropped the paper onto the kitchen table. It unfolded to reveal a national story regarding a retired football player that I'd never heard of until recently, O.J. Simpson. After evading police for ninety minutes as his friend drove him down the Los Angeles freeway in a white Bronco, he'd been arrested for the murders of his wife and her boyfriend. I shook my head and thought, *one too many concussions.*

In a small section of the front page, I read a local newsletter headline.

Campus Rapist Strikes Again

For over six months, violent sexual acts have plagued Midwest University that is located in the heart of the small town of Canby, Minnesota; however, according to authorities, twenty new rapes have been reported by older women in the community. He is no longer only attacking college age women. According to the descriptions gathered, the police believe the same man is responsible for all the attacks. The rapist has widened his perimeter which makes the entire female population at risk.

According to investigators, the latest victim was sixty-eight-year-old Gertrude Gunner, who was attacked last weekend while working at her daughter-in-law's downtown boutique. The rapist claimed to have come into the lingerie shop looking for a gift. When asked why she didn't report the rape right away (her police report was filed three days later, after the nineteenth victim came forward), Mrs. Gunner explained, "I know it sounds strange, but he genuinely felt bad about what he was doing. When he was done, he wiped tears from his eyes. He told me he was leaving the front door unlocked, and the next person who came into the store would find me. He said I wouldn't be tied up too long." Mrs. Gunner also commented that she didn't report it initially because she didn't think anyone would believe her since she was old and not attractive like the other victims.

Mrs. Gunner was unable to provide a thorough description of her attacker. She hadn't been wearing her glasses that day. She informed the detectives that he smelled like mint.

Authorities are baffled by this ongoing case, urging women to be proactive. Police Chief Jay Nelson warns women of all ages. "Don't walk alone. Always tell a friend where you are going. Buy a can of Mace."

If you were a victim of a crime, please call 911 immediately.

I shook my head. A man was raping innocent women and then apologizing for doing so. The wires in my brain were tingling with the possibilities. If this man was caught, I'd love to question him and understand his thought process. There were so many questions.

It had been a year since I finished my Abnormal Psychology paper on Tony Shade, and sometimes the news that more creeps were still not behind bars alarmed me. As a single woman, I feared for my safety, but as a psychologist, my curiosity grew.

Chapter 24

Joining the police academy seemed like the right career fit for me, and I was determined to become the highest-ranked recruit. As a child, I was always testing boundaries until they pushed back. Furthermore, becoming a police officer seemed like a perfect fit for my curiosity about criminals and how their minds work. My obsession with criminals and their crimes would come full circle.

During police academy training, my desire to hurt women subsided. The thoughts didn't disappear, but they did lessen. For eight to ten hours a day, I was either training to apprehend bad guys or I was studying laws and regulations to keep our community safe. After class, I worked out or studied. There wasn't enough time in the day for my desires. If I could continue this exhausting schedule, perhaps I could overcome my twisted cravings.

The physical exertion was addicting, and I enjoyed feeling the blood in my veins pump and my muscles swell in my biceps. Being physically fit was an important aspect of a rookie cop. We would be the ones working the streets and chasing the criminals. I became the most fit I'd ever been. Running up and down six flights of stairs didn't even wind me. I felt great.

While rehydrating after a required six-mile run, I met Michael. He accidentally bumped into me at the water station, knocking the cold cup of water down the front of my already sweat-soaked T-shirt.

"Dude, sorry about that. Michael is clumsy."

I looked around. Who is Michael? And why is this big oaf grinning at me like a clown?

"I'm Michael. Michael Bass. Nice to meet you." The big oaf stuck out his hand.

I shook it as I eyed him up and down. Is he slow? Why did he refer to himself in the third person?

He leaned over me to grab a cup of water. "Six miles and you aren't even out of breath. Are you Superman or something?" He was still grinning as he gulped down the water.

Being referred to as Superman was a great way to win me over. I flashed him a small grin. "Superheroes are more than just a pretty face."

He laughed. "Right on, man." He slapped me on the back. "Batman and I are going out for a few beers after we shower. Superman should join us."

I joined them and marked this time in my life as my introduction to alcoholism. Because I'd been a loner for the last ten years, socializing and drinking had not been a priority for me. When my high school classmates were sneaking out to get drunk on a lonely gravel road, I was sneaking out to peek into women's windows, trying to catch a glimpse of them exposed. I could feel in my bones that I was different than other kids my age, so I avoided contact with anyone. Of course, that didn't stop them from making fun of me or calling me weird names, but it kept me from saying or doing something I'd regret.

When Michael invited me to hang out with him and a few other guys from our police academy, I jumped at the chance. Even though I didn't like to think about it, I was lonely. Plus, the police academy was giving me confidence that I didn't know even existed. I pretended that I was a cocky jock like the rest of them. Physically I fit in. My biceps were sculpted, and I worked hard on developing a six-pack. Even though the inside of me still was the same awkward kid with wicked thoughts, the outside was healthy.

To guys my age, being twenty-four and single meant working hard during the week so we could party every Friday and Saturday night. We were blowing off steam. Every weekend, I joined Michael and the guys at a different local establishment. We didn't frequent the same one because "we need to find just the right flavor," explained Stan, who Michael had nicknamed Batman because his skin was as dark as Batman's suit.

"Stan, you have to quit seducing a new chick every week. This town only has so many bars." Michael teased.

Stan taught me that even a normal guy likes a lot of flavor. "I can't limit myself to just Vanilla when there is Rocky Road, Cotton Candy, and Cherry Nut available. I need to sample them all before I settle on just one."

"Stop talking about women and ice cream. You're making me hungry."

Stan also introduced me to tequila, which in turn introduced me to alcoholism. Each weekend morning, I'd curse the worm, but each weekend I'd engulf her again. It was a battle, one I didn't try very hard to fight. It felt good to let loose and have some fun. I almost felt normal.

However, alcohol also fueled my desire for things I couldn't have but felt I deserved. One Saturday night, after about six months of the same routine, I got tired of Stan always scoring with the women. I decided to give it a go myself. An attractive blonde strolled into the bar with a circle of friends. Even to her friends, she seemed to be the center of attention. Michael, Stan, and I were playing pool near the door when the group walked in. As the blonde walked by the table, Stan stuck out the pool cue to stop her from advancing. With it blocking her path, she looked at Stan, who was holding the cue. Her expression was a dare.

"Take me to bed or lose me forever," muttered Stan.

She threw her head back and laughed. "Are you kidding me right now? Is that the best you've got? Every woman in the tri-state area has seen Top Gun. *I think I'll pass." She raised the cue over her head and walked by Stan, shaking her head.*

Michael made a crashing noise. "Stan, you crashed and burned, my friend." He laughed at Stan's expense. "But damn, that was a blast to watch."

I blamed tequila for letting me think that even though Stan was shot down, I had a chance. After my fifth—or maybe it was eighth—tequila shot, I noticed the blonde woman exiting the bathroom alone. I excused myself from the table and walked quickly toward her. At first, my lopsided grin and overly confident eagerness were enough to charm her.

We talked for about twenty minutes before I pushed her into a small dark corner of the bar and kissed her hard on the mouth. She responded, and we made out for another five minutes before she pushed me away.

"This was nice. You're a great kisser, but I'm not interested."

"Not interested in what?" I teased back as I leaned in to kiss her again.

"In you. In taking this any further." She dodged my advances and kept pushing me away.

Fury rose in my clouded brain. "Fucking cock tease." The words sounded through my clenched teeth.

"Possibly. More like an uninterested cock tease." She ducked under my arms that were pinning her against the wall and started to strut away from me.

Ten feet to my left was a small door that I assumed led to a storage room. In a matter of seconds–before I could change my mind or let her get any further away–I grabbed her wrist, pulled her back, and yanked her into the closet that I'd opened with my other hand. As soon as I slammed the door shut, we were standing in darkness. The only light in the room was coming from under the closet's door, giving it a faint glow.

"What the hell!" She was mad and caught off guard. I covered my open mouth with hers, trying to force her into submission. She pushed me away. "This ain't going to happen. You must not take rejection well, but I'm not going to change my mind. Now, open the goddamn door and let me go."

Her voice was filled with anger, and I could feel the heat rising within. Red-hot fury. What color was fear? Would the touch of her skin turn cold once she realized I wasn't fooling around?

With one forearm pinning her against the wall, I used my free hand to unbutton my jeans and drop them to the ground. I kicked out of one pant leg. I hadn't bothered with underwear.

Again using my free hand, I ripped off her shirt, sending the buttons flying in every direction.

"What the fuck! What are you doing?" There was the sound of fear again—fear that ignited every extremity. I put my hand on her cheek to see if her temperature was decreasing. A bit maybe, but nothing completely noticeable yet. "Let me go... please."

When someone is angry, that emotion is all-consuming. There is no room for anything else. But fear allows other emotions to surface, like worry, sadness, and desperation. That aspect of a person piqued my interest. I lived to witness all of those at the same time. Worry is the trembling voice and sudden stillness of the body. Sadness is the tears in her eyes, and the tickle of her sinuses causing tears to well in her eyes. Desperation is the last resort, begging and pleading to change the inevitable.

I enjoyed witnessing these stages in my victims.

"What's your name?" I whispered in her ear as I tugged down the thong under her skirt.

She was crying now and didn't answer.

"What is your fucking name?" I asked through clenched teeth. I slapped her, jarring her to attention.

"Jenny."

"I'm sorry, Jenny."

Jenny and I spent ten minutes in the bar's cleaning closet. It was a thrill to take charge, beat Stan at his game, and finally explode months of pent-up rage.

However, those ten minutes changed the course of my life. A life that was going so well. I blamed tequila for giving me the confidence to think I could get away with it. I blamed tequila for making me forget all the hard work I'd achieved by being sneaky. This was the reason I hadn't gotten caught before. I'd always been calm, cool, and sober.

My life was about to hit a dead-end.

Chapter 25

2 years later - 1996

I couldn't stop myself from looking toward the door every ten seconds. I'd never felt so rejected and embarrassed. I was smarter than this. I'd never been stood up before.

Maybe he got in a car accident. That's why he's late. Something tragic must've happened.

Did he show up, see me, and run? Do I look as pathetic as I feel right now?

Match.com was a brand-new method of meeting people, promising to find someone special with similar interests, desires, and dreams. Initially, my curiosity was solely for research purposes. However, when one of my classmates shared her experience of meeting her current, high-quality, low-mileage, and shiny boyfriend on the website, I decided to give it a try. I wasn't meeting any quality suitors at the library or in class. And unlike Kitty, I didn't want to be alone forever.

What could it hurt? Naturally, I hadn't considered the possibility of a semi-blind date ending in a no-show.

This new trend of meeting your soul mate intrigued me. I'd always been a curious person, and I figured, why not? After answering twenty random questions, this computer program guaranteed it would select quality candidates to match my interests. I understood narrowing the possibilities with common interests, but sparks and attraction couldn't be measured, or so I believed. I was open to letting *Match.com* prove me wrong.

How bad could it be? For $9.95 a month, I paid a fee to browse a catalog of single men, discover their hopes and wishes, and chat with them to see if there was a spark. I knew the possible suitors were doing the same to me, judging me by my profile picture and the profile description, but I didn't care. Human nature interested me.

The dating program matched me with Gabe Paul, a twenty-something college graduate who preferred dogs to cats, enjoyed reading the newspaper on Sunday mornings with a strong cup of coffee, and wanted to find a partner who could also be his best friend.

Ummm, hello! Perfect.

That was, until fifteen minutes ago, when he didn't show up for our first date. We'd emailed for a month before I finally agreed to meet him. I'd been afraid of meeting up with a perfect stranger because he could be a serial killer or rapist. I was skeptical, but Gabe assured me that if we met publically, everything would be fine. I hadn't even considered that he might see me and run.

"I'm such a fool." The whisper escaped my lips as I sat belly-up to the bar.

"You sure don't look like a fool," commented the bartender who'd poured my first and second glass of wine. I contemplated ordering my third. He raised his eyebrows up and down in a teasing fashion. "Not sure what a fool looks like, but it isn't you."

"Sorry, I didn't mean to say that out loud." I cleared my throat and straightened up on my bar stool. I didn't need another stranger to realize what a loser I was.

"You aren't the first one I've overheard talking to themselves. Lots of crazies come in here."

"Are you saying I'm crazy?" I hadn't meant to include as much edge as I did.

It was his turn to clear his throat. "No, that isn't what I meant." He nodded toward the barstools. "These barstools are magical because they cause people to confess shit and talk about things they wouldn't even tell their best friends. You wouldn't believe the stuff people tell bartenders. We're unpaid therapists."

I looked him up and down. Standing about six feet tall with a full head of wavy, black hair and a name tag that read Ford, his expression proved he hadn't meant to kick me when I was down. While a smirk played on his lips, attempting to convey his manly confidence, his beautiful blue eyes showed his concern. That touch of vulnerability warmed my scorned heart. Stella would've labeled him a tall glass of water on a hundred-degree day.

"It seems I have some time to spare, so why don't you entertain me with a few examples?" I flashed him a small, humor-me smile but crossed my arms across my chest.

Because it was the opening he was looking for, his little smirk turned into a full-blown smile. He leaned against the bar and looked at the ceiling to collect his thoughts. "Well, every bar has a Norm–"

I nodded. "Like Cheers?"

"Yep, our Norm's name is Victor, and he uses a lot of phrases that start and end with the f-word. And typically those phrases offend ninety percent of the bar. Instead of an overweight, roly-poly guy like Norm, Victor is rail thin, and a lit cigarette permanently hangs from his wrinkled, pierced lips."

"Lung cancer?"

"Not that I've heard. Victor claims he'd rather drink a bottle of Jack for supper than inhale a grease-bomb cheeseburger that is sure to cause an early heart attack."

"Victor sounds like a gem." I glanced around the cozy, dimly lit bar. It was five o'clock on a Thursday, and no one that fit Victor's description was present. "Why isn't he here now if he's your Norm? Is he home with his adoring, but nagging wife, Vera?"

"Nope. Not married. Ever. On Thursdays, he takes his momma out for an ice cream cone."

I volunteered a small chuckle. "Is this Victor available? He sounds like a keeper."

"I'm not sure. If you leave me your number, I can ask." He winked as he slid a napkin and a pen from behind the bar toward me.

"Wow. You had that pen ready to go." Reading his nametag, I responded, "Ford? That's an interesting name."

"Not really. My mother wasn't very creative. I'll tell you the lame story that'll make you forget about your date not showing up if you give me your name."

"Tara." I held out my hand to shake his. "How did you know about the no-show?"

After our quick handshake, he tapped his forehead. "Remember these barstools are magic. Plus, I can read minds."

His wit and charm worked. He earned a genuine smile. "Mind reader, huh? Two can play this game. How about I guess the origin of your name?"

"Tara, I already told you it isn't a great story, but go for it." He pulled his hand back and cleaned the used glasses under the sink.

Again, I looked him up and down. Using the basic people-reading skills I learned in my psychology courses, I said, "Your mother was sixteen when she found out that she was pregnant with you. She raised you alone because her parents wouldn't help her since she broke their cardinal, strict rule of having sex before she was married. You don't know your father, and you don't care to. Your mother told you he was in the military and doesn't know where he is, but that's all a lie because she doesn't know much about him either since they only had sex one time. She named you after the kind of truck you were conceived in."

He looked dumbfounded. "How did you do that?" Ford had grown pale.

"Sorry. Sometimes, I get carried away." My lack of a filter often hurts other people's feelings. It was one of the reasons my college advisor told me being a therapist might not be the best career for me. I backpedaled with a flirtatious smile, hoping it would help smooth things over. "Seriously, I have no idea if that is true or not. I was just guessing."

He continued to give me a blank stare for ten seconds too long. Finally, he shook his head to rattle himself back into the present. A second later the smirk was back on his face as he regained his composure. "Well, if you must know, she was seventeen, not sixteen. You got that part wrong."

"My bad."

"By the way, the guy who stood you up is a complete idiot." He flirted. "You're the total package—pretty, smart, and funny."

It was my turn to smirk back at him. "If I use my mind-reading skills again, I'd say you're hitting on me right now."

"You're partly right. I want to ask you out, but I thought I'd wait until after you ordered your third glass of wine so my chances of you saying yes were slightly higher."

"Pretty smart for a guy named after a rusty old truck."

This night hadn't turned out as planned, but I couldn't deny that Ford's attention was flattering. Silently, I thanked Gabe Paul for not showing up for our *Match.com* first date. Maybe this was karma delivering something I deserved—a nice guy.

Chapter 26

A month ago, during one of our routine Sunday night phone calls, Kitty invited me on a mother-daughter trip. While growing up, vacations weren't in the cards. Because she was a single mother and owned a small business, Kitty couldn't afford to be away from the cafe for more than a few days. If the cafe was closed, she explained we made no money, and that wasn't something she could afford. There were bills to pay. When we did venture outside of Normal to get away, we'd pop down to Des Moines for a night. We would treat ourselves to a five-star hotel that supplied white plush robes for their guests. After devouring every item on the room service menu, we wandered the streets soaking in the hustle and bustle of the big city. I cherished those adventures when I had Kitty's undivided attention. We giggled until our sides ached, ate candy until the sugar high made us giddy, and vowed to always stay close. We didn't need expensive vacations when we knew how to make every second of a twenty-four-hour road trip into something memorable.

Therefore, when she suggested a three-day road trip, I didn't hesitate with my approval. She advised me that she'd already started planning. Hank offered to cover the restaurant, and his sister Susan couldn't wait to 'play waitress' for a couple of days. All she needed was a confirmation from me, and we'd pack our bags.

Two days after we made our reservations and agreed on an itinerary, she unexpectedly changed plans.

"Tarasue, my aura has been clouded. I need to tell you something," she explained.

"Oh no. Not your aura." Even though I respected Kitty's unconventional belief in nature's energy, I enjoyed making fun of it. "Kitty, you know I don't appreciate your sudden psychic revelations. They cause stress headaches and avoidance of my real feelings. As a therapist, I need to follow the advice I give, and your cosmic energy makes me test my best practices."

"Oh, Tarasue, you've always had a flair for the dramatic."

"Um, hello. *Hey, Kettle! You're black.*"

She giggled. "Are you racking up my phone bill, like I do to yours when I call rambling on and on?"

"What do you think? Have I ever been known to treat you to a dose of your own medicine?"

"You *are* my child." From the tone of her voice, I imagined the corners of her lips turning up. She enjoyed my sass and didn't expect anything less. She'd raised me to question things, voice my opinion, and defy authority, even hers.

"Making the trip to the Black Hills is two-fold. I desperately want to spend some quality time with you since you're so busy with your fancy career and young woman adventures, but Camille is celebrating her seventh birthday that same weekend, and she invited us to come. They live in Miner City, so we could just pop there for a bit since we'll be in the area."

> Lying by omission—a form of manipulation that occurs when someone purposely omits important information that changes the truth of a situation.

Over the past few years, I've grown quite familiar with this psychology term. By leaving out the original reason behind her great idea for a trip, Kitty had been able to control both the situation and me. I shook my head. One of my professors advised us that we'd learn a lot if we could break down scenes from our own lives. My mother would be appalled if she knew I was doing it to her right now, which made it even more enjoyable.

She never mentioned this detour when she initially sold me on the weekend trip. A 'mother-daughter adventure' was the label she used. She knew I was a sucker for hiking, nature, and the beauty of the Black Hills. In the back of my mind, I was skeptical, but my heart was stronger and leaped at the invitation. When would I ever learn?

After disclosing her teenage trauma, Kitty recounted the awkward friendship she'd formed with Lisa Shade when she still lived in Normal. She frequently stopped by the cafe asking my mother what to do with her life. Even though she wasn't a licensed therapist like I was, the whole town sought out my mother's advice, so that didn't surprise me. The residents of Normal pegged her as more of a witch or a healer.

Kitty frequently visited Lisa while she was serving a year in jail following Tony's arrest. "I wanted to make sure she kept her spirits up. Prison is hard, especially for a weak, tortured soul. Tony alienated her from everyone she knew. She had no one else."

When Lisa was released, the two friends kept in contact, and Lisa revealed how Camille had been deposited on her front step. I'd never met Camille, but my mom had talked a lot about Lisa and Camille. Read me the letters they sent. She showed me the drawings Camille made her, and she even framed Camille's school pictures and placed them on the mantel.

Growing up in Normal, I'd met Lisa Shade a few times. I recognized her name and remembered her and her infamous husband—whom I now knew was my biological contributor—running the Bible camp I attended with my best friend, Stella, in middle school. Beyond that, I didn't *know* her, but I swore Lisa was a magnet for drama just as my mother was a magnet for the wounded and broken.

Did I think it was strange that my mother was friends with her rapist's ex-wife? Yes, of course. But then again, I shouldn't put anything past my mother. Ordinary rules of society didn't apply to her. She didn't care what others thought. Kitty did what Kitty wanted to do, no matter what. Even if I questioned some of her decisions, I respected her.

"Well, this sure is a pickle." Sarcasm was one of my best qualities, or so Kitty joked.

"I know what you're thinking, Tarasue—"

"–Of course you do; you're psychic."

"But I have the best intentions." She ignored my interruption. "If you don't want to go to the party, we don't have to. It's your special weekend."

"So, if we disappoint a seven-year-old little girl, it'll be all my fault?"

"That's not what I'm saying."

It was *exactly* what she was saying. Another psychological term for control was referred to as emotional blackmail.

> Emotional blackmail–a form of manipulation that uses guilt to persuade a choice. Studies showed that mothers use this type of manipulation to persuade their children to make the correct choice by letting them believe they are making their own choices.

Wow! This short conversation tested many concepts I learned.

Even though I agreed to go on the road trip and attend Camille's birthday party, I gave Kitty the silent treatment as we made our way across the state.

> Silent treatment–by withdrawing from the situation, a person shows their disapproval. This form of manipulation withholds communication or affection to prove they are not pleased.

I was aware that I was being as manipulative as my mother, but I didn't care. It felt good. I stewed about how much I did *not* want to be here, and she let me pout. The silence didn't bother me. It allowed me to think, but as *she* liked to remind me, I needed to get out of my head, enjoy my surroundings, and communicate with three-dimensional people. But I found satisfaction in my own company. Maybe that was why I majored in psychology. I preferred to observe, figure out the *why, and* discover the *who*. I learned so much by watching.

It had been a quiet road trip. The expansive plains of South Dakota that dominate the middle of the state remind me of the opening act before an alternative rock band commands a stage in a crowded arena filled with enthusiastic fans. You listen to the less talented, less exciting, and less famous bands while impatiently waiting for the main act, which you're sure will be worth every second of wasted time.

Like little dots on the horizon, small towns littered the interstate every fifty miles or so. These towns were essentially abandoned, featuring only a single gas station. The public restroom was located in an outer building and required a key which you had to request from the manager to access. Traveling on Interstate 90 across South Dakota was the foreplay before the main event–the gorgeous, worthwhile Black Hills.

For about five hours, annoying static dominated the FM radio stations. Kitty clicked off the radio and the air conditioner since it was struggling to keep up with the heat of the summer sun and rolled down the car windows. We listened to the swishing sound of the wind as it whipped through the interior of the car via the open windows.

When I did open my mouth to respond to one of Kitty's mundane questions, I spewed a saucy comment. I was acting like a child, but I couldn't help it. Another thing I've absorbed through my college courses is that people tend to regress to childhood behaviors when triggered by similar situations. Therefore, I couldn't be one hundred percent accountable for my responses. I blamed regression because this was our typical mother-daughter routine.

"Let's stop at Wall Drug for donuts. Lisa mentioned that Camille digs the maple ones. Plus, I've seen about ninety signs advertising free ice water, and now I'm thirsty."

"Why are you trying so hard to impress these people?"

"I'm not trying to *impress* anyone. I'm being thoughtful."

"Seems to me like you're kissing their asses."

"Tarasue, trying to be kind wouldn't kill *you*." My mother–always the optimist, the one who saw an injured blackbird and nursed it back to health–still gave me advice even though history proves that I've never listened.

"Because they are family, right? You've mentioned that several times. But in my opinion, blood doesn't make a family. People who are there for you no matter what, up and down, high or low–those are the people I consider family. Hank is family. My friend, Stella, is family." I paused one second before adding, "You, Kitty, are my family. I don't need anyone else."

Kitty inhaled deeply. She always counted to ten to calm herself while she collected her thoughts. She was getting in touch with her natural aura. Becoming one with her thoughts and mind.

This was another example of why the residents of Normal thought she was a witch. This meditation she performed in public. Plus, she was very good at reading people. Thankfully, she couldn't always read me; otherwise, she'd know that I'd communicated with Tony Shade–her rapist, my biological contributor, and Normal's notorious pastor. If she knew my plan to interview him for a paper, she would've done everything in her power to stop it. I planned on keeping that secret to myself for as long as I could. It wasn't likely that she'd ever read *Psychology Today*.

Kitty wasn't afraid of anything, except her ex-stepbrother, Tony Shade. Not that I could blame her. After getting to know him, I couldn't agree with her more.

As she flicked one of her long, signature chestnut braids over her shoulder, she said, "Tarasue, I know you're angry. Your aura is jet black." She grabbed at the air between us and threw the negative energy out the window. I rolled my eyes. "I realize you aren't thrilled with all of this hullabaloo, but I need you to be receptive to these people. Give them a chance. They don't want anything from you. After this weekend, if you never want to speak to them again, that's your prerogative."

"Really? You aren't going to bully me into a relationship with a bunch of people who share my DNA like you bullied me into detouring to a birthday party with people I've never met before? You wouldn't guilt me into pleasing you because, as my mother, you know better?" My tone was teasing, but I also had history to prove that my point was valid.

"Yes." She held up her right hand, extending two fingers. "Scout's honor."

"You know that statement holds no value because you aren't an actual Boy Scout."

"I'm trying to make a point." She put her hand down and nodded to the upcoming interstate exit. "So, Wall Drug donuts sound yummy, right?"

Chapter 27

When we pulled up to Lisa and Camille's house, I tried my mother's calming technique. I closed my eyes, breathed deeply, and silently counted to ten. Like a spoiled child, I immediately concluded that it was ridiculous. As if a mere ten seconds of peace could reduce my anxiety.

I wasn't thrilled about this situation. Ever since learning that the sperm I thought was injected into my mother via a sperm lab was actually from her ex-stepbrother, Kitty shared more revelations that tipped my level of sanity. As soon as I was able to feel a solid footing under me, she yanked out the rug from below my feet.

Hey, I didn't pick your biology at a sperm bank from a file labeled 'Rocket Scientist's sperm'.

Hey, not only do I know who your father is, but he raped me.

Hey, not only are you the product of rape, but he was legally my stepbrother at the time.

Hey, the only other person that knows about this is your deceased grandmother, Tammy.

Oh hey, I'm friends with my rapist's ex-wife. Jump in the car because we're going to visit her and her family. It'll be fun.

If I wasn't working for my master's in psychology, I would've spent a shit-ton of money on a therapist. Instead, I applied what I learned to my own life. If I didn't stay ahead of the drama, it would do irreversible damage to my future relationships. Logically, I understood that even though I was created by a violent act, it didn't make my life less valuable. I didn't do this. The only one responsible for the rape was the rapist. Even though I was a result, I had no control over my genetics. Kitty didn't raise me to be a victim. Just like my mother, I've always been a survivor.

Years later, I learned that the man who supplied half of my DNA was a complete monster. Before he was locked up and put behind bars, he owned a modern-day brothel that specialized in acts of violence against women. The women whom he recruited were young and naive. Sure, he illegally paid them for their participation, but most of them couldn't fathom the violence that he had planned for them.

My stomach was in knots. I was about to meet a room full of people who were also survivors of the same evil. I was about to attend a very odd support group with balloons and cake. I had nothing to share with these people. Technically, I wasn't there when he forced himself on my mother. I arrived nine months later. These women were physically touched by Tony, except for Camille, who luckily, like me, never had a relationship with him either.

"Kitty, you came!" The woman, who I assumed was Lisa, pulled my mother into a big bear hug after she squealed with delight.

Kitty didn't enjoy public displays of affection. I could only imagine how much she wanted to escape this overly polished, perfumed woman's embrace. That brought a smile to my face.

Thirty seconds later, the man who answered the door cleared his throat. The two friends dropped their arms to their sides, remembering that other people were in their presence. Kitty said, "Lisa, this is my daughter, Tarasue."

I recognized the woman hugging my mother from the few church services that I'd attended in Normal. Standing in the doorway wearing a matching pink tracksuit, she appeared painfully thin. Because she hardly had an ounce of fat on her body, her bones seemed to poke through her clothing. Her hair, which was still cut in a stylish bob, contained speckles of gray. Even though she was smiling, the joy didn't reach her hazel, blank eyes, which were surrounded by dark, gray circles. Her tight smile made her look like she was in physical pain, or perhaps she was on some medication that curbed her enthusiasm. It was possible after everything she'd been through.

Always the formal one, I stepped forward with my right hand outstretched. I wanted to make the first move before Lisa felt it necessary to embrace me as well. "Nice to meet you, Lisa."

Thankfully, she understood by my stiff, formal posture that I wasn't interested in a hug. She held out her palm and shook mine. "The pleasure is all mine, Tarasue." Even though I feared the wind could blow her over, her grip and handshake were firm. Her mannerisms seemed robotic.

"Please call me Tara. Only Kitty calls me Tarasue."

She glanced in Kitty's direction and responded, "Tara it is then." She stepped aside and gestured toward the man behind her to offer his introduction. "This is Howard."

"Tara." Howard extended his hand. Like Lisa's handshake, his was firm and solid. Howard was a balding middle-aged man with a twinkle in his eye. His dark eyebrows and mustache were bursting with hair, leading me to wonder if they had somehow sucked up the magic hair growth that prevented it from growing on the top of his head. When he smiled, wrinkles creased his forehead and around his eyes. "Kitty. It is wonderful to meet you both. I wish we'd known you were coming. We already let Camille open her presents."

"I didn't let Lisa know we were coming, so the fault is mine."

This was news to me. I assumed that our attendance was expected and never thought to ask any questions regarding that fact. I shook my head. Kitty never ceased to amaze me, and I knew that later she would weasel herself out of this mess with a valid excuse. She had a gift of being able to make anything that she did wrong not her fault. I did not have that ability; in fact, I was the opposite and always told the truth even if it wasn't necessary.

"Please come in." With a classic Vanna White hand gesture, Lisa invited us into her house. As she stepped aside, I noticed the chaos in the living room to the left of the entryway. The scene reminded me of what happened when your VCR paused in the middle of a scene. Like confetti, brightly colored wrapping paper was tossed all over the room. Pink, purple, and yellow balloons, hanging from every door handle and drawer pull, bounced back and forth to the room's invisible airflow. Discarded paper plates and pink paper cups littered the coffee tables. Among the birthday party decor sat four people frozen in the scene, all staring wide-eyed at the occupants–us–in the entryway. Only one expression turned quickly into a smile.

After subconsciously clearing her throat, Lisa announced, "Everyone, I want you to meet Kitty Brady and her daughter, Tara."

The eyes of the young women darted to each other and quickly returned their attention to Lisa.

The smiling one recovered first. "Welcome!" She jumped to her feet and walked toward us with her hand outstretched. Thank goodness it wasn't another awkward hug I needed to dodge. "I'm Ivy Bass. I think we probably met years ago somewhere or another." She shook Kitty's hand and then mine. "My sister Jolene and I grew up in Normal. Perhaps you remember my parents, Isabella and Walter."

I assumed Jolene was the woman still sitting on the floor with the little girl, whom I recognized from pictures as Camille. From the look on Jolene's face, I understood she felt the same way about this situation as I did. Skeptical and not thrilled. Several angry lines creased her forehead, and her eyes narrowed as she checked us out. *I understand that woman.*

Suddenly, my legs were wrapped in an embrace.

"Thank you for coming!" squealed the cutest kid I've ever seen. Since she was the only seven-year-old in the room, I assumed she was Camille. "Did you bring me a present?"

"Camille!" Lisa raised her motherly voice. "That is not polite."

After releasing my legs, Camille put her hands on her hips and eyed me. "It's more unpolite to not bring a gift to a birthday party."

"The word is impolite, and I agree." I corrected her. I was going to like this kid. "We brought something better than a gift."

"Not possible," she fired back.

I stepped back out onto the front step and retrieved the box of donuts that I'd set on the entryway bench. As soon as they were visible, the fresh smell of baked goods wafted into the room.

"Wall Drug donuts!" She squealed again. "You got the light brown ones, right?"

"Maple. Yes, just what the birthday girl ordered."

Her arms wrapped around my legs again. "You're my new favorite person."

My mom cleared her throat to grab my attention. I looked up and smiled at her. I hoped that she did have the ability to read my mind now because I was thinking that this kid was my new favorite person too.

Chapter 28

After the awkward initial introductions, we meandered into the house. I asked Lisa several first-time guest questions, like how long they'd lived there, what her neighbors were like, and her favorite thing about the property. She gave me a tour of the house with Howard at her side. Kitty had already abandoned me when Camille asked her to check out her new Barbie doll. As Lisa pointed to different rooms, Howard followed her around the house like a guard dog. His display of affection was more like a labrador than a pitbull, though. The palm of his hand often rested on the small of her back.

As Lisa recounted how she'd found the property, I looked around the modest, ranch-style home. Besides Camille's most recent school photo–the same one Kitty had displayed at her home–the home was void of personal effects. Not one picture hung on the walls. Not one thirsty plant rested in the corner of a room. Lisa lived modestly and was ready to run at the first sign of trouble.

When the tour stopped in front of the sliding patio doors attached to the kitchen, Lisa extended her long, skinny arm toward the horizon. "Camille walks to school. It takes about ten minutes."

From the adjoining living room, Camille voiced her opinion, "But I hate walking in big snow boots and puffy snow pants. I look ridiculous. Like a marshmallow."

Lisa smiled. "Yes, she reminds me every winter morning that she doesn't like the cold and hates it when the brisk wind blows on her face. Otherwise, it's a very convenient location. We're only minutes from everything we need."

I got the feeling that the 'everything' she was referring to included the police station, should Tony ever find her.

Howard cleared his throat and added, "Howard is only fifteen minutes away in his bachelor bungalow."

It was my turn to smile. It was hard not to instantly like Howard. He was a simple, genuine man smitten with Lisa. Plus, Kitty had told me about his cute habit of speaking about himself in the third person.

I followed Lisa and Howard into the kitchen, where we joined Ivy and Jolene, who were dipping their donuts into coffee. Kitty and Cooper, who I was told was Ivy's son, helped Camille build a Lego set. I plopped down in a vacant kitchen chair next to Jolene. Small talk and easy-to-answer questions filled the room even though a proverbial elephant was still sitting in the corner.

Lisa, the obvious matriarch, was responsible for keeping the conversation flowing. "Tara, your mom told me that you're a therapist."

"Could make a shitton of money on this family alone," Jolene mumbled under her breath.

"What a rewarding job. Did you always want to be a psychologist?" Lisa finished.

As soon as I finished swallowing my last bite of the donut—which was amazing—I answered. "No. As a kid, I wanted to be a vet. I love animals, but in researching that career, I discovered that twenty percent of the job is putting family pets down. That was a deal breaker. I don't think I could do that several times a day."

Kitty added, "When she was a kid, she couldn't even swat a damn fly. Broke her heart to think she ended its life."

"Got a weak stomach, huh?" Jolene piped in.

"It's not my stomach that is weak. It's my heart." I shot back at her.

Jolene was the type of person who would treat another person with respect when they earned it. I was up for the challenge. It was a coping mechanism, and she was right. I could dissect her brain for hours.

"What is it that you do, Jolene?" I decided to share the microscope. When I said her name, the urge to sing it like Reba McEntire did in her hit country song, *Jolene,* was strong. I bet that would annoy the crap out of her. I tried to contain my grin.

"I'm a waitress," she answered. I could tell that she wanted me to discredit her occupation or put her down somehow. She did not want to like me, which was completely understandable. If only she knew how badly I didn't want to be here either.

"That's a hard job. At Kitty's Cafe, we fulfill all the roles—hostess, waitress, cook, clean-up crew, and counselor. No one warns you about that part. It's exhausting. Whenever I go home to visit Kitty, she schedules me to work, and I sleep like a rock after just one shift."

Jolene eyed me up and down, simply nodding her approval.

After Ivy took a small nibble of her donut, she asked me, "Tara, we know what you do for income, but what do you do for fun? Are you single or married? Do you have kids? You know, all the good stuff." She smiled.

If Jolene was the guard dog–the mean, ready-to-attack Rottweiler–it was obvious that Ivy was the happy-go-lucky Golden Retriever.

Ivy's question shouldn't make me as uncomfortable as it did, but I didn't have a suitable answer for her. My personal life was lacking because I did nothing outside of work and school. I rarely spend time with the few close friends that I have, but that depressing declaration wasn't for a first-time meeting.

Instead, I answered, "I'm not married. No kids." Whenever I gave that response, I watched the sadness on people's faces as they imagined how empty my life was. Ivy and Jolene's expressions were no different. Ivy's brow creased, and Jolene's lips pursed as if thinking, 'I knew it.' Before I could censor my next words, I added, "I recently started dating someone."

Kitty glanced up from her Lego-building task with Camille and stared at me, indicating that she'd heard my announcement. During our five-hour drive, I hadn't mentioned this fact, and now, I knew I'd never hear the end of it. My dating someone would be the topic of the five-hour drive home.

With excitement in her voice, Ivy responded. "Interesting. Who is this mystery man? What's he like? Where did you meet?"

"It's in the very beginning stages. Too soon to give details." I smiled. When I noticed Ivy's disappointment, I added, "I don't want to jinx it." I shamed myself for opening this can of worms.

"I love the getting-to-know-you part of the relationship. Every touch ignites a spark. You can't stand to be apart. You want to know everything about him." Ivy leaned her head down onto her chin as she gazed dreamily at me. "Tell me everything," Ivy begged.

"Geez. Someone is all horned up," muttered Jolene, who probably hadn't been on a date since the invention of sliced bread.

As I thought about Ford, I couldn't help but miss him. Ivy was right. After only a few weeks, I couldn't seem to get enough of him and his giant bear hugs. Even though our relationship was still in the PG stages, he was addicting. He told me to call him as soon as I arrived home because he wanted to cook dinner for me and hear all about my trip. He'd been so excited for me that I almost considered inviting him, but it was way too soon. Since I've been comparing everyone to a dog, Ford would be like a young Labrador Retriever. Jumping up and down for attention. Lapping up every morsel of information. *Where are you hiking? Do you have one hotel room and two beds? These people you are meeting—are they from Normal, or how does your mother know them?*

Before I could reply, the front door opened, and in walked a handsome face that I'd memorized—literally memorized—only a few months before from his dating profile.

Gabe Paul.

I blinked rapidly to make sure my eyes weren't playing tricks on me. I'd recognize him anywhere. Gabe Paul was the *Match.com* man who stood me up the night that I'd met Ford.

The man who'd been messaging me for a month before our planned date. The man who told me he was afraid of getting hurt again, so if we hit it off, we'd need to take things slow. The man who enjoyed reading the Sunday newspaper with a black cup of coffee. The man who wanted to meet that special someone to become his best friend. The man who talked me into meeting him in a public place to help deflate my insecurities about meeting a stranger. The man who never showed up.

Gabe Paul.

He was even better looking than his *Match.com* profile with a dimple on his left cheek, a big white smile, and dark eyebrows that accentuated his dark brown eyes. Not only did his appearance check the boxes, but his personality won me over. His messages were full of charm and witty quips, and we shared lots of laughs. I fell for him, even though my brain told me that I needed to wait until I physically met him to see if there was chemistry.

After chatting for thirty days, we made plans to meet at a local bar for a cocktail. I'd done all the right things before I went to meet him—I told my roommate, I left the details of our date on a tablet in my room, I carried Mace in my purse, and I drove my own car. I was careful; I was cautious, but I wasn't prepared for him to not show up.

And now, we finally were under the same roof. Not at a bar in Canby, but hundreds of miles away on the west side of South Dakota at a stranger's birthday party. *How can this be?*

What should I say? My cheeks flushed, and I started to sweat.

He was even better looking in person.

Without putting the paper sacks down, he used his foot to kick the front door closed. Walking toward me was the smile and dimple that had stood me up on the night I met Ford. I was one hundred percent sure of it.

Casually, he grinned at the entire household as if he belonged there, as if this was his family. In each hand, he carried a bag of groceries. As he set down the bags on the counter, Lisa stood up and made her way toward him. She patted his bicep and began unpacking the bags. "Thanks for getting these things, Michael. Camille wants me to make caramel rolls for breakfast tomorrow, and whatever the birthday girl wants, she gets, apparently."

"I heard that, Mom," Camille yelled from the living room.

He belongs here. What is going on?

Ivy looked lovingly at ~~Gabe~~ Michael, who was making his way over to the kitchen table.

Looking back and forth between these two strangers, my eyes bulged out of their eye sockets as I stared and tried to regulate my breathing. I didn't know what to do or say.

Michael neared the kitchen table and meandered toward Ivy. When he reached her, he kissed the top of her head, quickly grabbed her last bite of donut, and tossed it into his mouth. "Honey, remember when we were dating? You couldn't keep your hands off me."

The smile grew on Michael's face, and his bushy, dark eyebrows went up and down. "The good old days."

Adoringly, Ivy looked up at Michael and then quickly realized he hadn't been introduced. "Sorry. Michael, this is Tara." Ivy pointed to me and then Kitty in the living room, "And that is Kitty. Ladies, this is my amazing, very patient husband, Michael."

My mother lifted her head and said a polite hello while I was dumbfounded.

Without a flicker of recognition, Michael politely responded, "Nice to meet you both."

He showed no sign of recognizing me, so I'd either not made an impression on him through our *Match.com* conversations, or this man was Gabe's doppelganger. I was guessing the latter. I was *praying* for the latter because this little family dynamic had already been created by so much drama that I didn't want to add to it. Plus, I reminded myself that nothing had happened. Even if Michael and Gabe were the same person, it was my fault. If he was married, then he shouldn't have created a *Match.com* profile. Regardless, I didn't want to be the one to break the news. I decided to take his lead and pretend I had no idea who he was. I'd figure out this crazy twist of fate later.

"If things don't work out with you and this mystery man, Michael has a good buddy from the Police Academy who lives in Canby. He could set you two up. Right, honey?"

I almost choked on my Wall Drug donut.

"I have no idea if he is single," Michael said as he grabbed a maple donut. "That isn't something guys talk about. We're simple creatures. We normally just grunt, burp, and fart."

Everyone laughed except me.

Jolene said, "Like cavemen."

***

While we were gathered around the dinner table about to indulge in cheese pizza–Camille's favorite–Lisa led us all in prayer.

"Dear God, please bless this patchwork family. We need your presence in our lives as we try to navigate through our own healing and bridge relationships with each other. Even though we have been brought together by a web of trauma, let no man break us apart. Amen."

"Amen."

Camille leaped from her chair and grabbed the first slice of pizza as the warm cheese stretched and broke. Howard quickly wiped up the grease that dripped from the pizza onto the table. Lisa just smiled at everyone.

Patchwork family? That sounded about right. It was a great analogy for this group of people. Everyone looked a bit different, but we were all sewn together by one common stitch. Unfortunately, the stitch was sewn by a monster.

Chapter 29

As I watched the bright summer sun settle itself behind the thin, tall pine trees that populate the Black Hills, I enjoyed the reprieve from the summer heat. I'd retreated onto Lisa's back deck. I never noticed how nature could be so quiet and beautiful simultaneously. It was as if Earth was breathing in its wonder and calming every occupant. When the sun dipped a drop lower, the horizon became a beautiful shade of pink-purple that only God could create.

I couldn't help but feel a little of the same peace. Even though this was the last place I had wanted to be at the start of my day, my attitude shifted a few hours later. Not only did I feel welcomed here, but I also felt comfortable and a sense of kinship with them. These people were part of my therapy group. We'd all experienced a loss of innocence at the hands of Tony Shade. Whether we liked it or not, he had stolen a piece of us.

The fact that Michael looked like the man I'd been chatting with online faded from my worries. It was a weird coincidence. Ivy and Michael had been married for years, and I didn't notice one flicker of recognition from him. Michael wasn't Gabe.

The birthday party had ended when the birthday girl returned from the bathroom dressed in her *Teenage Ninja Turtle* pajamas and asked Kitty to read her a bedtime story. I looked adoringly at Camille. She must have dressed herself because she'd skipped a button on her top, causing it to gather awkwardly above her belly button. With her mother's urging, she told everyone goodnight and thank you in between a set of yawns. As she rubbed her eyes with her whole fist, she said, "This was the best birthday ever."

My heart melted.

As Kitty and Camille climbed the steps up to Camille's bedroom hand in hand, the rest of the guests picked up the disarray left from the party excitement. After throwing out the last paper cup, everyone said their goodbyes and retreated to their lodging except me who patiently waited for the birthday girl to succumb to slumber. I ventured through the sliding glass doors and into a slice of God's Country, Howard's nickname for the Black Hills. I tipped my head back in one of the Adirondack chairs.

Luckily on the west side of the state, mosquitos weren't prevalent, so I wasn't swatting any bugs while I enjoyed the cool night air. For a few minutes, I contemplated the idea of moving to the Hills. It was a stark contrast to the flat plains of the east side of the state, where straight-line winds caused tumbleweeds to blow for a hundred miles on any given day.

The sliding glass door creaked as it opened, and I glanced up to see Lisa making her way through the doorway. Her appearance was still perfect. No wrinkles in her pantsuit, not a hair out of place, makeup was fresh and not worn off. I wondered if her appearance was part of a control issue, like if she appeared flawless, people wouldn't notice the scars inside.

"We never truly know what's going on in someone else's mind, what they're capable of, what they're thinking, or how they truly feel. Do we?" Lisa fired off the strange comment as she pulled the patio door shut. She sat down in the matching chair. "In the five seconds that it took me to say that, your brain fired off at least a dozen questions regarding my sanity. Is she referring to Tony or herself? What is she capable of? Did she do something terrible?"

My eyes bugged out, but I didn't respond. Her little speech caught me off guard. She was reading my mind.

Lisa continued her strange conversation. "I understand these questions more than you think. They're bouncing off the walls in my brain, too. I question my sanity. I wonder how far I'd go to keep Camille safe. What would I be capable of if I needed to protect her?" Lisa looked down at her hands, which were slightly shaking. She quickly tucked them under her thighs to control the movement.

"If you're curious, I'd do anything and everything. She's my whole world." As she stared off into the distance of the black of night, a single tear raced down her cheek. She didn't bother to wipe it away. "Without a doubt, I'd die for her. Kill for her."

I wasn't shocked by her proclamation, but I was curious as to why she was telling *me*. We'd only met a few hours ago. I allowed the silence to fill the space between us.

"It's called motherhood." She was looking at me now. "There is nothing like the love between a mother and a child, but children can't return the love with the same power. Yes, you love and respect your mom, but you'll never fully grasp that deep love until you become a mother yourself."

I wanted to interject that I've studied relationships in tons of my psychology courses, but I also knew that studying something and experiencing it created different outcomes. I was curious to see where she was going with this conversation.

"I'm sure you've accepted what happened and why your mom kept it a secret for so long, but I hope you understand her primal need to protect you. She did what she did because she loves you unconditionally."

"Lisa, why are you telling me this?" She started to make this strange conversation personal.

"I've enjoyed your mom's company and friendship for years. In the beginning, I sought her out because I was curious. During every visit, I sat on the edge of my seat waiting to hear her wise words. Her words fueled me and gave me a sense of peace. And now, years later, I have Camille, your half-sister, and I feel an even stronger bond with Kitty. Your mother is an angel, a true blessing. I wouldn't be here without the compassion she showed me years ago. I completely understand wanting to shield your child from the harsh reality of her beginning. That kid is joy—pure joy. I don't want to be the one to crush that."

Lisa sipped the amber liquid in her glass.

"I think Kitty did a wonderful job raising you, especially all alone. What happened to her could've left her forever broken, yet she chose to overcome it. She's inspiring. I thought I should tell you from a mom's perspective that I plan on doing the same thing Kitty did. I'm not telling Camille who her father is until she is a mature, well-rounded adult. You may have felt that your mother was lying to you, but she wasn't. She was protecting you. There is a difference, and it's the reasoning behind it that makes the timing so important. Hopefully, you'll still be around when I tell Camille so she can lean on you."

I sat back in my chair, silence filling the air. I let Lisa's words penetrate my heart.

"Your mother amazes me. When I found her at the cafe, she was nothing but receptive, helpful, and compassionate. I'm not sure if I could have been as strong as she was. A strange woman shows up at her workplace dredging up a bunch of feelings that were buried. The mere mention of his name prompts her to confront her old feelings and memories.

"I'm blessed to have your mother as my friend. Without her support, I wouldn't be where I am now. I wish I would've been stronger back then and left him sooner, but then Camille wouldn't exist. I struggle with the guilt I feel for the women he was hurting. However, if I'd said something sooner, she wouldn't be with me now.

"When he started to physically and sexually abuse me, I felt so alone. Ashamed. I was too absorbed in my own pain to think that there might be more going on. But now I know that what he was doing to me behind the closed doors of our home was only fueling the fire. He craved more power—more thrill.

"When we moved to Normal, I learned Tony had family in town—an ex-stepsister. I kept waiting for him to invite her over for supper so I could meet her. That never happened. Then I overheard him bragging about the 'pranks' he played on his ex-stepsister to a man who was visiting. I was appalled. I couldn't understand why he'd do this to someone who had once been his family or any person for that matter. Every week, he'd leave her candy bars in her mailbox that had some weird tie to their childhood. He'd call her house, breathing heavily into the phone before hanging up. A few times he broke into the cafe. He'd bring one of his women there and take Polaroid pictures of them having sex on the counter. He'd leave a used condom in a booth. There were no limits to how repulsive he could be.

"I couldn't understand his obsession with a woman who was his sister for a little over a year. He had me so brainwashed that I blamed *her* for his obsession. Sick, right?" She paused and shook her head. Quickly, she wiped away another tear that skirted down her cheek. "One day, I stomped into the cafe determined to tell her to leave my man alone, pressuring her into telling me why he moved us to the town where she lived. But instead, I made a friend." Her laugh was deep and awkward. "Ironic how life works sometimes."

Lisa's words resonated with me. I'd been hurt when my mother-daughter trip had somehow morphed into a ruse intended to introduce me to strangers, but now, strangely enough, I felt a kinship with them. Life was ironic.

Chapter 30

I've heard the old saying that your hopes and dreams come true when you least expect it. I felt that this perfectly encapsulated the events between Ford and me. I'd been stood up by a blind date–an online blind date, which by my standards was even worse. Still, Ford managed to win me over with his genuine kindness, wit, and charm.

When I returned from my weeklong trip to the Black Hills with Kitty, Ford was waiting on the front steps of my apartment with a bouquet of wildflowers. We'd only been dating a couple of weeks, so I described my trip as a mini-vacation with my mother, stopping along the way to meet one of my mother's friends. Telling him that I was meeting a room full of my biological contributor's victims didn't seem like a discussion to have at the beginning stages of a relationship.

As he helped me unpack my bags, he asked me how the trip went, what I thought of everyone, and what else Kitty and I did for fun.

I answered the easiest questions first. "My mom and I found the cutest little restaurant called Cheyenne Crossing located on the rim of Spearfish Canyon. Everyone was so friendly, and the place looked like you were stopping by your grandma's for lunch. That is if your grandma lived in a homey, little log cabin in the woods. But best of all, the food was delicious. Homemade and rich in flavor. I could've eaten there all weekend."

"You're making me hungry."

"I devoured an Indian Taco made with fresh bread dough. The fresh lettuce and tomatoes came from their own garden. And thank goodness, we went hiking around Roughlock Falls after that to burn the calories that I consumed."

"Isn't that where they filmed a scene from *Dancing with Wolves*?"

"Yes. It's breathtaking. If I lived out there, every day would be an adventure. I'd go exploring all the time." That thought had occurred to me every day while Kitty and I were there. The Black Hills had an innocent beauty. Thankfully, large vacation resorts hadn't capitalized on the area and taken over. People waved to each other on the road, and everywhere we stopped we made new friends.

"Was Camille as adorable as your mom made her out to be?" he asked, dropping my duffel bag on the floor in the laundry room.

I was surprised that he remembered all the names I'd mentioned before I left.

"Yes. In fact, she was more adorable than my mom described. The kid is not only cute and smart, but she's also humorous and clever. I can't believe she's only seven years old. Is it weird that I want to be her best friend?" I rambled on about funny things Camille had said, only to realize I'd been talking nonstop for ten minutes. "Sorry. How was your weekend? Did you hear back about your promotion?"

Ford's search for the perfect job was a never-ending quest. He was working security detail at a large company, but the hours and wages left a lot to be desired. His dream job had been to be a police officer, but an ex-girlfriend had filed a false police report. Under the advice of his attorney, Ford resigned from the police academy weeks before he was due to graduate. The scandal cost him his future. He'd explained that he had no ill will toward the woman, just that he wished she sought professional help. From his stories, she sounded like a perfect patient for a budding therapist, and we joked about how I could counsel her.

"Unfortunately no. I left another message, but I don't want to sound too desperate. I'm not losing sleep over it. It'll work out." As he popped a mint into his mouth, he threw my dirty clothes into the washer and added detergent. I hadn't even asked him for his help. He was a wonderful boyfriend. Almost too good to be true.

"What about Lisa, your mom's friend? Did you get along with her?"

"Yeah, she was welcoming. Kind of an odd duck, but then again, my mom attracts all kinds of wounded souls."

"How is she wounded?" Ford looked up from the duffle bag as he set my makeup bag on my bed.

"Not physically wounded. Mentally. I don't know the whole story. Just bits." I wasn't ready to unload my issues onto Ford, but I also didn't want to lie to him either. I opted for a safe way to introduce Tony. "Her ex-husband is currently incarcerated for several sexual offenses, I heard. Supposedly, she'd been brainwashed into committing the crimes with him. It's a whole mess."

Ford followed me out into the living room, where I plopped down on the couch. I missed my space. It was good to be home.

"Damn. Poor lady." Ford sat down next to me, put his arm around my shoulders, and gently pushed my head down to rest on his shoulder. "What kind of sex crimes?"

As we sat side by side, he played with a few strands of my hair.

"Rumor has it that they ran a brothel right out of their house. When her husband was arrested, Lisa agreed to hand over evidence to incriminate him and a bunch of other powerful men. I think the whole experience did a number on her. I mean, there isn't a protocol for how to handle this kind of scandal, and I have no idea how someone is supposed to move on. I truly hope she invested in some counseling."

"A brothel? Really? I didn't think brothels were still around. Seems like an 1800s kind of thing." Ford paused for a moment trying to search for the correct response. When he couldn't find a suitable answer, he proceeded. "I'm curious about what kind of things they were doing. I mean I know what they were doing, but why the need for a brothel? When I was a kid, I saw a book at the library about the Kama Sutra. I bet they took those positions to a whole other level." It was Ford's turn to ramble. "Where did he find hookers who agreed to be locked in the room all night? Did he tell them all the details beforehand? How much did he charge the men? What did the hooker make? Are they all having sex simultaneously, or do they watch each other and take turns? How does the topic of a sex room come up in conversation with other dudes?"

I sat up and looked back at him. I raised my eyebrows and smirked at him. "Ford, is there something you need to tell me?"

His skin color changed from a tan-brown shade to a milky cream color. "No. Why?"

When I sat back down next to him, I nudged him with my elbow, "You haven't laid a finger on me yet, but you've read a book about the Kama Sutra. That's some intense reading."

His laugh seemed a bit forced. "Honey, you must've heard me wrong. I never said I *read* it. It's more of a picture book."

***

Even though he revealed that he knew about the Kama Sutra, Ford was a complete gentleman. After eight dates, he still hadn't tried anything more than second base. However, if I was completely honest, I wondered *why* he hadn't tried anything more. It led me to question my sex appeal. Maybe he didn't find me attractive, and that was why he hadn't pushed me to go further. I was overthinking the situation, but my pride pushed me to bring up the topic.

While we were driving home from a nice dinner at a local hotspot, I invited him into my apartment for a nightcap.

"Not tonight. I have to work a double shift tomorrow, and I need to be rested, or I'll never make it until midnight." He had his left hand on the wheel while his right hand held mine. He squeezed it as he looked over at me.

I couldn't meet his gaze. Before the night began, I convinced myself to ask him again even though he turned me down every time. I'd thrown myself at him multiple times when we had been alone in the car. I didn't understand.

As he pulled his car over to the side of the road in front of my apartment, he put the car in park and adjusted himself in his seat to face me. "Tara, this was fun again! I can't believe how lucky I am."

"Why don't you want to sleep with me?" I blurted.

"What?" My question caught him off guard. "Why would you think that?"

"You've never once accepted my invitation to stay overnight. You're a perfect gentleman. You never try *anything*."

"I'm sorry?" It was a question more than an apology. "I thought women wanted a gentleman who treated them with respect. Am I doing something wrong? Tara, I don't understand."

The way he said it made me feel like a complete idiot. Of course, I was being an idiot. I knew it, but I needed to explain.

"Oh, Ford, I've never been treated *this* respectfully before." After I pulled my hand away from his grip, I used both of them to cover my face. Through the cracks of my fingers, I asked, "Do you find me attractive?" My insecurities caused me to revert to a twelve-year-old's thought process—*do you like me? Check yes or no.*

When he laughed at my question, I pulled my hands down slightly so I could catch a glimpse of him. My expression was deadpan.

"Oh! You're serious. Sorry I laughed, but that seemed like a ridiculous question. I find you very attractive and honestly out of my league. I like to hold your hand all the time to prove to myself that I'm not dreaming and to make sure you won't run away. So, yes, I find you very attractive."

"Why don't you want to have sex with me?" I threw the question out there again. I was apprehensive about the response I might receive, but I hoped that by surprising him with the question, he wouldn't be able to give me a deceptive response. I needed to know.

His eyes widened. "I do want to have sex with you, Tara. I don't know where you get the idea that I don't. This is like our ninth date in two months—"

"Eighth."

"Our eighth date in two months. I stand corrected. I think about being intimate with you all the time. I wouldn't be human if I didn't."

"Then why don't you say yes when I invite you to come up? Why do you pull away when our kiss is just getting so good? Why don't you recline this car seat and show me that you find me attractive?"

He looked down at his lap, shifted in his seat, and answered, "I do want to... it's just... it's just..." He was struggling to find the words.

"You don't like me like that?" *Rip off the bandage. Reject me quickly. Get it over with.*

"No, I'm just nervous, I guess. Sometimes, I have... issues... with... performance. I was waiting until I felt more confident in our relationship before I told you. I guess that time is now." He tried to make a joke and threw in a fake laugh. "After my ex-girlfriend Jenny made that false report about me and spilled all of our dirty little secrets, I'm... I'm just a little scared to be intimate with someone again."

He still hadn't looked up at me. He was embarrassed and anxious. I pushed him into disclosing a painful secret out of fear of rejection. I felt like a jerk.

I *was* a jerk.

I wiggled closer to him in the car. I reached over and pulled his face, which was covered in a sexy five o'clock shadow, up toward my gaze.

"Ford, I'm so sorry. I had no idea. I immediately assumed it was me. I never even considered something else. I guess I wanted to reject you before you rejected me, so I picked this fight." Because his car had bucket seats, I wasn't able to get as close to him as I wanted. I kissed the top of his hand. "Please accept my apology for being a pushy jerk."

As a smile grew on his lips, he teased, "A sexy, pushy jerk."

I raised an eyebrow and considered the extra adjective. "Well, I'm glad to know you think so." I smiled. "Dude, I feel like a big slut now, always pushing you to go farther. You almost had to beat me away with a stick."

His smile grew, and I saw a small white mint in between his teeth.

"I won't push anymore. I'll be a proper woman and wait patiently for your advances. At least you'll know ahead of time that I'll be willing." I winked at him. "I'm an easy lay."

Chapter 31

After our confessionals–mine about wanting to rip off his clothes and his about being unable to get it up when he was nervous–I relaxed and enjoyed my time with Ford. Who knew that if you removed sexual tension from a relationship, your bond could be even stronger? Not me! In the past, whenever I dated someone, intimacy solidified our relationship. With Ford, the connection was deeper. He was easy to talk to, and he was curious about everything. Dating him was like being in a relationship with an excitable middle schooler who wanted to try new things, touch everything, and talk about anything.

Whenever Ford and I shared the same day off from work, we'd spend the day together. Sometimes, we would go for long walks along the river, watch old movies, or talk about our childhoods. One afternoon after a walk in the rain, we snuggled on the couch at my apartment, and Ford picked up a frame from my end table. He studied the photograph for a bit before asking, "This is either an older, hot sister who you haven't told me about yet, or it's your mother."

The picture of Kitty and I had been taken in the parking lot of a church minutes before I left on the weekend Bible retreat where

I'd been groped by Tony. We were standing under a big oak tree. Its branches were populated with big green leaves and stretched out over the tops of our heads, casting shade on the front lawn of the church. Tucked under one arm, I held my lumpy pillow covered by a flowered pillowcase while I gripped the handle of my overstuffed duffle bag. Looking at the faded picture, I could see the striking resemblance between Kitty and me. We both had long, wavy, chestnut-colored hair that fell to the middle of our backs. Our eyes were the same almond shape, and both of our smiles reached higher on the left side. Because the photograph was poor quality, the colors were fading, and it was difficult to see that my eyes were blue and Kitty's were brown. But otherwise, I was the spitting image of Kitty, only fifteen years younger.

"She'd love to hear you say that." I took the frame from him and peered down at it. "That's my mom. Everyone calls her Kitty."

"Funny nickname." Ford purred. "How did she get it?"

I set the frame back on the end table. "I don't remember all the details, but she earned it from rescuing cats."

I remembered the story, but it involved Kitty's stepbrother, who was my biological—I *don't like to say that word about him*—the man who contributed to my DNA. It had been three years since I learned that information, and I still didn't like thinking or talking about it. I never told anyone. Not even Stella, my best friend. What was the point? I couldn't change it, and I knew anyone I told would ask a lot of questions that I didn't know the answer to.

"A crazy cat lady, huh?" As Ford did his best imitation of a purring kitten, he pawed at me.

"Not really. She wasn't allowed to bring any rescues home because her mom, my grandma Tammy, was allergic. So she brought them to this big abandoned house a couple of blocks away from our house. She babysat and completed odd jobs for the neighbors to pay for cat food. Kitty has always been a sucker for the needy and wounded."

"When do I get to meet your mom?" He raised an eyebrow at me.

"I don't know." I rose from the couch and walked into the kitchen for a glass of water. For some reason, I wasn't ready to take our relationship to the next level, where we introduced each other to family. Plus, Kitty could read anyone like a book, and I was slightly afraid of what she would say about Ford.

***

Later that day, we walked hand in hand down the road to have dinner. After we'd ordered our food, an elderly couple stopped by our table to tell us that we were adorable together.

"Excuse me." The sweet, little lady who was probably in her seventies tapped the end of our table to get our attention. "Even though my husband wants me to leave well enough alone, I had to stop by and tell you two lovebirds what a cute couple you make."

"Well, thank you. That was sweet of you." I let go of Ford's hand that I'd been holding across the tabletop and self-consciously tucked a strand of hair behind my ear.

The elderly woman glanced toward her husband and said, "Did you hear that, Grumpy? She said I was sweet." She turned back to us and grinned. "My only advice is to make sure you're not related before you fall in love." She nodded to her husband. "Grumpy is my second cousin. Grossed some people out, but we didn't want kids, so we figured it was fine. Plus, it kept the wedding smaller since we shared a lot of the same relatives."

She laughed at her story while I smiled at her uncomfortably. I looked over at Ford, who looked more than uncomfortable. The color had washed from his cheeks.

"Well, have a great evening." She turned and walked away.

As soon as she was out of earshot, a giggle escaped my lips. I quickly covered my mouth to not disturb other diners. "Oh my goodness!"

"TMI, if you ask me." Ford didn't laugh, but his smile reached his eyes. "She reminds me of my mom. Always saying something a bit off-color and inappropriate."

"Your mom sounds like a hoot. I bet you miss her."

Previously, Ford informed me that his parents were deceased and he had no siblings, but I didn't know the details.

"Yeah, she died from cancer. Her death was a blessing. She suffered a lot at the end."

"I'm sorry. What about your dad?"

"He died a few months before she did. Sudden heart attack. It happens." He focused a smile back on his face. "What about you? Tell me more about your mom, Kitty."

I could tell that was all the information I was getting for the moment on his family. I understood. We were in a public place, and we were in the get-to-know-each-other stage of our relationship.

"My mom owns a little cafe in our small town, kind of like this one." I looked around the restaurant and wondered which ones were the regulars and which customers were first-timers like us. "Her business is her life. She hardly ever leaves Normal."

"What about your dad?"

"No dad. Never has been. When you meet my mom, you'll understand. She isn't conventional."

"So, I *do* get to meet her." Again, he raised his eyebrow to tease me.

We didn't talk much more about our families that night. Honestly, it was only a few months into our relationship, and I don't think either of us wanted to divulge that much about our families just yet. The loss of his parents seemed still fresh, and there was no way I wanted to tell a guy I just started dating that my father was a serial rapist who resided in prison. Seemed more like a ninety-ninth-date revelation or a relationship ender.

Chapter 32

Meeting Lisa, Ivy, and Jolene at Camille's birthday party reignited my initial curiosity about Tony. He stole something from each of us–innocence–and it wasn't something you could grow or replace. Once it was gone, you could never fully get it back. Jolene believed that Tony had something to do with her father's car accident. She had no proof but Lisa's suspicion. There was something more to Jolene's hatred, but I didn't think I'd ever know what it was. She was a hard egg to crack.

Tony and his friends stripped Ivy of her virginity and innocence, but she refused to allow the trauma to negatively impact her life. Even though the result had caused the worst-case scenario–pregnancy–she loved her son and didn't regret him for a second.

Lisa's situation was the hardest for me to stomach. I blame my mother. I was brought up to be a strong, independent woman, never allowing anyone to diminish the stubborn, bright light that was me. Even though Lisa didn't possess a mean bone in her body, I saw her as weak. She never spoke up. She never stopped it from happening. She stayed married to this monster. She could've avoided so much heartache if she'd been stronger.

Kitty informed me that I was being too harsh on Lisa. She was probably right, but I couldn't help feeling the way I did. I didn't see her as a helpless victim like I did Ivy. I saw her as a weak, passive woman who allowed herself to be victimized. She could've stopped so much tragedy from happening.

Maybe that was why I couldn't stop thinking about all the crimes Tony committed. There were too many years that women didn't stand up to this man, and I felt like it was my job to defend the powerless and cowardly. Sure, I was being harsh, but I was taught to stand up for myself. It didn't matter if I was being bullied or if someone else was. I was just as guilty as the bully if I didn't say something.

I one hundred percent believed that was why I chose psychology as my degree. Kitty believed it was because I needed to learn that my perspective wasn't the only one—that I wasn't always right. The world isn't just black and white. There's a lot of gray. My hippie mother always interjected, "There is a whole kaleidoscope of colors that you don't see." She wasn't wrong. "If you see the same situation through another lens, you'll see something different. It helps build empathy."

Because I enjoyed arguing with her, I responded, "However, if I want to be a great therapist, I need to logically help my patients, not sympathize with every ounce of their drama. Hand-holding is not the reason I majored in psychology, Kitty."

"As your mother, I'm well aware of your strengths, Tarasue, but to be truly great at something, especially helping people, you need to understand where they're coming from. That, my sweet girl, is your weakness. If you don't feel their pain, you'll only look at them like a textbook study. Patients are more than just a statistic or a financial asset. They're people who'll come to you for professional advice, not a robotic message about what the University of Phoenix discovered when they polled two hundred residents."

***

Two months after we'd returned from our Black Hills trip, I went home for the weekend to visit Kitty, and like usual, I helped out at the cafe. Even though I teased her that I'd love to come home and just relax once in a while, I enjoyed waitressing and catching up with the locals. This was an extension of my home. Kitty's Cafe had been part of my life for as long as I could remember.

That Saturday afternoon, as I was scrubbing down the tables and refilling the salt and pepper containers, Tommy Baker walked through the front door. Bible Camp boyfriend Tommy. It had been years since I last laid eyes on my first crush. His beautiful auburn hair was cut military short, but his signature chestnut-colored freckles still speckled his cheeks. He'd grown another six inches since high school and stood heads taller than anyone in the cafe. He was dressed in a pair of faded blue jeans and a gray sweatshirt.

He dropped into a seat at the counter and opened a menu. As I wiped my hands on my apron, I strolled his way.

"I'm sorry, but we don't serve alcohol, Sergeant Baker," I teased as a way of greeting him. Tommy joined the Army after high school.

Tommy looked up from the menu he'd been studying, and his face broke out in a grin.

"Tarasue? Damn girl. You turned into a royal fox." Tommy never had much of a filter, but now as an adult, he stammered to correct his politically incorrect greeting. "I mean, not that you weren't good-looking when we were kids. But now, you're a full-blown hottie." He whistled for effect.

Never one to take a compliment well, I muttered, "Ah, thanks." I put my hands on my hips and looked at him. He hadn't aged besides his height and his short hair. His wit and personality hadn't changed much either. Tommy had always been everyone's friend. Easygoing and happy.

After I took his to-go order of a cheeseburger and fries, we exchanged the typical small talk about what we'd been up to and who we'd heard from since graduation. As soon as there was a break in the conversation, I blurted out a question that I'd wanted to ask him for years.

"Tommy, this question may seem like it's coming out of left field, but bear with me."

"Well, now you have me very curious."

"Nothing like that. I assure you. Something from our teenage years."

"So, it has a PG rating?"

I smiled. Tommy and I had only 'dated' for a few months, but during that time we hardly talked or spent time together, much like a lot of junior high crushes. We were friends and hung out in the same social circles in high school, but we never dated again.

"Wait! Let me guess." Tommy's eyes grew wide and serious. "Do you have a baby? Am I the father?"

"Cute. Considering that we never had sex, I'd say that is highly unlikely." As I shook my head, I smiled bigger. Tommy's personality and sense of humor were what attracted me to him many moons ago, definitely not the fact that his ears were too big for his head.

"Not technically. No. But I had plenty of wet dreams about you. Some people might consider an intense wet dream almost like having actual sex. You've seen *Basic Instinct*, right?"

"I don't think it can be called sex if the girl isn't even in the same room." I shook my head. I decided if I wanted to know his answer before he started joking about some other childhood memory, I'd better spit it out. "Do you remember Bible Camp when you asked me to be your girlfriend?"

"Yes. You were the hottest girl. Everyone wanted to bag you, but I asked first, so I won." He licked his finger and made a pretend point in the air.

"Gross and thanks, I think? Back to my question, we were supposed to meet that night at the lake, but you never showed up. What happened?"

"Yeah, I always knew you hated me not showing up on the beach that night. I figured that was why you broke up with me months later. You were so out of my league."

"What happened? Why didn't you meet me?" I didn't want to talk about leagues, and I didn't remember any specifics about why we broke up. It was just a crush. I probably started crushing on someone new. That's what twelve-year-olds do.

"After the hike, the group split up. Most of the boys were fishing, and the girls were playing in the water. As we were fishing, I bragged to my buddies about how you and I were sneaking out to play a little tonsil hockey. Pastor Tony overheard the conversation. He pulled me aside later and thankfully didn't embarrass me in front of my friends. He asked me who I was meeting and when. He seemed so excited about it that I thought it would be fine to tell him. Once I confessed the plan, he got upset and told me that meeting you without a chaperone would be against camp rules, and he'd be forced to remove me from camp immediately. I didn't want that, so I agreed to not tell anyone about my conversation with him. He said he'd talk to you and explain why our plan was sinful and wrong.

"Years later, when we were friends again, I thought, *Oh good, she isn't still mad at me for being a lame ass.* I totally would've kissed you that night. I even practiced with my hand." He held out the palm of his left hand. "Wanna see?" he teased.

I punched his shoulder. "You're a class act, Tommy. I appreciate the truth and that you were willing to practice on yourself." I laughed. "Not many guys are so worried about it that they would practice first," I said.

"Yep, that's me—a real ladies' man."

***

The conversation with Tommy caused a queasy feeling in the pit of my gut. Even as a kid, I knew it was bizarre that Pastor Tony had shown up on the beach that night. I suspected something fishy, but suspecting something and knowing the truth sometimes doesn't jive.

That Sunday night when I returned to my apartment, I woke up in the middle of the night. Something was bothering my subconscious. Over the weekend, I didn't sleep well in my childhood room, but I assumed it was because I was used to my apartment. I'd been so excited to return to my bed after spending the weekend in my small twin bed in Kitty's house that I tossed and turned for fifteen minutes, willing myself to succumb to slumber again. Despite my body sinking into the mattress and my head comfortably resting on my pillow, my mind would not rest.

I reached over to switch on the lamp next to my bed. On my bedside table, the light beam illuminated the stack of paperwork I'd collected on Tony Shade. Three years ago, I'd interviewed this monster for my psychology paper, but I never stopped collecting evidence and studying the case against him. I reassured myself that it wasn't an obsession, more like a hobby.

Hobbies don't haunt your sleep.

My sassy subconscious voice sounded like my mother's logic.

I sat up in bed, pulled the file onto my lap, and paged through the papers I already knew by heart. I scattered copies of various pieces of evidence that I'd been collecting. The copy of the police report detailing the death of my biological grandfather caught my attention.

I'd read through the report before almost having the details memorized, so I wasn't sure what I thought I was missing. I studied the photo of the inhaler that Gus had for his asthma. I understood why the police didn't look further into this death after they discovered he had died of suffocation. It was a common cause of death for someone who suffered from asthma for years. Gus hadn't been a healthy man. He was overweight and ate mainly TV dinners, according to the contents of his fridge. His doctor even said he recommended heart medication the last time he saw him for his asthma, and Gus had refused.

When I looked at the inhaler, I read the label, "RX1044-09." It listed the pharmacy that filled the prescription and the date of the refill. Five refills were available until Gus needed a follow-up appointment with this doctor.

"Shake the inhaler. Empty your lungs. Press down on the canister and take a deep breath in. Hold for 5 seconds. Repeat."

"CVS, 46624 Prairie Drive, Marshall, MN, Date filled October 13, 1978." He picked up his prescription two days before he died.

October 15, 1978, Deceased Gus Everett Shade, Sergeant Lilianna Winston

On October 15, 1978, at approximately 0800, I responded to a death report at 515 Wildwood Ave, apartment 2B. The 911 call was made by his daughter-in-law, Lisa Shade, who was in town visiting, but not staying with the deceased. The deceased, Gus Everett Shade, age 59, was found face up in the middle of his queen-sized bed wearing a pair of red plaid boxer shorts. No jewelry. He was lying on top of a fitted sheet; the top sheet had fallen onto the floor. One standard-size pillow was resting under his head. Beside his bed on the nightstand lay an empty inhaler prescribed to the deceased, a half glass of water, an unopened bottle of Tylenol, his wallet, and a box of tissues. In the drawers, we found undergarments, socks, and an address book.

His wallet contained eighty dollars in cash, his driver's license, a grocery receipt, and a picture of a woman. The items listed on the receipt matched the contents found in his stomach (verified by his autopsy on October 20, 1978) as well as in the refrigerator. Lisa and Anthony Shade, the daughter-in-law and son of the deceased, reported that the apartment's front door was unlocked and all windows were open with the screens intact. No sign of forced entry. The son, Anthony Shade, verified that he and his wife had attended dinner with the victim but had left the apartment around 2100. They had plans to meet the deceased for breakfast that morning. When he didn't show up at Perkins (2601 S Villanova), they drove to his apartment to check on him. According to Mr. and Mrs. Shade, they discovered the victim dead in his apartment bedroom and promptly called 911.

No signs of a struggle. No property theft except possibly one pillow from his queen-sized bed.

What am I missing? What was everyone missing at the time of Gus' death?

My spidey senses told me there was something here, but I needed caffeine if I was going to do some major brainstorming at three in the morning. I set the file folder on the nightstand and shuffled into the kitchen to make coffee. Coffee would help. It would ignite the sparks that were waiting for a flame.

The fresh smell of coffee beans wafted through the air as I waited for it to finish brewing. I inhaled deeply, letting the smell itself wake my insides. As I breathed in the aroma, I thought about how scary it would be to die of suffocation, not being able to take a breath. It was something a healthy person took for granted. Stella had asthma as a child, and I remember she clenched her chest when she couldn't catch her breath. Her inhaler had been lifesaving, and she'd never gone anywhere without it.

I ran back to my room and grabbed the police report again. Stella told me that her inhaler would last her two or three months. Gus' inhaler was empty after only three days. That didn't make sense.

Chapter 33

For some reason only my subconscious knew, I wanted to ask Tony about his father's death before I delivered my assumptions to the police. Maybe it was the fact that he was already in jail that I didn't feel the need to rush to the police with my discovery. Plus, Gus was already dead. Maybe I wasn't one hundred percent certain and didn't want to run to the police like an amateur sleuth until I confirmed my suspicions. Or maybe it was out of morbid curiosity. Honestly, it was a combination. As a therapist, I desperately wanted to understand his reasoning. As a naturally curious person, I yearned to be proved right, but as his offspring, I wanted to be wrong. Tony had already done so many terrible things that adding murder to his rap sheet might throw my worries about nature versus nurture into overdrive.

Whatever the reason, I called up a phone number that I'd memorized years before. The familiar, husky voice of the woman I'd grown to respect, Haley Gorski, answered on the second ring.

"Well, ain't this a blast from the past! Hello there, Miss Brady," she chirped.

I held the receiver out and looked at it. *How did she know it was me?*

When I placed the receiver back up to my ear, I heard her say, "Caller ID. Welcome to 1996! You should invest in that feature. It's so nice to know who is calling before you answer it. I hardly answer my home phone anymore. After I see that it's either my ex calling or my mother, who wants to complain about my father, I let the machine pick it up. Hell, I ain't got time or patience for either of that drama."

I laughed. Haley Gorski was a breath of fresh air for that prison.

"Okay. You got me. I lied. If I ain't on the rag, I answer the booty call, but not my mother!" Haley admitted.

"Hi, Ms. Gorski. You're right; I should invest in Caller ID. I'm surprised the Warden splurged for that fancy feature."

"The feature is only on my line. Hell, he probably doesn't even know. He'll sign anything I put in front of him." I heard her chuckle at her control over her boss. "In my line of work, it's a good idea to be able to jot down all incoming calls in case we get a bomb threat or something."

This information was good to know for the request I was about to make.

"Ms. Gorski, do you think the Warden would allow me to visit Tony Shade again?"

"Did you not earn your degree yet? Don't tell me that you failed. I didn't peg you for a quitter."

"No. I mean yes. I graduated." I paused for a second to consider how much information I wanted to reveal. "Honestly, I keep thinking about the conversations I had with Mr. Shade and have some follow-up questions that would help me sleep better at night, but I don't want to make a big deal about it."

"Girlfriend, no problem at all. In fact, Warden Jespersen doesn't even need to know you're here. I'll add you to Mr. Shade's visitor log, and you'll be good to go."

"Really? That's it?"

"I'm a witch, girl. I wave my magic wand, and I make things happen." She released a small witch cackle.

"You're amazing, Ms. Gorski."

"Call me, Haley; all my friends do."

***

The following day I drove to Fort Madison Correctional Facility to meet with Tony. I didn't want to lose my nerve or have the Warden find out. I put gas in my car, stocked up on snacks, and drove. I was on a mission. The whole time I was pumping myself up and repeating, *You have nothing to lose*. It was a conversation with a total creep I already knew.

Nothing to be worried about. No big deal. Tying up some loose ends.

And sure enough, at the beginning of our meeting, he made the scariest horror movie reference, creating shivers to travel up and down my spine, but I refused to show any weakness.

"Quid pro quo," Tony slurred.

"This isn't *The Silence of the Lambs*. I'm not Clarice, and you aren't Hannibal."

"Wow. You're comparing me to Hannibal Lecter. I'm not sure if I should take that as an insult or a compliment."

"I did not compare you to Hannibal, and if you see it as a compliment, I doubt we'll ever see progress in our relationship."

"Are we building a *relationship*? I had no idea. A relationship is kind of a big deal. I'm touched. I figured your endless questions had something to do with another psychology paper. Did you fail the first one?"

"I'm not here to talk about my education. I'd like to ask you a few questions that have bothered me for a while now. Things that don't add up."

"I'm speechless and thrilled that you've been thinking about me all this time. What has it been? Two years? I must've left quite the impression, but then again, I tend to do that to women. I'm sure you've heard," he teased.

I hated his cocky grin. I imagined slapping it off his face. I despised his self-assurance, aware that his actions had an impact on me. I wanted to tell him that I hadn't been thinking about him. I wanted to lie. I wished everything he said wasn't true. To get what I was hoping for—the truth—I swallowed my true feelings for a little bit longer.

I dove right in. I'd driven hours and prayed that this trip wasn't a waste of my time and knew that the less time I spent with this man, the better. "I read the police report filed after your father's death. Did you know he had asthma?"

Tony eyed me suspiciously. "Gus? This is what brought you down here to visit me. You want to know how well I knew a man, who I'd had very little contact with, had asthma?"

"Yes, you summarized that correctly. It's the beginning of a list of questions that I have."

As he crossed his arms over his chest and leaned back in his chair, I understood that I'd already bored him. Time had not softened him into sharing information. I'd hoped loneliness would be on my side.

"I'm sorry to disappoint you, but you need to do the hard work yourself. You kids nowadays think everything should be easy. A snap of your fingers and you get your answers. That's not how real life works, Pretty Young Thing."

He hadn't forgotten me and the nickname he'd given me. Maybe I'd left more of an impression than he was willing to admit.

"I'd prefer it if you called me by my given name. Did you know that when you give someone in authority an inferior nickname, you're actually revealing that you feel threatened? Just an observation by a licensed psychologist." I explained. I removed the gloves that cushioned the blow. "It's okay if you can't remember the answers to all my questions. You're getting old, Mr. Shade. Not in the prime of your life anymore."

"You're trying to get under my skin, aren't you?" He laughed. "I missed this little banter we had. I'm so glad that you think I'm interesting enough for you to come back. It was my charm, right?" Before he answered a single one of my questions, Tony wanted to make sure that he made me as uncomfortable as possible. "I get that a lot. Chicks are drawn to me for my looks, but it's my award-winning personality that has them begging for more."

"Mr. Shade, I don't care what you believe. I know the truth of the reason I'm here. I think you know it too, but you can tell yourself whatever you want if it helps you sleep better at night in this hellhole."

"I have a question for you, Tara. If you answer mine, I'll answer yours. Sounds like a deal?"

"Tempting."

"I think you came back because you missed me, but I don't think the Warden knows you're here. I think you skipped the proper channels so that you could ask me your questions your way."

"Was there a question in there?"

"I believe I've found my answer based on the smile on your face. I can read you, Tara."

"Great, but I didn't smile. Now that we've covered your question, answer mine."

"No."

"No, you didn't know your father had asthma?"

"Correct. That was the question, right? I'm old, so my memory is shot." He eyed me through a narrow opening in his eyes.

"Did he ever use his inhaler while you were visiting him the weekend he died?"

"I just explained that I didn't know he had asthma; therefore, I think you can deduce from my answer that he didn't use an inhaler in my presence." His response reminded me of how a teenager responds when they are bored and uninterested.

"According to the police records, you and your wife told the police that you were with him Friday night from approximately six until midnight and all day Saturday until you left after dinner. Is that right?"

"If that's what the record says, then yes."

"And never once did he use his inhaler?"

"Why are you asking the same question in different ways? I answered your question. Tara, have you earned a detective badge in the last two years since I saw you? Or maybe you've watched too many *Magnum PI* shows lately."

I smiled. I did love Magnum, but then again, what woman didn't?

"I just found it odd that Gus filled his inhaler prescription three days before you visited, and when the police inventoried his apartment, the inhaler was empty. Just surprised me that it would be empty so quickly. One inhaler should last about five months or 200 puffs. Since you spent the entire weekend with him, I find it interesting that you never saw him take one of the 200 puffs."

An evil smile grew on his lips, but his eyes remained narrow. "Quid pro quo: Why do you care, Tara? You didn't even know Gus."

"I never said I cared. I believed that the facts held interest and merited further investigation."

"You mentioned you had more questions. I'd *love* to hear them, but I hope they are better than the first."

"Why did Daisy Armstrong's appearance at your trial rattle you? One of the local newspapers reported that your skin was drained of all color and you suddenly looked like you were going to throw up."

"Daisy is dead. She was never in that courtroom."

"Correct, and you knew she was dead, so why did you mistake her daughter for Daisy?"

He shrugged his shoulders. "Maybe I missed her. Maybe I was actually in love with her. Maybe I believe in ghosts."

"Or maybe she knew something that you were hoping she took to her grave? And when her daughter showed up at your trial, you were afraid she'd have something to add that would put you away for life."

I hit a nerve. His smile faded.

I forged ahead. "Daisy had something over you. She threatened you with it, and you didn't like that."

"Pretty Young Thing, how old are you? Twenty-something? You think you know how the world works. Well, you don't. Some things are better left unsaid so that you can sleep at night. Don't ask me questions if you're afraid to hear the answers."

"I won't learn anything new from you, Mr. Shade. I'm only here to rattle you. I'm here to force you to acknowledge things that you haven't admitted yet."

"You think you're better than the police at probing and getting information?"

"I never said that. I don't care what the authorities do with the information I discover. Everything we discuss here is hearsay anyway. They aren't going to take my word for it."

"So, you've already tried telling the police about our interviews." He smiled again.

"Maybe. Maybe not. I'm here discussing this crap with you because you're partially right. I'm not sleeping well, and I think figuring out the extent of your involvement will help me sleep better. I'll be able to rest knowing that I did everything I could to bring justice to your victims."

"You use the word 'victims' like they had no say in what happened to them. They had plenty of say. No one is innocent in this. The majority of the women who attended my parties were there to either pay off a debt, make some quick dough, or experience dark fantasies as I did."

"You tell yourself that to help *you* sleep better."

"Believe what you want. I don't care." And with that lie, he stood up and informed the guard our meeting was finished. "Have a great day, Ms. Brady."

Chapter 34

All week I stewed over my conversation with Tony. I felt like I was making a morsel of progress.

As I drove to Fort Madison Prison again, I thought about the innocent question that Ivy had asked me when we first met–*What do you do for fun?* The answer to that question was sad. Today was my only free day, and I was driving three and a half hours to talk to a man whom I detested. In my daydreams, I often imagined slicing off his balls to pay for all the sick and twisted things he had done. Prison didn't seem a strong enough form of punishment. Physical deformity seemed more fitting. This man and all of his heinous crimes caused me to think about him for more hours in the day than he deserved. Yet, I couldn't seem to rest without feeling that I had uncovered the whole truth about the monster he truly was.

Something in my blood–his blood–knew there was more.

When Tony entered the room, he looked back at his guard and said, "She keeps coming back for more. She can't get enough of me. Kind of twisted and sick, right?"

His new guard glanced at me and returned his attention to locking the door behind them and chaining Tony's ankles to the floor. To meet in a private room, these were the necessary precautions of this prison. I felt like it was excessive and unnecessary; however, I could admit that it made me feel better knowing he wasn't going anywhere and he couldn't touch me.

"Good morning, Mr. Shade."

"What's good about it? You could at least bring me an Egg McMuffin if you are going to keep badgering me."

"This isn't a social call."

"I never said anything about it being social. Just thought it would be polite." He opened the palms of his hands. "So, what do you think about the president being reelected? Did you vote for him?"

"I'm not going to tell you who I voted for."

"Right. Did you know that I knew Bill? We ran in the same circles back in the day." Tony bragged.

"No, I did not know that."

"Yep." He smiled at the memories floating around in his head. "That man has a talent for telling people what they want to hear. And he *totally* inhaled." Tony threw his head back and laughed. "He inhaled a lot and often. I don't know why he made such a big deal about it. He did worse than that. Much worse."

While I found it fascinating that Tony had been friends with the President of the United States, I wasn't here to reminisce about his glory days.

"We had that in common—a talent for telling people what they wanted to hear. He begged me to go into politics with him and said I'd be perfect as his right-hand man." Another smirk played on Tony's lips. "I wasn't interested in playing second fiddle. While he'd get the pick of the litter, he offered me his rejections. No thanks." His eyes met mine again as he added, "You think I'm messed up? You just wait. I'm predicting he won't be able to keep it in his pants. The man loves power. He gets a rise out of it. I guarantee that he's used that power to bed more than a hundred women so far in his presidency." He shook his head.

Despite Tony's apparent desire to share further details about the President, I remained focused. Our time was limited. "I have a couple of follow-up questions that I wanted to ask." I pretended that I was referring to some notes in a manila folder I brought along. "Your ex-wife Lisa told the police that you'd been acting strangely the morning that you found your father deceased."

He eyed me skeptically. "I'd just found my father dead. Of course, I acted oddly. It isn't an everyday occurrence. You only get one father." He paused as he pronounced every syllable of the last sentence.

"She said this happened *before* you found Gus' body. The report says that you'd gotten into an argument with your father the evening before. You two left his home abruptly. Then Lisa noticed you were missing from the hotel room in the middle of the night. She said at the time she thought you might be using the bathroom or went to the vending machine for a snack. However, the next morning when you ripped the watch off your father's wrist, you showed no emotion regarding his passing. She was suspicious."

Suddenly, Tony sat forward in his chair and tried to grab my manila folder, but the wrist cuffs–that I was tremendously thankful for–held him back. I didn't want him to see my notes because they were old college notes. Furthermore, Lisa had never told the police that information, only me when I called her after my last visit with Tony. She'd wished me luck on breaking Tony.

"Lisa told the police that, huh? Interesting. It never came up in trial."

"Must not have been enough evidence to back it. However, maybe if I tell them what I think happened, this report will make more sense."

"And what do you think happened, Pretty Young Thing? Oh, please tell me. I'm dying to know," Tony laced every syllable with sarcasm. He sat back again in his chair, proving that he wasn't worried about what I was about to say.

My nostrils flared as I took a deep breath, attempting to calm myself. The accusation wanted to burst from my mouth, but I knew the delivery needed to be as powerful as the words themselves.

"You killed your father." I paused for effect, but Tony showed no signs of surprise. "You argued with Gus about something that night, and after you and Lisa stormed off, you decided to kill him. You snuck out of the hotel room, broke into his apartment, grabbed a pillow from the extra bedroom, and smothered him in his sleep. You made it appear like an asthma attack by emptying his inhaler to indicate he'd been using it excessively that weekend."

Tony and I engaged in a staring contest while I waited patiently for him to formulate an excuse.

He slowly started to clap his hands. As the beat of the clapping increased, so did the corners of his mouth. "Bravo. Bravo, Miss Brady. You should write fiction. That's one helluva story."

Even though I didn't expect him to suddenly confess, I was disappointed that I didn't receive a stronger reaction. "I would also like to discuss what I touched on during our last visit. Daisy Armstrong." Because Tony normally chose to end our sessions whenever things got too heated, I decided to jump right in. I knew that his patience was rapidly diminishing. "We already determined that it wasn't Daisy but her daughter Lily. I wonder why her presence affected you so strongly."

His jaw clenched before he gave his version of the truth.

"I'm not sure why I feel the need to tell you this. Maybe so you stop looking at me through those judgmental eyes of yours. Daisy wasn't innocent. Far from it, actually. She believed that she was the muse. I let her believe it." He threw his head back and laughed as his memory took him back in time. "She played the part of whatever role was requested. If someone wanted a dominator, she called all the shots. Upped the stakes. Pushed every limit. But if a client wanted a scared, innocent virgin, she was down for that, too. She cried. She screamed and fought back until she was finally overtaken. She was an amazing actress.

"Then one night, our fantasies went too far, and a girl had a seizure in the Room. Daisy panicked. She'd been restraining the girl as two men were pleasuring themselves, and suddenly, the chick's eyes rolled back into her head and she went limp. I admit even I was shocked.

I didn't know what to do. So, we did nothing. We just stared at her and didn't try to save her. Daisy and I had to dispose of her body. The men who were in the Room paid good money for issues like this to be taken care of without involving them. We completed the dirty work.

"Daisy was never the same after that night. She stopped enjoying the role-playing and entertaining men. Something inside of her died that night. She came to me and threatened to expose everything we'd built. She had nothing to lose. Her husband was dead; her daughter despised her. She didn't care if she went to jail or if I killed her. She just wanted out.

"Honestly, I was fine with her leaving. I was over her sad, depressing attitude. Our business was growing, and we were getting clients from all over the country. I knew she wouldn't talk if we let her go. She wasn't like that. Plus, I knew she loved me. She thought I'd come crawling back to her and beg her to come back. I never did that, but Lisa did. Totally surprised me when Lisa was more upset about Daisy leaving than I was."

I struggled to remain calm, and not show my alarm and shock at his revelation. When I heard the words leave my mouth, I hoped Tony didn't notice the shaking. "Who was the girl?"

He looked at me blankly, like he didn't know who I was referring to. A woman's body was nothing more than a vehicle to get what he wanted. He had no respect for human life.

"The girl who died? Who was she? What was her name?" I clarified.

He smiled his signature bone-chilling smile. "I don't know."

The silence that fell between us was filled with significance. He'd supplied more information than he ever had before. He got cocky and was showing off. He wanted to intimidate me or impress me. However, what he perceived as an insignificant event and confession turned into a shocking and heartbreaking revelation to me. He admitted that he was an accessory to a murder. He hid a dead body. Was her family still looking for her? Had she been reported missing all those years ago?

As his smile widened, he laughed, and his amusement caused bile to rise in my throat. This was all a game to him. He noticed that I was sweating and struggling with the information.

"Just kidding, Tara." A bellowing laugh escaped his lips again, making the guards take notice. "You should see your face. I didn't think an Indian princess with your gorgeous skin tone could turn to ash, but I was wrong. Gray isn't your color."

"You're lying."

"About which part?" He shook his head, portraying the most innocent expression his devilish face could project.

"You're not kidding. You killed a girl. I believe it." My gut told me he wasn't lying. He was too proud of it. He wouldn't have just told me all of that to rile me up.

Or would he?

Chapter 35

I jarred awake in the middle of the night. In my dream, I was replaying the last conversation that I had with Tony, trying to figure out what I was missing.

He called me Miss Brady. Not Tara or Pretty Young Thing.

He used my last name in conversation. I'd never told him what it was. Did he know I was Kitty's daughter? What else did he know?

Chapter 36

"When am I gonna meet this smoking hot unicorn?" Stella stopped again as she rolled through town.

For the past six months, I'd told her stories of Ford and how we hadn't been intimate yet because he preferred to wait. She called him a unicorn because he sounded like a mythical creature–a man whose main goal wasn't to have sex every chance he got. Those men didn't exist in the real world. I hadn't yet told Stella that we had broken up last week. I'd never been the one in a relationship who pushed to be more intimate. It was odd being on the opposite side. I didn't like it.

Ultimately, the relationship ended amicably. He admitted that he wasn't ready for anything more, and I didn't want to be with someone who wouldn't take our relationship to the next level. Before he climbed into his car and drove away, we hugged. It was a giant bear hug like one you'd give your uncle. When I walked up the sidewalk to my apartment, I shook my head. I didn't think the six months were a waste of time, but I truly had been hoping for more. The psychologist in me wondered if he subconsciously preferred men, and maybe I'd intellectually challenged him. My education taught me never to take things at face value. There must be more to the story, and possibly something that the person didn't even realize.

Ford was good-looking, charming, and an extremely nice guy. I wished him no ill will. But as a young, active, sexual woman, I could admit that I'd been ready for the next step in our relationship, intimacy. During the day, every woman wants to be cherished and treated like a princess. I wanted my hand held in public, doors held open, and the palm of his hand resting on the small of my back as he guided me into a room. After making breakfast together, out of the blue, I wanted a kiss to be planted on the top of my head. Ford checked those boxes.

At night, I wanted to be ravaged. His desire for me would be all-consuming. I yearned for him to be unable to keep his hands off me. His gentle kiss would turn into a fit of passion as his tongue opened my mouth. After he ripped my clothes off, he'd lick and kiss every inch of my body. In bed, I'd beg for what I wanted—what I needed to reach climax.

That part never happened.

Ford made me feel like royalty. Sometimes, he even called me princess. He handled me with white garment gloves as if I'd break or lose value if he touched me. At first, his excuse for not being able to perform made sense, but most of the time, I felt like I was his sister or a friend, but not his girlfriend. I wanted more. I felt guilty for wanting more, which in turn made me feel worse.

Other little things bugged me about Ford. Tiny, nitpicky habits. When he would come over, he always knocked on my door and said, "Knock-Knock. Knickety-Knock." The words sounded strange coming from a grown man. When I asked him why he said it, he told me that it was his mother's coined phrase when he was a kid. Even though his reasoning was adorable, something about those words coming from a grown man caused a shiver to envelop my spine. A weird gut feeling surfaced in the pit of my stomach that I couldn't put my finger on.

When a non-filtered person is in a relationship with someone more sensitive, there are bound to be disagreements. Our arguments were odd, to say the least. One night, after he made me a home-cooked dinner, he asked what I thought of the meal.

"It's good." I wasn't a big fan of pork, and I couldn't fake my enthusiasm. He'd wrapped a pork tenderloin in bacon and sprinkled brown sugar and honey over it. The effort and the combination sounded like a mouth-watering combination, but I didn't love pork. He must've read that on my face.

"Good? Just good?"

"Yes, it's good. Not one of my favorites, but it's good. I appreciate the effort you put into it."

Instead of being mad at me for not simply saying I enjoyed it, Ford apologized.

"I'm sorry you don't like it. I should've asked you first what you wanted. You don't have to eat it. Let me take it." Ford stood up from his seat at the table and tried to grab my plate.

I batted his hand away. "No. No, it's fine. It's good. I want to eat it. I just gave my opinion, which means nothing. You worked hard on it. Let's enjoy our supper."

"I'm sorry that I didn't make you something that you liked."

It was an unusual conversation, one that left me thinking. Why did he feel the need to apologize to me because I didn't like something? I didn't understand. Kitty had raised me to always be honest, but sometimes my filter needed to be turned on. I should've tried harder to show my appreciation, but being less than honest was a struggle at times.

I explained my reasoning to Stella. "I know this will sound like it came out of nowhere, but I had to end it." Stella and I were enjoying a cup of coffee at my apartment in our pajamas. She'd arrived after midnight the day before, so this was our first chance to catch up.

"You don't have to justify dumping a guy because he didn't want to rip off your clothes and hump you on the kitchen counter. Girl, I get it. An old-fashioned gent ain't for everyone."

"Something like that." Stella always had a way of saying it like it was but in a fun and kind way that made me laugh. However, I wanted her to truly understand my point of view. "You don't think I sound like a complete whore since I broke it off with him because he didn't want to have sex with me?"

"Girl, if you are a whore, then I'm the entire planet's triple-crowned harlot with a frequently-visited va-jay-jay." Stella's sexual desire and sex life were *very* healthy. Sometimes I teased her that she should've been born a man, and then her appetite would've been more acceptable. Instead, she was often called a slut.

"True." I smiled. She tossed a throw pillow at me. "Normally, the guy I'm dating is all over me, and I'm fighting him off with a stick, denying him every ten seconds. When Ford wasn't like that, it was nice at first. I didn't feel the pressure. I felt like he wanted to get to know *me*, the real me, not just my body. But the more I got to know him, the more I wanted him to rip my clothes off and take me in the hallway because we couldn't make it to the bed. He was the most thoughtful, kind man I've ever dated. Genuinely helpful and considerate. Then my overthinking caused me to second-guess myself and his reasoning. I wondered if he was gay or worse–he wasn't physically attracted to me. We had the most insightful conversations. He was a wonderful listener. I bounced ideas off him all the time. I loved hearing how he viewed the world. He was unique and interesting."

"Maybe his man tool is broken?"

"He told me once that he did have issues with intimacy, but..."

I wasn't sure if I wanted to tell Stella what I witnessed. I hadn't breathed a word of it to anyone.

"I caught him masturbating once, so I knew he could get it up," I blurted out before I had a chance to overthink it.

"Well, that's good news, but weird that he told you he couldn't."

"He didn't say he *couldn't*. He said he had intimacy issues. I assumed that meant he couldn't get it up." I gulped a large swallow of my now lukewarm coffee and decided to tell Stella. She was my best friend. I could tell her anything. "Remember those dance lessons I told you that we took?"

"At the Hidden Valley Retirement Home for gray-hairs who needed to have their pulse checked?"

I shook my head. "Yes. The ones at Hidden Valley *Golf Course*."

"Did you learn to dirty dance? Air hump?" Her smile peeked behind the brim of her coffee cup. "Maybe the naked tango or the cha-cha-touch-my-who-ha?"

"Keep your mind out of the gutter for one minute. Is that possible?" I giggled despite my scolding.

"I will try." Immediately, she looked bored. "My dirty mind's switch is faulty, so you better hurry. You have sixty seconds starting now. Go!"

"We learned dances like the foxtrot and tango." Stella pretended to yawn and patted her mouth. I added, "It was fun. Don't knock it until you try it. One day after the lesson, Ford excused himself to use the bathroom. For at least twenty minutes, I mingled with some classmates and finished my drink, but Ford still hadn't returned. I wondered if he had an upset stomach or ran into someone and lost track of time talking. I decided to use the restroom before he returned."

As I started telling the story to Stella, the scene replayed in my head. To get to the bathroom, you needed to zigzag through the locker room. No door to pull open or shut behind you. The maze was the privacy obstacle. The locker room smelled like sweet, flowery perfume trying to mask the smell of old lady body odor. Club members freshened up in this room after a round of golf.

Before I could weave my way to the bathroom stall, movement in the back of the room caught my attention. His back was to me as he faced the wall and peered out the small window that was about four and a half feet from the floor. His dress slacks were sagging, which allowed the top portion of his ass to be visible. His right arm quickly jerked back and forth. Seconds later, his head angled toward the ceiling, and a white, thick liquid shot all over the wall in front of his waist.

Ford.

With my eyes and mouth widening in circular shapes, I silently turned around and sprinted out of the locker room.

What is he doing?

I knew *what* he was doing, but why? What had him so turned on as he looked out the window? Why did he feel the need to relieve himself at that moment?

I walked straight out of the golf club's back door and toward the eighteenth hole, the last hole on the course and nearest the clubhouse, where our dance lessons had taken place. I power-walked past four men standing near a golf cart as they added up their scores. I rushed past the beer cart gal, who yelled at me to stay on the path; otherwise, I would get struck by a golf ball. I kept moving.

I didn't understand. I understood masturbation, but I did not understand why Ford had to do it in a women's locker room, in the middle of the afternoon, in a public place where he might get caught when I was more than willing to satisfy him. I *wanted* to satisfy him. It didn't add up.

Think, Tara. Think. What have you learned about things like this in your classes?

Masturbation has health benefits for men, including improved sleep, boosted immunity, and reduced stress. Not only does a person feel physical pleasure, but a person's body awareness and self-esteem increase. A person's mood also improves.

However, it was the middle of the afternoon, so he wasn't going to be sleeping anytime soon. I wasn't aware of any health concerns that Ford had that would affect his immunity. There were only two logical explanations that made sense to me. Ford was either stressed about something or he didn't find me attractive.

As I slapped a mosquito on my arm, I looked up and noticed I'd walked to the thirteenth hole. I needed to turn around and find Ford in the clubhouse. He would wonder where I'd disappeared to. Ironic. I wasn't going to mention anything. I needed to digest the information myself.

Stella gasped and responded, "Gross. In public? Did he clean up his jizz from the wall?"

"I don't know. The point is that he has intimacy issues, and I didn't feel like I could be his girlfriend and his therapist."

"Damn right. I don't know one guy who would rather tell a girl that he couldn't get it up versus the truth—he's a freak in the sheets."

Only Stella could make an awkward conversation funny. I laughed.

"Do you still have his number?" She raised her eyebrows up and down.

Chapter 37

Sundays were my designated pajama day. It was the day I paid my bills, the day I did laundry for the following work week, the day I grocery shopped for the essentials I would need for my meals, and the day I made long-distance phone calls to check in. On Sundays, I reset my life, prepared for the week ahead, and reminded myself who I was.

One of my Sunday phone calls was to Ivy this week. Not only was she easy to talk to, but she was also open and receptive to forming a relationship. Her sister Jolene was another story. While Ivy was friendly and outgoing, Jolene was cold and harsh, and we'd probably never be close, and that was fine by me.

While Ivy and I were talking, we discussed the ups and downs of our mutual connection.

"There are things that trigger me, such as the smell of whiskey. I hate it. I think it's because I smelled whiskey on the breath of the men in that room. Michael's so sweet and hasn't touched the stuff since I told him. It's kind of like your mom. She won't eat a KitKat to save her life because that was the nickname Tony gave her back when they were kids."

A quiet, muffled sound escaped my lips to acknowledge that I was listening. I thought about correcting Ivy and telling her that he nicknamed my mom Kitty, not KitKat, but I didn't have a chance before she started talking again.

"But life is funny because as soon as you think you've moved on, gained some leverage on healing, reality slaps you in the face and throws you a curveball. I thought I'd moved on from the whole gang rape memory," Ivy said, followed by an uncomfortable laugh. "I was seeing a counselor, focusing on raising Cooper and adjusting to married life with Michael, the man of my dreams. I was happy. I'd moved on and was a better person for having survived that. One night, I was cooking supper for my perfect little family, and Michael nonchalantly asked me if I recognized the name Tony Shade. Damn, I remember that conversation like it was yesterday. Michael knew what happened to me and where Cooper came from, but I'd never told him the names of any of my attackers. That night, I felt the past I tried so hard to forget collide with my new picture-perfect life."

"Why did he bring him up out of the blue like that?"

"He got a call from a good friend who he'd met in the police academy. His buddy, who lives in Canby, where Tony was arrested, remembered that I grew up in Normal. He put two and two together and called Michael. He was curious if my parents knew him since they were about the same age."

"Wow. What a small world."

"Yes, it is. Even though at the time, telling Michael the whole story about the rape made me sick to my stomach, I'm glad he knows everything now. There are no more secrets. Oddly enough, I'm grateful that Ford called that day."

Did she just say Ford called? What are the odds that Michael's Ford was the same as my ex, Ford? It was a unique name, but it couldn't be the same guy, could it? Two 'Fords' from Canby, Minnesota?

"Ford? That's Michael's friend's name?" I managed to squeak.

"Yeah. Funny name, right? He's a nice guy. Michael and Ford became friends during their police academy training. Ford tried so hard to fit in, and he idolized Michael. They were just becoming friends when Ford got kicked out. Michael felt so bad, and Ford took it hard. That was years ago before I'd even met Michael."

I couldn't get myself to tell Ivy that I knew who Michael's Ford was. The comment was lodged in my throat, and I couldn't cough it up, like a loogie.

Instead, I asked, "How does a guy get kicked out of the police academy?"

"Yeah, it's not a great story. I guess the boys were at the bar relieving some stress after a long week of training. Ford wasn't much of a drinker, but that night he consumed more alcohol than the legal limit. According to Michael, he forced himself on a girl, and that girl pressed charges. Ford claims that it was consensual, but as soon as the charges were made, he was kicked out. I don't know. He's always been a great friend to Michael, and I've never witnessed him even get annoyed." Ivy paused as she took a deep breath. "Please don't share this information with the family. From time to time, Ford joins us for the holidays, and no one else knows this story."

Oh, my God.

"Hi, Tara. Bye, Tara." Michael's voice suddenly filled the phone receiver.

"Sorry, Tara, that was Michael. He says hello and that he misses you." In the background, I heard Michael rattling what I assumed were his car keys. "I gotta go. Cooper's basketball game starts in fifteen minutes, and I don't want to be late. Can I call you next Sunday?"

After hanging up the phone with Ivy, I dropped down onto my couch and stared at the wall. What a small world. I couldn't get over the coincidence that I'd briefly dated the same man who was friends with Michael. I started to run through the six months I'd dated him for signs that I could've figured out this revelation sooner. Maybe I didn't ask enough questions, but then again I wasn't looking for connections. For the majority of the time, I enjoyed his company until I decided I wanted more.

The fact that Ford had been accused of raping a woman shocked me. First of all, he never laid a hand on me and claimed he couldn't perform, so hearing that he'd attacked a girl at a bar seemed strange. It didn't match with the Ford I dated. Was he kicked out of the police academy before he was found guilty, or was the fact that he was accused enough for the academy to dismiss him? I wondered if he tried to fight the accusation, or if he just lay down and allowed the avalanche of destruction of his life to happen.

A light bulb ignited in my brain. Goosebumps rose on my arms.

I suddenly remembered a conversation with Ford about an ex-girlfriend who filed a police report against him. Was it the same woman who got him kicked out of the police academy? If not, being accused of rape twice seemed more than fishy. There had to be some commonality there. But what?

Chapter 38

2 years before

"Hey, Mikey. How's it hanging?"

"Low, loose, and full of juice." We both laughed. "My brother from another mother. How the hell are you? Michael misses your awkward embraces and off-the-wall comments."

Just hearing Michael's sunshiney voice made me wish I'd called him sooner. The dude was a breath of fresh air. Whenever we were together, I felt normal. It was as if in Michael's presence I was the best version of myself. Except for that one night. That one night tequila overruled all the good that was happening in my life. The night of Jenny.

"Seriously, you're still referring to yourself in the third person. You haven't grown out of that ridiculous phase?" I laughed remembering muscular, smiley Michael hitting on chicks and referring to himself in the third person. Ninety percent of the time, he received a response. Often his line was, "Michael hopes you know CPR because your beauty took his breath away."

The typical response was a giggle, and then the woman would ask who Michael was. His grin would spread across the bottom half of his face, and he'd jerk his thumb at himself. Again, he'd earn another laugh, and then, to surprise us all, he'd end up in a conversation with the woman. The woman might assume he was slow or something, but he'd always be rewarded with her undivided attention. As his buddies, we'd watch in awe.

"You hurt Michael's feelings. Take it back before Michael hangs up on you." Now, he was having some fun.

I cleared my throat. "Seriously, dude, I have a question for you. Have you heard of a man named Anthony Shade or Pastor Tony?"

"Tony Shade." He repeated the name out loud to himself, seeing if it rang any bells. "I can't say for sure. Why? What's up?"

After being kicked out of the academy, I moved to Canby, Minnesota, where I worked security for Allied Secure. I hadn't seen Michael since he was in town a few years ago for a training exercise for the force.

"The dude's name is everywhere right now in Canby. Supposedly, years ago he ran a nasty brothel, a whorehouse, out of the back of his home. And get this, he was the town's very popular, very friendly pastor."

"No shit." Michael's interest spiked.

"And his wife was in on it. She participated, enjoyed, and even housed some of the girls. It's a huge scandal. It all happened in your wife's hometown."

There was silence for a minute. "What?"

"Yeah, this pastor, Tony Shade, owned a modern-day brothel in Normal, Iowa, for years before moving to Canby, where our wonderful law enforcement officers arrested him for soliciting sex from a minor. That's where Ivy is from, right? Normal? He would've been about her parent's age. I wonder if she knew him. Ever met him? The situation is fucked up, man."

"Wow. I've never heard of him. But just wow."

"Yeah, the situation is completely fucked up. Can you imagine? He never got caught the whole time he lived in Normal. Chicks went in and out of his place, and no one was the wiser. I've been trying to keep up with reading the papers to see what comes out. It sounds like a messed-up movie. Girls of all ages worked for him. I guess it depended on what the customers wanted. I wonder if they ordered the girls from a catalog or something. Were the girls categorized according to their age, the size of their boobs, and the color of their hair? I'm just trying to wrap my head around it all."

I knew I was rambling, but as soon as I made the connection between the town and Michael's wife, I had to know more. When the news first appeared in the papers, morbid curiosity consumed me. This man had avoided authority for years, and it seemed like his desires were intensifying, just like mine. He couldn't contain them. As soon as I remembered that Michael's wife, Ivy, was from the same small town, I called Michael.

"Are you still there, man?" I hadn't heard anything from Michael for a few seconds.

"Yeah, just digesting this." Michael's tone of voice had lost the upbeat, chirpiness to it. "I hope to hell that Ivy didn't know the creep, but Normal is a small town, so that seems unlikely. I'll have to ask her. Thanks for the heads up, Ford."

When we disconnected the call, we promised to plan a visit for me to come to Mitchell. Maybe then I could ask Ivy myself about what she knew about the infamous Tony Shade.

Chapter 39

I logged into one of my fake dating profiles. Gabe Paul. *No new messages.*

I didn't expect her to message me back after I stood her up, but I was still curious. Gabe had only one prospect, Tara Brady, unlike my other accounts, Trey Pierson and Dylan Keith, who were chatting with several women simultaneously. Checking their profiles and keeping up with their online dating was time-consuming and required a great deal of organization. 'Trey' and 'Dylan' collected as much information as possible about their potential suitors to map out all possibilities.

Trey was a twenty-five-year-old restaurant manager who was looking for a woman who inspired and challenged him to be the best version of himself. He didn't drink or smoke and had never done drugs. Growing up as an only child, Trey was a self-proclaimed momma's boy and never turned down home-baked goods.

Good morning, Sara. How'd ya sleep?

Hi Trey! Good. Can't chat right now, though. I'm heading to class, and then I need to give my roommate a ride to work. I'll message you when I get home.

Bingo! *Sara would be home alone around 11 am. I knew this from past conversations. Sara had class from 9-11, and her roommate worked about twenty minutes away. We hadn't met yet, but she told me that she answered phones at a local dentist's office. One day after her shift, I followed her home so I knew where she lived.*

My ski mask was in the dryer. Perfect timing.

Dylan's Match *profile received a notification from Audrey.*

> Hi Dylan, I'm sorry I've been MIA this week. I have Friday off from work. I'm getting my hair done, but I could meet for coffee after that if you still want to.

> Hello, Audrey. Let me check my business calendar and get back to you about coffee. Where were you thinking?

> There is a new coffee shop near Judy's Cut & Curl called Roast. If 2 p.m. works, I could walk from my appointment and meet you.

Bingo! *It was turning out to be a busy week. Now, I knew where Audrey would be on Friday at 2 pm—alone waiting for Dylan—the divorced dad of two elementary-age daughters who indicated that he wanted to meet a woman to share his bed and his busy life—who wouldn't show. She'd end up walking home alone from the coffee shop, and I'd have her all to myself.*

It was almost too easy. I had my pick of women who were desperately trying to find their Prince Charming. These women had no idea how easy they were making the process of finding them. Of course, the initial chatting took great effort and patience on my part, but it was worth it in the end. We started with an elementary-type spark: 'I like you. Check yes or no if you like me too.' An innocent conversation would start online where we would discuss our interests, family, passions, and life goals. To avoid confusion, I selected distinct attributes for each character. Because I couldn't use my own photo, I chose pictures of my ineligible friends who wouldn't join Match.com because they were in relationships.

For Dylan's profile picture, I used an old photo of my dad when he was in his mid-twenties. His sideburns hung down just past his jawline, which accented the smile that had formed on the bottom half of his face. It was a candid picture that seemed to have caught him in mid-laughter. It had been taken outside, so the lighting made him look like a movie star. Because the photo was black and white, it gave off a classy, artistic vibe that attracted the older, more sophisticated women on Match. Plus, Dylan claimed he was a hopeless romantic who preferred Bing Crosby to the 'noise on the radio nowadays.'

Trey's photo was a picture of my friend Troy Pears, who was six feet tall and approximately two hundred pounds. When he let his hair grow out, he had a mess of curly black hair on top of his head, but it was his killer smile that grabbed the girls' attention—that and the fact that he had no idea how charming he was. His profile was my most active one. Thankfully, Troy was married and had a set of twin boys that were keeping him and his new wife Ava very busy.

I fondly remember the Saturday evening that I first heard about Match.com. I'd been watching television when the news outlet featured a new up-and-coming way to meet that special someone.

The nightly news anchor introduced the story. "Studies show that people are marrying later in life instead of right out of high school or college, setting career goals ahead of starting a family. We talked with Dr. Phillip McCracken, who has been conducting a poll through the University of Alabama to discover how this trend is affecting the American population."

Suddenly on my television screen, a homely man in his late fifties appeared. Small round glasses rested on the end of his long, pointed nose, and acne scars dimpled his cheeks. At the bottom of the screen were his credentials. My initial thought was, "This dude studies dating patterns because he can't get a date himself." A plaid bowtie peeked out from under his double chin.

"Men and women are placing career aspirations ahead of their family plans. In the last five years, the average age a person marries has increased from twenty-one to twenty-six years of age. This trend may be in direct correlation to the divorce rate increase. Perhaps these young people are products of divorce and decide to avoid that outcome by not marrying until life experiences have given them greater insight. Whatever the reasoning, the chances of meeting a special someone decrease due to the focus now being on career advancement. I don't see this trend changing unless something dramatic changes in society."

Dr. McCracken continued to explain as he nervously played with his mustache. "Match.com is an innovative way to eliminate the hassle and countless wasted hours of trying to find your perfect match. After someone answers questions about what is driving their search and questions about likes, dislikes, and preferences, Match.com *will filter candidates for a possible suitor."*

Images of famous couples throughout history flash on the screen. Fred and Wilma Flintstone. Sonny and Cher. Nancy and Ronald Reagan. Joanie and Chachi from Happy Days. *Lucy and Ricky Ricardo from* I Love Lucy.

"Gone are the days of the first date discovery. For instance, Joanie would already be aware that Chachi would rather stay home on a Saturday night than go out. Ricky would already understand that Lucy wants to be a star and will do anything to be taken seriously. The guesswork and the adventure of discovery are taken out of the equation. The mystery is removed from the equation. The potentials already know that they have things in common and will focus on commonalities."

As the TV camera returned its focus to the news anchor, I noticed that the bottom of the screen showed the information that the news segment was referring to.

Match.com $9.95 per month to help you find that special someone.

I powered up my home computer. As I waited for the green screen to warm up, I shuffled to the kitchen and mixed myself a double Jack and Coke. More Jack than Coke.

This might be fun.

There was an abundance of desperate, lustful, vulnerable women to pick from. These women were eager for love. Desperate even. Ripe for the picking. Totally my type. Was the creator of Match.com *someone like me? A misunderstood, assertive man thirsting to be challenged?*

As I swirled the little straw around in my drink, I imagined the upcoming adventures and grew hard in my pants. I typed in my passcode and searched for Match.com. *To create a profile, I needed a user name. I looked up from the computer, trying to think of a clever name because I couldn't use my own. My eyes landed on a newspaper clipping that I'd framed.*

Mitchell's Police Academy Recruits Win Annual Baseball Tournament.

Grinning from ear to ear, I stood wedged between my police academy classmates after we beat the local firefighters 3-2.

That was when I decided to use my married friends' names to see what I could get away with.

For months, I'd been meeting women on this website. I tracked their details on a spreadsheet and thanked my lucky stars that I'd watched the news that night. In my research, I found that if I initially told the women that I was leery about starting a relationship because I'd been hurt and I'd prefer to get to know them through online chatting first, they tended to let their guard down. The pressure was off. We could simply talk for a bit before taking it to the next level. By the time we scheduled our first physical date, we'd chatted so much that the fear of meeting a stranger had evaporated. We were old friends.

The day that I recognized Tara on her Match.com *profile was the day that a light bulb had burned its brightest. I immediately recognized her from the woman I'd crossed paths with a few years before. My gut reaction to seeing her caused all kinds of sparks that I didn't understand, so I ducked into the nearest store to avoid eye contact. At the time, I hadn't known why I reacted that way to her, but now I wondered if it had led me to this very moment.*

I recognized her name from an article that I'd read about Tony Shade. It had been published in a national magazine, and the local paper did a story on her. It was that article that helped me find Tony. It was her words that helped me understand why I was the way I was. I was one hundred percent sure that that was not the intent of her study; however, in my case, it helped me come to terms with my natural desires. They weren't my fault. It was nature.

Everything I'd done up to this point seemed to be preparing me for this moment. The woman who helped me find my father was also the woman with whom I had a strong physical reaction. What are the odds? It was fate.

I sat back in my chair and stared at the screen for a moment, willing myself to focus. Take a deep breath.

Name: Tara Brady

Age: 23

Location: Canby, Minnesota

Education: Current Graduate Student

Current Status: Single, never married

Children: none

Pets: none

Appearance (list everything you are comfortable supplying): 5'6"

Race: Caucasian, but everyone thinks I have native bloodlines.

Following my intuition, I created Gabe Paul, who was a twenty-something college graduate who preferred dogs to cats. Gabe was a loan officer who loved his job but hoped to be promoted soon. He was searching for a woman he could call his lover and his best friend. And I knew the perfect 'face' for Gabe—my police academy buddy, Michael Bass. Even though he was a fabulous, tough authority figure, he was a giant teddy bear. He was totally Tara's type.

Unfortunately, Gabe and Tara never met because Gabe didn't show up for their first date.

I did.

Chapter 40

1997

It felt like I was starting to get somewhere with my independent investigation and my interviews with Tony. When you knew the right questions to ask, it made the reward of answers so much more powerful.

Tony was very intelligent, so every little nugget of information that he was supplying me was strategically placed. He was the puppet master pulling the strings of my investigation. I was aware of it, but I didn't let it deter me from my end goal—figuring him out and proving that he was more than just a pedophile and rapist, as if that wasn't enough. The courts found him guilty of sexual acts against women and children, but my gut told me that there was more. Tony thrived on power, and once he gained it, he hungered for more. He'd do anything to get what he wanted.

I was researching to see if there were any missing girls from the Normal, Iowa, area during the time that Tony and Lisa lived there. So far, I hadn't found anything, but I wasn't giving up. My gut instinct told me to verify this information. After I uncovered more, I planned on calling Lisa with more questions.

But one Sunday, during my normal routine of preparing for the week ahead and checking in with loved ones, everything changed.

The first person I always called on Sundays was Kitty. She was the one to instill this routine in me. Kitty's Cafe was closed on Sundays, so I knew she'd be home doing a similar routine.

"Hello there, daughter."

My mother didn't have caller ID. She didn't have extra money to spend on things that were not necessary. She just knew my routine like I knew hers.

"Good afternoon, Kitty. How was your week? Discover any new recipes to share with your favorite and only daughter?" Kitty locked her recipes in a tiny safe in her office. Even though I was her only living relative, she wouldn't let me have copies of them until she closed the cafe for good or, heaven forbid, died. She preferred the latter. She was strangely protective of her recipes.

"You *are* my favorite. I only needed one child because I perfected it the first time." That was also an old joke.

"Mom, considering that I know who my notorious biological contributor is, you should come up with a new joke."

"Good point, honey. I'll work on that. Sorry."

I changed the subject to some small-town gossip. "Stella told me that Coach Knight is getting a divorce. Supposedly, Susan finally had enough of Coach's infidelity."

Clanking noises echoed behind her voice as she pulled out dishes from her cupboards. "Yes, Hank told me that, too. Poor Susan. She has a heart of gold, and that man used her innocence and loyalty to his advantage so he could become Normal's not-eligible playboy."

"I had no idea that he was that bad. A playboy?"

"You can't believe everything you hear, but rumor has it that he helped Tony recruit some of his students to work the Room. He may have even conducted a few 'tryouts' himself. Gross." She must have paused for a moment because I couldn't hear the clang of dishes landing on the countertop. Or she paused because she said his name. "No paper trail, so there is no proof of that. Just small-town, old lady gossip."

My mother heard more than her share of gossip by owning the only official restaurant in town. The bars offered fried food and pizza, but if you wanted to sit down with your family and enjoy a homemade, nutritious meal, Kitty's Cafe was the only option in Normal. If a farmer's loan to buy a new John Deere tractor had been approved, he'd celebrate with a cup of coffee at the cafe. He'd share his good fortune with others at the counter. The news would spread before he even made it home to inform his wife.

Kitty was a wealth of gossip, but she never revealed a source or disclosed a secret to anyone but Hank and occasionally me.

"It surprised me. I had no idea. Coach Knight seemed like a great guy. He was a great teacher. Plus, I remember how he helped Lily shave several minutes off her 3K. They were pretty tight for a while."

Now, when I paused to remember my high school years, Lily did pull away from him. At one point she refused to let him coach her.

"Unfortunately, a person's true colors aren't always visible."

Kitty and I talked for another ten minutes before we hung up, and I called my favorite eight-year-old.

"Hi, Camille. It's Tara."

"Tara? Tara who?"

This was our game. Every week I'd have to supply her with information to confirm my identity. Sometimes I gave her facts about my life, and other times I used information about someone else, like a cartoon character she was into or a superhero she'd heard of. With Kitty, I played a sounding board, the prolific daughter, and the wise therapist. When I talked to Camille, I was immature, giggly, and wildly popular.

"Oh, shoot. Do I have the wrong phone number? I was looking for Camille Aubrey Shade, the only eight-year-old who knows the capital of Greenland is Nuuk because she's obsessed with polar bears. Supposedly, she wants to move there someday. This Camille is an amazing kid. You should meet her. When she drinks Coke and laughs hard, the pop often shoots out her nose. Even though she says it burns coming out, it's hilarious. I love it when that happens."

She giggled. I loved her laughter. At her birthday party, I told bad middle-school jokes until she got a side ache. "It does hurt."

"So, it *is* you. Hi, Camille. What are you up to today?"

My mother had been right, but I'd never admit that to her in so many words. I adored Camille. Honestly, she made it hard not to. She was witty, eager, and wiser than her age. I'd never yearned so much for a kid's approval.

"Well, this morning Howard brought over donuts, the kind with jelly in them–"

"A Bismarck?"

"Yeah, those. So good. I spilled jelly all over my favorite *Ninja Turtles* shirt."

"Oh, bummer." Camille loved donuts and the *Teenage Mutant Ninja Turtles*. I didn't understand the latter.

"Mom will get it out. She is a master at laundry." Camille was always saying the funniest stuff, or at least I thought so.

"Master at laundry? Is that an award that she won? Maybe it's an Olympic sport."

"Anyway, when are you coming to see me again?"

After calling Camille, I threw my clothes into the dryer, emptied the dishwasher, took out the trash, and used the bathroom. Even though I dreaded the last phone call that I planned on making, it fueled me for the week. Each phone call had a purpose to serve. Talking to Camille warmed my heart. Calling Camille filled my bucket. Being in her presence, making her laugh, and hearing her excitement about something filled an emptiness in me. I missed the innocence of being a child. Not worrying about everyone else. Calling Kitty was a routine that filled our mother-daughter needs. I needed to hear how I was still loved and cherished, and she wanted confirmation that I was happy, alive, and successful. Kitty always said she had two goals for me to achieve every day of my life.

"Only two?" I teased her. Two seemed like a minimal requirement, and Kitty never took the easy way. So I kept asking questions to get the details.

"My two requirements aren't as easy as they sound. The meaning is deep and will help you throughout your life."

"Can't anything you do be normal? Why does everything have to hold such a powerful meaning?"

"Tarasue, I just want you to close your eyes at night and ask yourself if you were really happy today."

The final phone call I planned to make today would provide me with a sense of purpose. I wanted to prove that my gut had been right about Tony Shade. He was more evil than I first thought. I wanted him to rot in prison and never see the outside again. I planned to prove that he killed his dad, possibly Ivy and Jolene's father, and maybe even this girl he mentioned. I also wanted to prove that even though I shared his DNA, I was nothing like him.

Thankfully, I made a friend in Haley, the Warden's secretary, so she put me down as an approved visitor and caller on Tony's list. I couldn't make the three-hour drive every week, nor did I want to. Talking to him over the phone was stressful enough.

I sat back down on my living room couch and dialed a third number that I knew by heart. After validating my information, I was placed on hold so that the guards could collect Tony and bring him to the area where the phones were used. During these ten minutes, I tried not to think about my phone bill. I needed to look at it as another piece of a puzzle. I was getting so close.

But it wasn't Tony who came back on the line; it was Warden Jespersen, a voice I distinctly remembered from the years I worked on my research paper. Since Haley had helped me navigate the rules this time around, I avoided him easily. "Hello, Miss Brady."

I was taken aback by the lack of anger in his voice upon learning that I was still in contact with Tony and had not shared my interview information. The man was so incredibly power-hungry. I expected fire; instead, it was smoke.

"Hello, Warden Jespersen."

"I know you didn't expect to hear from me this morning but rather Anthony Shade. However, that is not possible." He paused. I imagined him taking a long drag from a cigarette or perhaps a long sip of his drink, but I knew it was for dramatic effect.

He waited for me to confirm my sin. "Yes, I was." If he thought I'd apologize for not going through the proper channels to meet with Tony, he didn't know me well. I didn't say another word.

"Well, like I said, that isn't possible because he's dead."

Chapter 41

What? How? Tony was dead?

Once he dropped his bomb, distinct pleasure radiated in the Warden's voice. He enjoyed shocking me into silence. I was sure it gave him great pleasure to be the one to break the news to me.

"Yes, you heard me correctly. Another inmate stabbed him. Unfortunately, things like that happen here. It is a dangerous place filled with dangerous men. That is why we have silly, trivial protocols to keep our visitors safe. Oh well, that wouldn't be a concern of yours anymore. I'll have my secretary mail you the gifts you've given Mr. Shade over the years. He won't be needing them where he is going." And with that, he hung up the phone.

Hearing that Tony was murdered should've brought me some peace. I thought I'd feel glad that he was no longer breathing. That he couldn't hurt another person. But I didn't. I felt robbed. I had goals and a purpose. In my imagination, I planned on shoving the knowledge of his murderous crimes in his face. I imagined laughing at him and making him sweat because he thought he'd gotten away with something. I wanted to wipe that smug smile off his face forever. However, another inmate did that before I could.

I wasn't mad. I wasn't sad. I was disappointed that I didn't get the closure I yearned for.

I couldn't decide if my research and proving Tony's guilt were even worth the effort if he was no longer alive.

Two days after I heard that Tony had been murdered at the prison, I received a surprise voicemail message from my mother. When I arrived home from class, the answering machine's red light was blinking. I pressed the speaker button as I dropped my car keys into the designated bowl on the entryway table. Over the distant noise of clinking dishes, I heard Kitty's voice asking me to call her. She was cleaning in the kitchen.

"I know it's not Sunday, but it's important, Tarasue. It can't wait. Call me back. I love you."

Often when I received a message from Kitty, she would ramble on and on about whatever prompted her call. She never gave a second thought to how long her recording would be or how long I'd need to stand in my entryway listening to her offbeat rambles. Sometimes, I think she needed to talk because she was famous for being a good listener. Leaving ten-minute messages on my answering machine was an outlet for her. Her messages would include stories about some regular customers, something she saw on the news, or a funny memory from my childhood. Because I was the planner and the one who liked a tight schedule, I called her on Sundays, while Kitty reached out whenever she had the urge. Her long-distance phone bill was insane.

I decided before I called her back I'd get a few things done. I used the bathroom, made my bed, threw a load of clothes into the washer, and swept the kitchen floor. If she said it was important, then I needed to be ready for a long conversation.

When I dialed my childhood home phone, she answered on the second ring. Kitty didn't have an answering machine. Although she loved leaving long messages on mine, she claimed she thought answering machines were a way for the government to keep tabs on us.

"Do you actually think the government would be interested in hearing what *you* have to say?" I burst out laughing when she told me her reasoning.

"Tarasue, I taught you to respect different opinions, not laugh at them." She tsked her finger at me.

"You can't truly believe that, right?" I was trying to take her seriously, but Kitty could sometimes be completely ridiculous. I respected when she cleansed my aura; however, I drew the line at thinking the government would be monitoring a middle-aged mother who was one hundred percent a make-love-not-war woman.

So, the fact that she answered on the second ring meant she was waiting patiently near the phone for me to call back.

"Lisa called me today. I'm not sure if you know, but her ex-husband Tony was sentenced to a maximum security prison for the crimes he was convicted of."

While Kitty talked, I rested the phone receiver between my shoulder and ear as I warmed up food from last night's casserole. She didn't like to refer to Tony Shade as her ex-stepbrother, her rapist, or my biological contributor, only as Lisa's ex or Lisa's mistake, which was fine by me since I preferred not to talk about him at all.

I assumed that she was calling to tell me that he'd been killed. I wasn't about to tell her that I already knew.

"Most of the men in the prison are bad eggs like Tony. They're also serving extensive jail sentences for horrific crimes. Because even the most hardened criminals don't approve of someone who has abused children, Tony probably focused on bragging about his sexual adventures and not mentioning the age of the girls. Anyway, he'd earned himself quite the following. I heard he was already planning his next brothel when he got out; at least he *believed* he'd be released. He was unbelievably optimistic about the ability of his charm."

As I listened to her ramble, I silently agreed with her description. Tony never seemed to understand that some women, like me, were repulsed by him. His charm and wit didn't seduce me but made me hate him more.

"Even though he was more of a monster than a man, I hate to tell you this, Tarasue, but Tony was murdered a few days ago. One of his fellow inmates stabbed him."

"Wow." Thank goodness we were having this conversation over the phone, because if we were face-to-face, Kitty would've recognized my fake surprise. "I'm not sure what to say."

"Like I said, Lisa called me today, and she told me. Obviously, she's broken up about it, but there is a little more to the story." Kitty paused a month before she continued. "Recently, she asked Howard to look into Camille's family–"

"I thought Camille's mom said in the note she left Lisa that both of her parents were deceased?"

"Right, but for some reason, Lisa didn't fully believe it, or maybe she just wanted to make sure. Call it a gut instinct. When she received the adoption paperwork in the mail a year later, Lucy's death certificate was enclosed, but nothing about the rest of her family. Howard still enjoys investigative work, so she thought, why not? You know Lisa; she probably wanted to give Howard a project, and that poor woman will probably never stop looking over her shoulder. Waiting for the other shoe to drop, or so they say."

I remembered Kitty telling me that Howard had been a police officer, then a detective, before retiring and becoming a private investigator. He was the one who found Jolene in California. I was sure it was hard to fully retire from solving puzzles, especially when he was good at it. However, I didn't understand what this discovery had to do with my sperm donor's death.

"Anyway, the reason I'm calling is because Howard found Lucy's parents."

I still didn't understand why she was telling me all of this unless she was trying to downplay the news of Tony's death. Trying to pretend that it didn't matter. I didn't know why I needed to know this so urgently, but I also knew Kitty wasn't one for dramatics, so I waited patiently. "That's good news, right? Camille has more family."

"Kind of. What Howard discovered is quite tragic. Molly and Earl never fully recovered from Lucy's suicide and the mystery surrounding their granddaughter's disappearance. They used alcohol to numb their pain. Supposedly, Lucy's parents were celebrating Tony's arrest at a friend's house, where they both had too much to drink. Earl shouldn't have been driving, but he did, and they got into a car accident. He never saw the other car. Their car had flipped on its side and caught fire before the first responders arrived at the scene. Molly was trapped inside, and Earl had been thrown out of the vehicle and was lying unconscious in the ditch about fifty feet away. They were unable to save Molly.

"The next thing Earl remembered was waking up in the hospital, and his body ached from head to toe. He went to raise his arm to massage his temples, and his arm was handcuffed to the bed rails."

I didn't know what Earl looked like, but I imagined a large, grown man waking up bruised and scratched up in a strange place. Then he realized he couldn't move. How awful that would feel. I couldn't even begin to imagine the thoughts running through his mind.

"Oh no. That's terrible." This phone call was getting worse and worse by the minute.

"That's not the end. Earl's blood alcohol content was three times the legal limit, and when they crashed, he hit a family of five head-on. The accident killed everyone but Earl."

I didn't know what to say. What does someone say? One decision, the decision to drive drunk, destroyed a whole family. I couldn't imagine the guilt a person would feel, but I also felt the weight that one choice–one bad choice–made.

As if she read my mind, Kitty said, "Earl was convicted of manslaughter and was sentenced to several years behind bars. I'm not even sure how many."

"How awful! He is mourning so many people, and now, he has to live with the fact that he killed people–his wife and a whole other family. I assume that Camille doesn't need to know about this tragedy."

Kitty ignored my comment and continued with her story. "In jail, Earl supposedly grew angrier and angrier. He was picking fights, harming other prisoners, and even attacking a guard. He was moved to a maximum security prison for his bad behavior. More years have been tacked onto his initial sentence."

I imagined gentle, timid Lisa hearing this news from Howard. Even though the woman wasn't a favorite of mine, I knew this news would've caused her enormous heartache. I was sure she regretted even asking Howard to look into them.

"The reason I need to tell you all of this, Tarasue, is because of what Earl did next." I'd assumed she was telling me this story so that I would know not to ask questions about Camille's family the next time we were all together.

I was no longer worried about my phone bill. I wanted to hear the end of this story. "Okay?"

"I know sometimes I repeat myself, but I'm gonna tell you this again because it's important. Earl believed that Tony had planted the evil seed of sin in his family. Everything bad that had happened was Tony's fault. First, he seduced his wife, Molly. When she rejected him, Tony set his sights on their youngest daughter, Lucy, to punish Molly for ending their affair. Unfortunately, Lucy ended up pregnant and giving birth to a little girl, our sweet Camille. Thankfully, Lucy realized how awful Tony was and ran, but she was never the same. The whole family was so angry and confused. Earl and Molly filed police reports and wrote formal complaints to the church, but nothing changed. Years went by, and nothing was done.

"They believed that Tony's arrest was the justice they were seeking, that they would finally find peace. He was off the streets and locked up. Lucy and Camille would be safe. But peace is much more complicated than that.

"Long story longer, Earl went to jail, and his life continued to spiral downhill. Then a few days ago, Earl was transferred to Fort Madison Prison. He found himself in the same prison as the man who created havoc in his family. He knew what he had to do. He told the police that he wasn't sorry for killing Tony. His exact words were, 'Hundreds of people have dreamed of doing what I did to that devil. I'm just the first one who had absolutely nothing to lose.'"

This was the first long-distance phone bill that was worth every penny.

Chapter 42

Walking was the exercise I enjoyed to release the stress of my life. Kickboxing would've been a perfect outlet and more appropriate for the feelings that swelled inside of me; however, I didn't like to sweat, and I'd never been very coordinated. So, I walked... and walked... and walked.

I hadn't told anyone about my phone call with the Warden yet. I couldn't tell Kitty because then I would've had to tell her that I'd been talking with Tony for years; I'd been lying to her for years. She would've been relieved, but for some reason, I couldn't admit that secret yet. Maybe I was still processing the information myself. It wasn't that I felt bad about his death; he deserved to be stabbed, especially by someone that he'd wronged. Honestly, I hoped he suffered. He'd caused so much pain for others around him that a long, slow, painful death was what he deserved.

Learning that he was killed by Earl, Camille's biological grandfather, did cause me some internal nausea. She didn't have memories of a grandfather playing cards with her or teaching her to fish. If and when she found out about him, he'd only be remembered for being a murderer. Like every adult around her, I wanted to protect Camille from everything that might cause her pain. Unfortunately, I saw a slew of similar questions like the ones I have about my biology haunting Camille when she learned this news. Hopefully, it would be years from now, and I'd be a professional therapist with years and years of experience to help her heal.

After making my three-mile loop, I arrived home to discover a small box had been delivered to my front step. I stopped in my tracks and stared at it. That was the box that the Warden said he'd be mailing to me with the supposed gifts I'd given Tony. I hadn't given him any gifts but at the time didn't care to correct him. Taking a few tentative steps forward, I walked up my sidewalk and gently picked up the box as if an explosive was inside. That was the closest thing I could compare it to–a bomb. I was afraid of what the contents would do. Rip my heart in two. Did he leave me a letter that would explain everything? Is his journal filled with sordid details of his conquests? After confessing his sins, did he want forgiveness? Or would I discover more questions? Would any of my questions be answered or only leave me with more?

With my arms fully extended in front of me, I carried the box inside the house and set it on the kitchen counter. I was torn between wanting to rip it open and wanting to burn it in a fire without opening it. One good thing about not telling anyone about his death: I didn't have their opinions on how to deal with it.

I decided to shower first.

***

The journal–legal pad–that I'd given him years ago when I was writing my first psychology paper was on top of the contents. I'd ask him to write down feelings, things only he knew, anything he wanted to get off of his chest. The entire journal was blank except for a poem on the front page and one on the last page.

The first one read, "Dear Tara, I love you, doll, with all of my heart. Together forever and never to part."

The last poem read,

Pretty Young Thing

You make my heart sing

Full lips I want to part

You're a sassy, little tart

Does your mother know where you are?

You travel so far

For answers that you'll never get

But I don't mind at all one bit

Even in death, this evil, vindictive man gets the last word! I felt like I needed another shower.

Every bone in my body hated him. If Earl hadn't taken his life, I wouldn't have given it a second thought if I'd ever been given the opportunity. I would've stabbed him just like Earl did so I could watch the life drain from his eyes.

If I were in therapy, I would've had to admit that I'd thought too long and hard about murdering him. Not healthy.

What did his last poem mean? Did he know who I was after I tried so hard to hide it? He mentioned my mother. Did he realize Kitty was my mother? Did I ever mention how far I had to drive to get there? I'd been careful. If I gave personal information, I made sure it wasn't completely factual. I made sure to provide just enough information to make it believable, but not enough to reveal that I was from Normal.

In my frustration, I started rummaging through the rest of the box. I'd only intended to look at the journal, knowing that it was the one I'd given him years before. Even though my head knew that I wouldn't find any journal entries, my heart held out hope. There was an impressive stack of handwritten letters addressed to Tony. I opened one that was on top of the stack. It was written by a woman named Tiff Richardson. She proclaimed her love to Tony, telling him that she knew he was wrongly convicted, and she would fight to free him. I crumpled up the letter and tossed it aside. However, Tiff wasn't the only misguided female who was interested in reforming a bad boy. There were more letters in the box, each adorned with little hearts.

I couldn't help but shiver as I imagined the excitement each letter brought to Tony. I could picture the smirk that would form on his face every time one came in the mail. His fans.

In more of a chicken scratch handwriting, I found a few letters that were not signed.

That handwriting looks familiar.

The first letter postmarked from Canby, Minnesota, told Tony that he was a big fan of his work, but not of his pastoral practice. "I fantasize about doing the things you did to women too, but unlike you, I don't enjoy it. Okay, I *enjoy* it while it's happening, but afterward, I feel terrible. I'm wondering if you ever dealt with intense remorse. I'm not sure how to stop." The author—who I assume was a man—asked if he could call Tony.

I wondered if those conversations ever took place. I folded the letter back up. The police might be interested in looking at it if this man was raping women. I unfolded the next letter postmarked two weeks later.

Dear Mr. Shade,

Do you ever wonder why you were made with exotic taste in sexual acts? I wonder all the time.

I wasn't abused. I wasn't abandoned. I wasn't treated poorly by any women. In fact, my mother was a lovely woman. She was smart, well-rounded, and funny. I had the best life growing up. I never felt neglected or like I was missing out on anything. She made sure I had everything I needed.

But somewhere inside of me, some strangely mutated DNA triggered by puberty hormones prompted some bizarre thoughts in my teen mind. I imagined things that I'd never seen or heard of before. At times I thought I was possessed. I fought it. Believe me, I tried.

I'm not sure why I am telling you this. Maybe you will understand. Maybe you will tell me I'm not crazy. Maybe next time you will accept my phone call.

The letter was not signed.

Dear Mr. Shade,

I thought you would find this article interesting. Since she quotes you throughout, I assume you gave her permission to write this article. Did she tell you that she received an A in her class and her paper was then submitted for this publication? Not only are you infamous, but you're also famous as well.

Maybe you'll accept my phone call next time.

Inside the envelope was a copy of my paper that was published by *Psychology Today*. That magazine ran the article in July, the first month they could print it after I'd graduated. I recognized the article because I had several copies clipped by friends. However, this time when I saw it, I didn't feel the normal sense of pride. I felt betrayed. This man who'd been begging Tony to mentor him had thrown my award-winning college paper at Tony to belittle me and threatened Tony to take his phone calls.

Tony had known when I came back to visit him what my full name was. He knew I was Kitty's daughter. Or did he think it was a common name and fail to make the connection? I didn't think so. I couldn't believe that he didn't see my last name and recognize the resemblance between me and my mother.

His eerie poem made more sense now.

But who is this man who wrote to Tony and tried to call him numerous times? And did Tony ever answer?

The next envelope contained a newspaper clipping.

Local Law Enforcement Urge Women To Stay Safe

Canby residents are asked to take necessary safety precautions. As soon as you enter your home, lock the door behind you. Lock your cars at night, and never travel alone. As of Saturday, three women have reported being victimized in public areas and two more inside their homes.

Police Chief Jay Nelson said at a press conference that this predator is a high-level, manipulative criminal. "He rips these women of their innocence and then makes them feel sorry for him as if he couldn't help himself. That's an intense level of manipulation." He urges the public to report anything suspicious and not trust someone you don't know. "None of the women recognized their rapist. They describe him as above-average looking, with a solid build, 5'10" to 6'0" tall." Police Chief Nelson confirmed that they are working on a composite sketch and will release it to the public as soon as it is complete."

Unfortunately for the authorities, this notorious man's behavior of treating his victims like he had no control over his actions has led the victims to rid themselves of physical evidence, making it hard for them to track him. One woman who didn't want to go on record said, "He cuddled me afterward, wiped away my tears, and told me that if I hadn't been so attractive and charming, he would've stayed away."

Written in red permanent marker in all caps, someone had written, "This is me. Impressive, huh? I think I'm above average in the looks department, but not going to dwell on one incorrect fact."

The newspaper article was dated April 11, 1993.

The Campus Rapist had been writing to Tony, possibly talking to him.

I needed to give this information to the police. Why hadn't the Warden turned it over to the police instead of me? Knowing him and his need for control and recognition, I did not doubt that he read every one of these letters before boxing them up and sending them to me. Maybe I needed to read the rest to get the full picture.

When I removed about fifty handwritten letters, I stacked them and discovered a small vintage tin at the bottom of the box. As I picked it up, I heard things jiggle inside. I pulled the lid off and found a rosary, a guitar pick, a KitKat, and a bluebird.

Instantly, I recognized the little stone bird as the one I'd buried in the sand at Bible Camp thirteen years before. I'd been waiting for Tommy, but Pastor Tony showed up instead.

Chapter 43

"Good evening, Tarasue. I've been trying to get a hold of you all day." Kitty cleared her throat.

"You didn't leave a message." I looked over my shoulder at my answering machine to make sure I hadn't missed a blinking red light. I hadn't.

"I figured it was my turn for one of our conversations to be on my phone bill."

I smiled. "Thanks, Kitty. Yeah, you get windy sometimes."

"Bug, I hate to tell you this over the phone again. I wish–"

"–I lived down the road. I know, Kitty. Tell me what?"

"Anyway, when the authorities cleaned out Tony's prison cell, they found something." I heard the ice jingle in her glass. If Kitty was having a cocktail while making the phone call, it meant this was extremely difficult for her. "I wish I didn't have to do this over the phone. So impersonal. I wish you'd move back to Normal or at least live in a neighboring town."

"Kitty! What did they find?" Maybe this was the missing piece of the puzzle. Maybe Warden Jespersen stole something before mailing me the box. I wasn't sure why or how Kitty would have the missing information, but I wasn't about to shoot a gift horse.

"Oh, sorry." She took a deep breath. I silently counted with her. Six, seven, eight, nine, ten. She spat out, "You have a brother. A half-brother."

I almost choked on the sip of Diet Coke that I'd just taken. That wasn't what I was expecting her to say at all. I was anticipating a further revelation of his monstrous nature, perhaps another crime he'd committed, or the confirmation that she knew I'd been in contact with him. I hadn't expected the blow of information to land softly.

A brother?

I had another half-sibling. If he was anything like Camille, I wasn't worried. Our instant bond had surprised me, but Camille was a breath of fresh air, and I couldn't imagine my life without her. Another kid would be fun to add to our dynamic. I remembered the dreaded pit in my stomach and the nerves of anticipation as we drove to the Black Hills to meet Camille for the first time. I hadn't been prepared to like, let alone love her.

I didn't understand why Kitty was being overly dramatic. As I wiped off the spit from the phone receiver, I waited for her to fill in the blanks.

"According to the prison, he is thirty-one years old."

Another shock. A brother about my age. Well, I wasn't worried. We could spoil Camille together. I was optimistic after the last relationship that Kitty forced me into.

"His name is Ford Raven."

What? What did she say?

The gut punch that knocked the air right from my lungs.

"And I hate to tell you this, but your half-brother Ford was arrested today as Canby's Campus Rapist."

As the receiver fell from my hands, I dropped to the floor. This couldn't be happening!

Chapter 44

For the last eight years, I studied to be a therapist to help people make sense of everyday drama. Never in a million years did I consider that I'd apply *all* of the knowledge to my own life.

One of my ex-boyfriends was my half-brother. In what universe does that even make sense?

And he was the notorious rapist in my small town? I couldn't make this up.

Having a father who was a rapist and a pedophile and then having an ex-boyfriend who was also a rapist and your half-brother does a number on your psyche. This situation was more than messed up. My brain told me that none of this was my fault. But my heart wondered if I attracted these messed-up kinds of people.

What was it about me that damaged individuals gravitate to? Am I a magnet?

When I was younger and decided to be a therapist, my natural ability to listen and decipher problems had been an asset. My career choice was clear to me. However, I made that choice before discovering that Tony Shade was my father and the man I dated was my half-brother. My education told me to not let those things define me, but my wounded heart begged to differ.

I also knew that it was healthy to occasionally have a pity party and then get over it. That's what I was doing when I ran into my old professor, Beth Doyle. I'd ridden my bike along the river when I decided to stop and enjoy the gorgeous afternoon. After laying my bike in the freshly cut grass, I plopped down on a bench that faced the brook. As I was sitting there letting the tears flow freely down my cheeks and drop onto my thighs, I heard footsteps behind me come to a quick stop. Quickly, I wiped away my tears and straightened myself.

"Fuck. I hate exercise."

The female voice sounded familiar. When I turned around, I noticed she was bent at the waist trying to catch her breath. As she raised her head, I recognized Professor Doyle, who taught Abnormal Psychology. Even though she'd lost weight and cut her hair into a fashionable bob, I still recognized my favorite professor. She wore skin-tight shorts, a crop top, and a sweatband wrapped around her head.

"Hello, Professor Doyle." When I greeted her by name, she looked up. I smiled at her and scooted over on the bench to leave space next to me. "Yeah, sweating and breathing that hard should be reserved only for sex." I wasn't in the mood to filter my words, but I decided to apologize anyway. "Sorry, just saying." I heard Kitty's voice in my head telling me that just because I was having a bad day, I didn't need to project it onto others. Once again, my mother was right.

She laughed. "I remember you. Brady, right?"

"Yes, Tara Brady. I was in your Abnormal Psychology class back in '94."

"Oh yes, that was the class where I learned that students were keeping track of how many times I pulled my hair into a ponytail only to let it drop. That was eye-opening. I did it fifty times during one lecture." She shook her head. "So, I chopped off my hair to stop that annoying habit."

I laughed.

"I learned a lot about myself that year. I'm sure you heard all the rumors that my husband left me. Huge scandal. I felt ugly and cheap and decided to make everyone around me pay for it by looking at me in all those awful old man clothes that I picked up at Goodwill. 1994 was my grunge era."

It was my turn to laugh at her. "You had your own *style?*" I asked it like a question because it was the topic of much campus gossip. "The outfit that you wore on Lecture Mondays was my favorite."

She smiled up to the sky, feeling the sun's warmth on her face. "Ah yes, the homeless man's flannel, holey stocking cap, and a pair of oversized boots. I thought I was starting a trend."

"Oh, I think you did. I heard Homeless Harry traded in his dirty baseball cap for a MU stocking cap." Homeless and harmless Harry was a staple of the Midwest University campus. Rumors claimed he'd been a previous student who'd been poisoned by his roommate and was never the same. Other people believed he'd been a very active fraternity member who dabbled in some narcotics that permanently affected his brain. Sadly, no one bothered to find out the truth.

Professor Doyle dropped down beside me on the bench and gazed out at the water. "I know we get paid to help people sort through their problems, but if they'd take a moment to enjoy nature, they'd understand that being active outdoors and getting fresh air is sometimes all the therapy they need."

"I see a few issues with your revelation." I held up my index finger. "Income. Unless you decide to give them tours of the nature trails and take them on hikes as a tour guide, then you aren't going to earn a dime." My middle finger extended to show two. "Winter. What about snow? I don't think twelve inches of snow piled up on the streets is considered therapy."

"Oooh, a fellow winter hater." She held up her hand, indicating she wanted to high-five. I slapped the palm of her hand. "What caused you to be upset and sulking here along the river, Brady?"

I looked over at her, gave her a small grin, and asked, "Do you want the short, tailored version or the slap-you-in-the-face truth?"

"If you spit out both, I bet I'll learn quite a bit. We can learn a lot from what people *don't* say."

"The poetic summary is everything that I thought was the truth turned out to be a lie."

She nodded for me to continue.

"The medium version is that I'm being dramatic. Even though the lie was told to protect me, it rocked my foundation." I indicated the area around me and my baggy attire. "You're crashing my pity party."

"I see you've read Julie Franklin's book on self-care."

"Get Over It, You Big Baby. Yep, I absorbed every word. I even laminated a few pages to protect them from my big, fat, ugly tears that threatened to wrinkle some worn, high-lighted pages."

Professor Doyle told me she wasn't my professor anymore, so I could call her Beth. She assured me that therapists needed therapists too, so I had every right to bounce off the feelings I was having. When I gave her the longer version, I witnessed her eyes widen, and she took a few deep breaths to absorb my drama. When I finished, she reached over and rested her hand on my shoulder.

"I know you know this, Brady, but sometimes we need to hear the words said out loud by someone you respect. Assuming you respect me, that is."

I smiled and nodded for her to continue. I liked this woman.

"Your feelings are valid." She paused as she squeezed my shoulder. "Normally, I charge a hundred dollars for someone to hear me say those four words." A therapist joke. A good one. "Thankfully, not a lot of people can say that their father is a rapist, as well as their ex-boyfriend. Only books and movies should be able to depict such drama. However, if anybody can deal with that kind of trauma, it's you. You're strong. You're smart, and you have a support system that'll keep you level. Never be afraid to let your feelings out. It's a good reality check. Life isn't always going to be roses. It's not healthy to live in a bubble, and because your situation is so unique, I'd love to offer you therapy, pro bono." She threw her head back and laughed. "Full disclosure, though, is that I'd write your biography. That shit could make me millions."

Epilogue

I convinced myself that today's visit was for research purposes. I need to understand. I want answers, and he holds the key to unlocking the mystery. Even though I've made this trip to Fort Madison Prison several times, this time I'm not meeting Tony. I'm visiting Ford, my ex-boyfriend and half-brother. That reality creates shivers up and down my spine. Those two descriptions do not belong together. Ever. But that's exactly why I want to see him; I need to see him so I can ask him why.

I'm a glutton for punishment.

Pulling up to the large gray fortress causes a backlog of memories to flood to the surface. Butterflies flutter in my stomach as my palms start to sweat. I don't want to be here. Everything about this place generates high levels of anxiety. Surrounding the cold stone building, a barbed wire fence stands at least fourteen feet tall, topped by a circular, electric web that would toss any escapee flying back down into the yard.

The last time I was here, I was visiting my biological contributor. I'd been naive and young, thinking that getting to know him wouldn't affect me, that I was stronger than any revelation he'd share. Writing my thesis paper on nature vs. nurture with him at the center opened many professional doors; however, personally, I was never the same. I hadn't planned on becoming jaded and less trusting, but it happened anyway.

After I make my way through the guarded gate, park my car, and am escorted into the building, I expect to see a friendly, familiar face at the front desk, but Oscar isn't there. His replacement is a young, stout woman with angry crease lines resting on her forehead. We don't make small talk. I don't ask her how the fish were biting, and she doesn't recount any adventures that I've missed since my last visit. I just hand over my personal belongings, fill out the visitor log form, and wait on the hard, metal chair that is bolted to the floor.

Sitting in silence, I remind myself that this is the last time I'll be at the prison. I don't need to ever return. My visits will not be a regular occurrence. I'm here for closure.

Once she confirms the approval of my visit, another guard unlocks the door to my right and gestures for me to enter. Following three locked door entries, I'm escorted into the visitor call room. I'd never been in this room. When I met with Tony, our interviews were conducted in a reserved conference room. The call room is used for spontaneous visits that need less supervision.

Lining one side of the room, big black phones are bolted to the wall. In between each phone is a set of glass that is three panels thick. The guard pulls out a chair to indicate where I'm to sit. He explains that when my prisoner arrives, I should pick up the phone receiver, and he'll automatically be able to talk to me. I don't need to press any numbers.

Instead of informing him that I'd watched enough movies to know the drill, I nod and thank him.

Before I can relax and gain my composure, the adjacent door on the prisoner side of the room opens, and Ford struts through it. The first thing that I notice is his skin color. Gone is the healthy, tan glow gained from hours of exploring the outdoors. His skin is pale, which makes the dark circles under his eyes more noticeable. However, I realize Ford is still very good-looking with his chiseled jawline, bright blue eyes, and thick head of wavy brown hair.

"Well, hello, Tara. This is a nice surprise."

"Hello, Ford."

"I'm going to take a wild guess and say this isn't a chance meeting."

"You're very perceptive."

He scrutinizes me closely, and I'm grateful that I opted for a baggy sweatshirt, no makeup, and a ponytail. I'm not looking to impress him. This isn't a friendly visit. But as his eyes travel up and down the top half of my body, I still get a sick feeling in the pit of my stomach.

"Stress and years have been good to you, *sister*."

It takes everything in me not to throw up or get up and storm out of the door that moments ago I'd just walked through. As my blood pressure rises, the hair on the back of my neck stands up.

How long has he known that we were siblings? His arrogance leads me to think that he was aware of our shared DNA from the beginning, a realization that fills me with a deep sense of unease.

"This is a fun, little reunion. While it's always a pleasure to see you, I'm curious why you are here, Tara."

"Honestly, Ford, I'm not sure. I was hoping to catch a glimpse of the nice, considerate guy I knew a few years ago; however, I'm quickly realizing that it was a facade. You're a fabulous actor. You fooled me. Did you know from the very beginning?"

"Did I know what?"

He wants me to say it–that we're siblings–but I can't. Giving a voice to this nightmare feels like a betrayal of the hope I'm still clinging to. It's something about saying the words that will make them true. If I say that he is my brother out loud, then I'd have to deal with those feelings.

As we stare at each other, I don't need to hear his answer. I can tell by the smirk on his face that he knew. He knew from the start, and it was why we met.

"I bet you're glad *now* that I refused to have sex with you, huh?" Ford throws his head back and enjoys a deep, hearty laugh. I quickly swallow a large lump–that tastes like bile–when he adds, "You were such a horny little bitch. Must've inherited that from our father."

A terrible sense of déjà vu fills me. As I stare at this man, I wonder how he could've turned out so much like Tony even though they'd never met. Was my theory about how nurture could dominate nature untrue? I'd believe it with my whole being as I researched the theory for my paper. However, now as I witness Ford in the same setting as Tony–our biological contributor–I realize I could've been wrong.

"You know, I'm glad you broke up with me. I didn't know how much longer I could stand listening to you whine about all your ridiculous problems or listen to you beg me to touch you. It was all quite repulsive. You were so needy, so desperate, so pathetic." His lips curl as he watches me crumble hearing him describe our relationship. "Are you still searching for Mr. Right? Is *Match.com* recommending you any more duds? I wonder what happened to the guy who never showed up for your date. What was his name again? Gabe Paul?" He chuckles.

I ignore his digs. One word forms in my head, and I ask, "Why?"

"Why not?" He raises an eyebrow, challenging me.

His two-word response is my answer. There is nothing he could say to make this situation any better just like when I was interviewing Tony years ago seeking an answer that would make sense to a normal person. These two men linked by DNA are irrefutably fucked up. No answer either of them could give me would satisfy my curiosity. I need to understand that. I'm seeking answers to bring closure to this mess, but I quickly realize that the only closure I need is my acceptance.

I decide that I'll enjoy the news that I'm about to spring on him.

"You idolized a man—a monster by society's terms—who wanted nothing to do with you. How does that make you feel?" I force the tears back, telling myself to save them for my three-and-a-half-hour road trip home.

"If he hadn't been murdered, I would've been able to tell him who I was. He would've realized that I did everything for him." Ford looks up at the ceiling. A small smile forms on his lips. "He would've been so proud. Damn, we could've shared tips and fed off each other's accomplishments."

I refuse to acknowledge that he described the abuse he inflicted on women as accomplishments. "The old, I-was-trying-to-impress-my-father excuse? That's the reason you raped and violated countless women? That's lame, Ford. You sound like a pathetic kid."

"I did impress him. You have no idea."

"I'm sorry to have to be the one to tell you this," I lie. I'm not sorry. I want to hurt him because he used and manipulated me and so many other women. It's my turn. "But he did know about you, Ford. He knew you were his son."

I watch the news sink in. I see his eyes searching mine, trying to figure out my angle.

I count the seconds in our silence. *Nine, ten, eleven, twelve, thirteen.*

"You're lying." He eyes me through tiny slits. "There is no way he could know about me. My mother didn't even know she was pregnant when she was dating him."

"Well, that may be the case, but he did know of your existence. Your mother contacted him..." I look down at the notepad I'd brought. "In 1980, your mother contacted him several times seeking child support. It looks like she had an address for him in California. In 1982, when he was living in Normal, Iowa, she made another attempt to contact him. Your parents were going through some financial heartache, and I bet she figured if she collected some back child support, it would help them break through their debt."

Ford stares at me, trying to let the information penetrate his brain. "I don't believe you."

"I don't care if you believe me or not, but it's true. I rummaged through Tony's things after his passing and found these letters from a lawyer seeking child support, along with a letter that your mother wrote to Tony telling him about you. She even sent him a picture of you from high school to prove how much you looked like him. You're a dead ringer except for the blue eyes." I hold up a class composite picture of Tony for a visual. "This is a picture of you, isn't it?"

Immediately, he recognizes his senior picture. While I let him process this news that I'm sure devastates him, I shuffle my visual aids back into the folder that had been preapproved at check-in.

As I shift into my therapist mode, I say, "Ford, I know you told yourself that you raped all those women because you couldn't help yourself. It was ingrained in your DNA to seek attention from the man you inherited the genes from, but Ford, you must acknowledge that you alone bear responsibility for your actions. You can't blame a man you'd never met–a man who wanted nothing to do with you, a man who resides in Hell. You're the master of your destiny. You control the ending of your story. You need to seek forgiveness and make amends. No one but you is to blame for the choices you made.

"I've spent countless hours researching this topic, nature vs. nurture, and you were raised–nurtured–by a set of wonderful, wholesome people. Even though you were educated and raised to make the right choices, you did not. No matter whose biology makes up part of our DNA, we're ultimately in control of our actions. No one else."

When I take a breath, I notice that Ford's eyes have glazed over. I'm unsure if he heard a word I said, but I didn't just say all of that for his benefit; I also need to give myself that allowance. Plus, if I say it out loud, it rings more true.

Taking my own advice on controlling my destiny, I hang up the receiver and stand up. I've said my peace, and I must accept that the closure I'm seeking isn't possible. Unfortunately, life is unfair and cruel sometimes.

As I walk toward the door that represents freedom, I visualize Ford and me as small seeds dropped into the dirt. We were given similar nutrients to help us grow, but through individual choices, one seed turned into a thistle while the other grew into a wildflower.

Bonus Epilogue and Recipe

Hi, Readers!

Not ready to be finished with drama in Normal, Iowa, send me an email to get a bonus epilogue.

emersynpark@gmail.com.

And be sure sign up for my newsletter to receive all the behind the scenes secrets.

www.EmersynPark.com

Swedish Meatballs

1 lb hamburger

1 egg

3/4 c seasoned bread crumbs

1 tsp brown sugar

1/2 tsp salt

1/4 tsp pepper

1/4 tsp ginger

1/4 tsp ground cloves

1/4 tsp nutmeg

1/4 tsp cinnamon

1/2 c milk

Mix ingredients and roll into 1/2-1 inch balls. Brown lightly in 1/2
T oil. Place in a greased 9x9 casserole dish.

2 T butter

2 T flour

1 c beef broth

1/2 tsp salt

Dash of cayenne pepper

1/2 t Worcestershire sauce

1 c sour cream

Mix and pour over meatballs. Bake at 350 for 45 minutes. Serve with
mashed potatoes or wild rice.

Acknowledgements

Actions speak louder than words.

That phrase is completely true; however, since you can't see me dancing for joy or hear me trying to sing the little poetic number that I wrote, this page will have to do.

Honey, we've been together for thirty years, and you know me and still love me more than anyone else. I appreciate your unwavering support and encouragement.

Boys, thank you for understanding my need to lock myself in my room to 'talk to the voices in my head.' And Bandit, my loyal sidekick, I'm glad you needed to stretch your legs and dragged me along. Lots of good ideas seem to develop when we are on a walk.

Witches, thanks for always having my back, and letting me use your names in my books! And a few lucky ones feed me stories that I use. Thanks for being my muse!

My Beta Team (Gena, PJ, Sarah, and Betsy), your eyes are the first to view the book. Your advice helped me create a book that I'm proud of.

Editor Caramie, you polished my jumble of words until they shine. You work *miles* outside of your job description, and I can't thank you enough for all you do.

ARC Dream Team (Denise, Stacy, Nancy, Farah, Susan, Jenny, Cindy, Chris, Ashley, Heather, Jaime, Kari, Liz, Lisa, Peggy, Tiffany, Katie, Monica, Mikell, Nikki, Samantha, Marla, and Krissy), I appreciate your passion for reading and helping me reach new readers. It's a crazy ride, and I'm grateful for your support.

Lindsey, I'm sorry you lost sleep, but I appreciate your feedback.

Jaidyn, as a psychology major yourself, your wisdom was greatly appreciated.

But most importantly, I need to thank *you,* the reader, for choosing my book. Thank you for supporting my dream job!

Cheers! ~Emersyn Park